FABLE

EDGE OF THE WORLD

FABLE®

EDGE OF THE WORLD

CHRISTIE GOLDEN

BALLANTINE BOOKS

NEW YORK

Acknowledgments

I would like to thank my tireless and encouraging editor, Frank Parisi, and the good Lionhead folks Ted Timmins, Ben Brooks, and Gareth Sutcliffe for their enthusiastic support. You all helped make my first venture into Albion a great deal of fun.

ISBN 978-0-345-53937-3
eISBN 978-0-345-53941-0

Printed in the United States of America

www.delreybooks.com

www.lionhead.com

2 4 6 8 9 7 5 3 1

First Edition

Book design by Christopher M. Zucker

This book is dedicated
to the memory of James R. Golden
1920–2011
You were and are my Hero, Dad. I love you.

EDGE OF THE WORLD

Prologue

The sun was setting, and Gabriel was comfortably tired. He made sure that his horse and friend Seren, who had pulled his caravan for many a year, was well tended before heading off to share supper with his fellow Dwellers.

It was, as most such gatherings were, lively and full of laughter and conversation. Yet Gabriel, a youth in his late teens whose arms and legs seemed a bit long for his body, did not join in. His thoughts were full of things other than weather, horses, customers, and the practicalities that occupied the minds of most other Dwellers.

Gabriel's thoughts, as they often did, concerned Heroes.

A tiny hand squeezed his knee as he sat a little ways away from the firelight and music. He looked down into the small faces of Peter and Anna, twins who were about six years old. They gave him conspiratorial grins.

"Gabriel," Peter said, "can you tell us more about Heroes?"

"Oh, please, please!" begged Anna, jumping up and down a little bit. "I want to hear about the old king and his beautiful queen!"

"Well," Gabriel said, "if you're very quiet, then yes."

"Hooray!" said Peter, who then covered his mouth at Gabriel's glare.

"That wasn't quiet."

"I know," whispered Peter.

Gabriel looked over to see if his friend and mentor Katlan had noticed. The outgoing youth was talking and laughing with some of the other tribe members.

"Well," said Gabriel, "do you remember what I told you about Heroes last time?"

"I do!" said Anna. "Heroes are special people in Albion. They have three kinds of abilities—Strength, Skill, and Will."

"Strength and Skill are pretty obvious, right?" The two children nodded. "Tell me about Will."

"The first Hero we know about was William Black," said Peter. "He saved Albion a long time ago by using magical abilities, which we call the Powers of Will."

"Very good. You've both been paying attention." Gabriel smiled as he saw three more children creeping up to listen. "And of course, it's very common for a Hero to master all three of these things."

"No it isn't, silly," piped up Gerald. "Only a couple of Heroes can do that!"

"And what makes them so rare?" Gabriel prompted. Gerald's brow furrowed as he seriously pondered the question. Anna stuck her hand up, but Gabriel waved her to silence. "Oh! Because they belong to the Archon's bloodline. Only true descendants of the bloodline can master all three things."

"Very good," said Gabriel, though he felt a pang. He was hardly a descendant of the Archon. He knew he could never be a Hero. Still . . . it was fun to dream.

"Penny," he said to one of the girls in back, "all Heroes are always good and helpful, aren't they?" Penny shyly shook her dark head but offered nothing more.

"No, of course not!" know-it-all Anna scoffed. "Our old king was a true Hero, and he was very, very good. But Mr. Reaver was the Hero of Skill, and he's very, very bad!"

"Gabriel!"

Gabriel started guiltily as he looked over at Katlan, who stood glaring at him, arms crossed. "Little ones," he said, gentling his tone, "go back to the firelight with your families. There will be singing soon."

The children cast sidelong glances at Gabriel, then did as they were told. Katlan sighed and sat next to Gabriel. The two were old friends, but recently, Katlan had been named leader of the Dweller tribe to which they both belonged. With that responsibility had come Katlan's increasing concern over what he called "Gabriel's daydreaming."

"You shouldn't be talking about such things."

"Our king was a Hero, Katlan," Gabriel said in a low voice.

"That's all well and good, but that was a long time ago. Talking about Reaver like that could get us in trouble if it gets back to him. He's a very powerful man."

"Because he was a H—"

"Because he has money and a lot of political clout!" Katlan interrupted sharply. "Look. I don't know who was a Hero and who wasn't. And it doesn't matter, not these days. What matters is that you're never going to be a Hero, nor are those children. So stop filling their heads with nonsense. And stop filling your own with it too, eh?" He grinned and squeezed his friend's shoulder, then rose and went back to the ring of firelight.

Gabriel watched him go. He would stay silent to the children. But he would never stop daydreaming about Heroes.

———————

Forty years ago, in the Land of Albion, a king ruled wisely and well....

The sound of shrieks issuing from unnatural voices filled the icy wind. Snow assaulted bodies as the cacophony assaulted ears. Most of the refugees were dead by now, victims of avalanche, exposure, or things far, far worse. Only a handful remained: a handful of the two dozen who had fled Samarkand—was it only three days ago?

Shan blinked eyelashes long since frozen and encrusted with ice, trying to clear his vision as he climbed hand over hand. His father had died early, at the hands—claws?—of the things that followed them. Shan shuddered and blotted out the memory. His little sister had been too weak to go on, and they were forced to leave her behind. Both his mother and infant brother had died even before they left the city of Zahadar. Shan and his older sister, Lin, were all that remained of his family.

The thick furs wrapped about body, feet, hands, and heads weren't enough to keep out the snow that attacked like bullets of frozen water. Most of the rations they had all so carefully packed had been abandoned early on, the extra weight proving too great. What remained wasn't enough to sustain them. The picks and tools weren't enough to carry them forward. The guns and other weapons they had brought weren't enough to protect them. Nothing would have been enough for anything, not over the Sakur Pass. There was a reason that the pass had never been crossed in living memory, even in the bright warmth of summer. To do so now, in midwinter, was to die.

But to have stayed would have been worse.

The howling still filled the air, but it had changed, subtly, and Lin, climbing steadfastly beside him, whimpered.

"The sha—" she began.

"Be quiet!" Shan snapped, his voice raw with exhaustion and terror. He didn't even care how he sounded. The *things* in pursuit of them—and *she* who directed them—were all that mattered.

He breathed in air that was frigid even through the wrapping that covered all of his face but his eyes. His muscles quivered as he continued to slog forward, using the ice pick for better purchase. There was no energy to spare for comforting his sister, not if either of them was to survive.

Six others climbed in grim, terrified silence and agonizing slowness alongside Shan and Lin. No one helped anyone else, not anymore. Now, no one had strength to spare for anything but his own survival. At least it was still daylight. Before, they had been fortunate enough at night to find shelter of some sort, be it a cluster of pines, a cave, or even a sheer rock face that prevented attacks from at least one direction. More precious than food or even furs was the oil that kept the darkness—both natural and unnatural—at bay for those soul-racking hours.

Shan's numb fingers managed to find a ledge. He tried to pull himself up. He couldn't. His muscles were too cold, too weak, too starved, and all they did was quiver uselessly. A second effort, a third, and this time panic flooded him and with a growl of sheer will he hauled himself over the edge and lay there, shaking and gasping.

"Shan!" cried Lin. He forced himself to roll over and reach out to his sister's grasping hand, bracing his feet against a rock outcropping. His fingers were so numb, he couldn't really even feel her hand clutching his.

"Come on, Lin, you can do this! There are footholds that can help you! Try to find them!"

She turned up a face wrapped in protective furs. The only thing Shan could see were her soft brown eyes huge with fear.

"I can't feel anything with my feet!" she cried. "Shan, please! Help me!"

Tears stung his eyes only to freeze as they tried to slip down his face. He braced himself more securely, willed his legs to stay firm, and pulled with all his might.

Her mittens came loose. He heard her shriek even over the howling wind, over the cries of the *things* that were hunting them, and heard his own scream of horror as he watched her tumble back down.

I have to get her. I have to climb down and get her. She's all I have left. Lin . . . !

He managed to roll over onto his side before unconsciousness claimed him.

Shan awoke to the comforting warmth and, almost more important, the orange light of the torches. Someone had propped his head up and was trying to feed him some thin broth. Disoriented, Shan sipped hungrily for a moment, then memory returned like a thunderclap.

"L-Lin!"

"Easy, Shan," said Kuvar. "It's too late for Lin. She died hours ago. Don't follow her."

Shan closed his eyes in pain. He had been too weak to go back for his sister, and no one else had done so. He couldn't blame them. He had had to suspend judgment about others' choices days ago. It was a marvel that he himself hadn't been tossed over the edge, much less be offered food and shelter. He would be on his own on the morrow, though; that much he knew.

"How?" was all he could manage.

"The cold," Kuvar replied. Shan nodded, relieved. Better to

freeze to death than to be injured and die in pain, or attacked by—

The Shadows rose up, just beyond the ring of firelight. Shan stumbled to his feet, forcing his fumbling hands to grasp the pistol, which he fired into the lurching, dancing shapes. Numb fingers struggled to reload while others charged forward, their katanas flashing in the torchlight. The black shapes with gleaming red eyes pressed in from all sides, even from above; the firelight, and the weapons wielded by the refugees, were all that was keeping the fiends from utterly wiping out the party. The Shadows moaned and cackled, and occasionally, gratifyingly, screamed in what sounded like annoyance as they died.

They had never before pressed their attack at night. Always, they had terrorized from a safe distance, an arm or a wing occasionally venturing into the light in a threatening manner before being quickly withdrawn. But now—now they fell upon the refugees as if done with toying with them and intent upon ending the game.

A scream to his right. Kuvar dropped his katana, his hands reaching up to clasp at the black, translucent tentacles that were wrapping around his throat. They squeezed, and Shan stared, frozen not with cold, not this time, but with horror as he watched Kuvar's tongue bulge and his eyes pop.

He felt a sudden iciness that had nothing to do with the natural elements brush against his face. He whirled, screaming incoherently, and fired.

Click. Click.

The Shadow laughed.

Using energy he didn't know he had, Shan dove for Kuvar's abandoned katana. He rolled as he hit the stone ledge and slashed out with the elegant sword; the Shadow that was reaching for him howled in pain. Heartened, Shan got to his feet, wielding the weapon not with any kind of expertise but with the sheer desperation of survival. All around him the sounds of battle raged. He swung the sword wildly, sometimes cutting air, sometimes cutting something else, too crazed to even realize what he was doing.

And then he became aware of the silence. His own heartbeat a drumbeat in his ears, his panting ragged and loud. He looked around, keeping his weapon in front of him, and realized that he was the last one standing.

Six bodies lay at his feet. They looked like discarded dolls, their limbs bent at odd angles, their faces bloated and locked in expressions of horror.

Shan looked up at the hovering Shadows. Suddenly anger filled him. "What are you waiting for?" he shouted.

The lassst one. It was barely audible, and for a moment Shan was convinced he had imagined it.

Yessss, another whisper agreed. *We have a purposssse for thissss one.*

Shan had thought he had tasted the depth of terror. But now he dropped to his knees. Any "purpose" they had in store for him had to be the most—

He suddenly turned the katana around, placing its point at his midsection. But before he could plunge the elegant blade home to prevent their doing whatever they had in mind for him, a black tendril snatched the sword from his hands.

Be at eassse, one of them said in a mocking tone. *You shall live, Shan of Ssssamarkand.*

"Wh-what do you want?" Shan said. He was mortified that he was sobbing but could not control it.

You will ssscale the mountains, if you are sssstrong enough. We will not hinder you. If you ssssurvive, then we have a messssage to give to Ssssabine of the Dwellerssss.

"What?"

Tell him . . . and they began to laugh.

"What!" screamed Shan, feeling insanity hovering at the edges of his mind.

We are coming.

Chapter One

"My lord, if I may?"

Jasper's voice was slightly high-pitched and filled with suffering so long tolerated that it was no longer even felt. In other words, he sounded completely normal.

The monarch looked into the mirror as he fiddled with his crown. The cursed thing never seemed to fit correctly on his head. His eyes met Jasper's in the mirror and he nodded.

"Please. And if you can do anything that makes this ermine stole feel less as if it's made of armor, I'd be grateful for that too."

"Alas," said Jasper as he stepped beside the young king he had tended since the monarch's birth, "while it is indeed in actuality merely the weight of two stuffed minklike creatures, I can sympathize with the symbolic weight it places on Your Majesty's shoulders."

"It's the crown, not the wedding outfit, that has the symbolic weight," the king shot back good-naturedly. "I can't wait for the ceremony."

"Then may I say that Your Majesty is among the very, *very* fortunate few," noted Jasper.

The king chuckled. "It's nice to have you back, Jasper."

Jasper, once the king's butler, had spent the last few years serving in a different capacity. He was now the steward of a magical, and quite secret, Sanctuary. Established by the late king, the Sanctuary was the present king's birthright as he was both the son of a Hero of Albion and a Hero himself. When the then-prince, sickened by his older brother Logan's cruelty to his own people, had chosen to lead a rebellion to take the crown, the loyal if acerbic Jasper had fled with the future king and Sir Walter Beck. Together, the three had found the Sanctuary, which had served as a sort of headquarters for the rebellion. Once Logan had been overthrown, Jasper had remained there, continuing to probe the mysteries of the place.

But for this occasion—a royal wedding—he had been recalled to his old duties. And while he attempted to appear much put-upon, the monarch knew Jasper well enough to realize that the old butler was secretly quite pleased.

So, for that matter, was the king himself—and, he dared believe, his entire kingdom. Nine years had passed since the monarch had stood against both his brother and the darkness that had threatened to wipe out all of Albion. The king had not been quoting a cliché when he spoke of the symbolic weight of the crown. His days gathering followers and fighting hobbes, balverines, and the occasional gap-toothed bandit seemed like a stroll in the garden compared to the very gray duties of ruling a kingdom. He had made choices he was proud of, and some he was not, and not one of them had been clear or simple. More lives had been lost than he would have wanted, but in the end, his people were now safe, happy, and well on their way to regaining prosperity without having to make deals with the devil.

Speaking of devils . . .

"No whispers of Reaver returning?" he asked of Jasper, who

seemed to know everything about everyone. "It'd be just like him to try to spoil today."

"I can honestly say that I have not heard a breath of Mr. Reaver's whereabouts, and I am buoyant with delight at the fact."

"Ben Finn's just gotten back from wandering about, and Page's network hasn't heard anything either," the king said. "We may just have gotten lucky."

"I would touch wood when you say that, Your Majesty. Repeatedly."

The king grinned. He glanced down at the other "old friend" who sat patiently at his feet, as he had done for over a decade. His border collie, Rex, had been a faithful ally on the long road to rule. Now that he was growing old, he slept more than he played, but was still alert and healthy. Rex's eyes were fixed on his master, and he barked happily as he saw the king smile.

"Good dog," said the king. "The best dog ever."

Rex pranced a little at the praise, then sat down attentively. The king surveyed his reflection in the mirror and liked what he saw. Like Rex, he too was older, and time had begun to make its presence noticed in the crinkles around his brown eyes and the occasional thread of silver in his hair. His face was still strong and, if the blushing and giggling ladies of the court were to be believed, handsome. But he didn't care what they thought. There was only one woman whose opinion mattered, and today, she would become his queen and his life's companion.

"You do look happy, Your Majesty," said Jasper, and there was an unusual hint of warmth and pride in his voice.

The monarch turned from the mirror. "I am, Jasper. My kingdom is content and growing, we are at peace, trade with Aurora is good, and I am about to be wed to the most wonderful girl in the world. And," he added, whispering conspiratorially, "I'll be happier still tonight."

"One should hope so, Your Majesty."

Chuckling slightly, the monarch clapped his old friend on the shoulder. "Let's go. Can't keep the love of my life waiting."

Rex trotted after them, tail waving, as the king and his butler left the room.

The throne room was exquisite testimony to the majesty of the castle's design. Stairs covered with rich blue carpeting led up to a raised dais, upon which the throne itself was seated. The walls were lined with portraits of former royalty, and the whole was illumined by colorful light filtered through three stained-glass windows. The room's formality had been gentled through the use of flowers adorning the walls and fixtures, and a white canopy that draped from the ceiling. The throne was still present but had been moved back slightly to make room for a small table presided over by an elderly robed woman. All the guests had arrived and were chatting quietly among themselves. Over to the right, a quartet played.

A slender blond man stood by the door, peering into the room and fidgeting as the king and Jasper approached. The king grinned as the young man tugged on a collar that was apparently too tight. Even from behind, Benjamin Finn looked quite out of his element. As indeed he was. Finn, who had been one of many who had helped the monarch claim the throne, came from common roots and had spent most of his life as either a soldier or a mercenary. Nonetheless, the king knew the man's worth. Finn was brave if a little reckless, and a master sharpshooter, and the king appreciated his wit and rather tall tales. Despite his devil-may-care attitude, Ben Finn had a great heart.

"You look so anxious, one might think you were the one to be married today," the king said casually. Ben started, then glared at him.

"Crikey, don't *do* that. I'm likely to drop the rings, and it'd be all your fault."

"No, no, my best man would never do that, not if he doesn't want to start posing for 'Wanted' posters again."

"Too right," Ben muttered, but the king noticed nonetheless that the soldier put his hand in his pocket with an overly casual movement, making sure the rings were still there. As he did so, he glanced up at his friend and liege.

"Thank you again for the honor. I know that there would have been someone else you'd have picked if you'd had the chance though—and I would have cheered it."

The king sobered. Ben was right. One very important man was missing on this special day—his friend and weapons tutor, Sir Walter Beck. It had been Walter who had guided the then-prince on his quest, from that night when he, Beck, and Jasper had fled the castle, up until Walter's tragic demise. While Captain Jack Timmins had taken over Walter's role in things martial, no one had ever been as loyal as the knight, and the king knew he would never have quite that same kind of bond with anyone again.

"Walter would have been very happy today, wouldn't he?" the king said quietly.

"Your Majesty—wherever he is, I suspect he *is* happy."

The king nodded and took a breath. Ben was right. Walter was the last person who would have wished to cast any pall over his king's wedding day, and so, the king would not let that happen.

"Ready, sir?" asked Ben.

"Yes."

"You're sure? Because you know, you're the king; if you don't want to go through with it, if you're getting cold feet or anything like that—there's no one who's going to force you to do it, now, is there?"

"You're babbling, Ben."

"Oh. I am, aren't I?"

"Come on. Let's go."

As they walked in, Rex trotting behind his master, they saw many familiar faces. Sitting in the area reserved for special guests of the kingdom were two others who looked as out of place as Ben clearly felt. One was an extraordinarily large and powerfully built man with a long, curling black mustache. He wore a thick-brimmed hat and his wide leather belt was adorned with a skull and crossbones. To look at him, no one would guess that he had a soft spot a mile wide for animals. This was Boulder, the taciturn bodyguard of King Sabine of the Mistpeak Dwellers.

Sabine was as different from Boulder as could be imagined. Little more than half the big man's size, he could best be described with words like "knobby" and "spry." His beard was as pointed as his hat and his strange, upturned shoes. Propped up beside him as he sat was a staff that his gnarled hands gripped tightly. Affixed to the top of the staff was a purple bottle that served Sabine as a pipe. Smoke usually rose from its opening as Sabine puffed away on a long stem, but for the occasion, the Dweller leader had grudgingly agreed not to smoke.

The Dwellers had been the king's first allies and had remained loyal friends. It was quite a trek from Mistpeak to Bowerstone, and the monarch was pleased to see that the cranky old man had made the journey.

Another who had made an even longer journey was the exotic Auroran leader, Kalin. Her only concession to the cold climate of Albion in winter was a cloak currently folded in her lap. Otherwise, her body and garb proclaimed her origins proudly, from her shaved and tattooed head and arms to her green, gold, and red robes. She was here not only as a true ally but as a countrywoman of the bride-to-be. Indeed, Kalin had been the one to introduce the couple. Kalin caught the king's eye and gave him a sweet, fond smile. He returned it, then turned his attention to the front of the room as he and Ben walked up the stairs and stood on the priestess's left. As it had been important to his fiancée to have the wedding performed in the traditional manner of her people, the elderly and wise Priestess Mara had accompanied Kalin across the ocean to officiate.

The music changed. All eyes now turned from the present king to Albion's future queen. The king's breath caught, as it did every time he saw her.

Laylah.

Tall and slender, delicate of feature with wide, doelike eyes, her lips curved in a smile that made his heart leap. The dusky golden brown of her skin and her ebony tresses contrasted with the creamy white of the formal gown. In her hands, she held a bouquet of native, riotously colorful Auroran blossoms.

Walking behind her as her maid of honor was the only true Bowerstone native besides the king himself—Page. She resembled Laylah slightly although her skin was much darker, her features fuller, and her long hair tightly braided in rows. The leader of the Bowerstone Resistance during Logan's reign, Page had taken a great deal of convincing before she had come to believe that the current ruler could be trusted. And he supposed he couldn't blame her.

He was delighted that Page and Laylah, though from completely different backgrounds, had become such fast friends. Laylah could not be called a true innocent. She and her people had suffered, terribly and terrifyingly, from the dark horror known to them as the Nightcrawler. It was this darkness the king himself had helped to defeat, first in Aurora and later in Albion proper. But even though she had endured much, Laylah had a certain naïveté about her.

This could not be said about Page. She was as hard as Laylah was soft. A shrewd observer of people, Page knew how to motivate and inspire her friends and stand up to her enemies. Her "organization" was still largely intact though now she offered what she knew—at least *most* of what she knew; the king suspected that she still kept a few things close to her vest—and had proven to be an invaluable resource. Page was that admirable though often oxymoronic thing, the pragmatic optimist. He was glad that Laylah had found not only a friend but one who could help her understand Bowerstone and its populace, both good and bad.

But all that, important though it was, could wait. All he saw now was the brave but gentle girl who had won his heart. Her cheeks turned a dark rose as she ascended the steps to stand beside him, and her eyes were bright with joy.

Most of the wedding ceremony was a blur to the king. He uttered his name when needed to, happily vowed to love, protect, and be true to Laylah, and had a moment of panic when he heard Ben swearing as he fumbled for the rings. Laylah extended her slender hand, and the king slipped the simple gold ring on the fourth finger.

Out of the corner of his eye, he saw a bearded Dweller standing outside the throne room, arguing with a guard. The guard was shaking his head, but Jasper quietly intervened and led the messenger as discreetly as possible to where King Sabine was seated. He heard Sabine's distinctive yapping for an instant, then both he and the messenger hastened out.

The king's heart sank. Something bad had obviously happened, and he was selfish enough, at this moment at least, to hope it was something Sabine could handle by himself.

He had a feeling it wasn't.

Oh well, he thought as Laylah slipped a ring on his own left hand, *such is the life of a king.*

Even, it would seem, on his wedding day.

He clasped Laylah's hand and turned to face the applauding crowd as Priestess Mara presented them as King and Queen of Albion. Laylah's arm was slipped through his, the new royal couple nodded, smiling, to the well-wishers. But the instant they stepped through the doors, the king felt the strong grip of Sabine's clawlike hand.

"Your Majesty! We must speak right away!"

"Unfortunately, I fear King Sabine is correct," said Jasper. "This matter is indeed demanding of your attention. I suggest you, Mr. Finn, Captain Timmins, Miss Page, and the lady Kalin take a few moments now to converse. I shall take our lovely new queen to the reception and—"

"No, Jasper," said Laylah. Her musical voice was soft, as always, but firm. "I am, as you say, the queen now. My husband has said he wished me to share in the duties as well as the pleasures of ruling. If this matter is so urgent, I should like to hear of it." She turned to the king. "If His Majesty agrees?"

He sighed. "I had hoped you would get to enjoy more of the pleasures of being queen before you were forced to share its duties, my love. But yes—come with us. I would have you all know that Queen Laylah is my true partner, as well as my wife."

She beamed, and again he wished that this "urgent matter" could have waited until tomorrow, at the very least. He kissed her hand. "Jasper, I trust that you will keep the crowd entertained until we rejoin you. Tell the others to meet me . . ." He hesitated for a moment, then acknowledged the seriousness of the matter. "To meet me in the War Room."

Chapter Two

The king and his new wife arrived first. Rex followed obediently, heading straight for his favorite corner, where he turned nose to tail and promptly fell asleep. The others trickled in as Jasper was able to find them. First to arrive was Ben, already undoing his collar and shrugging out of the formal coat, flinging it casually on a chair. "Jasper said something's up with Sabine."

"Your guess is as good as ours," said the king. "I saw someone come in to speak to him and Jasper said we should all convene."

Ben bowed to the new queen. "You had him all to yourself for about two minutes, Your Majesty."

Laylah leaned in toward her husband, who slipped an arm about her waist. "More than I expected to have, truly. Do not worry, Mr. Finn. I understood the import of my choice in who I loved."

"Ben, please. I'm glad to hear you understand. But if you'll pardon the language, it still stinks."

Laylah smiled. "So it does."

Page hurried in. Kalin followed her, her brow furrowed in worry. Laylah embraced Page tightly and smiled at her countrywoman, who, the king noticed, did not return the expression. Page drew back, smiling sadly. "I did warn you," she said.

"Everyone did," Laylah said. "I am more concerned with whatever is going on with Sabine than in having the day interrupted. We are married, and to me, that is all that matters."

"Spoken like a true Auroran," said Kalin. "I pray this is all not as dire as it seems."

"Hate to interrupt the romance, my lord," came the gruff but warm voice of Jack Timmins, the captain of the guard. "Sabine's right behind me, and from the way he and Jasper are behaving, we'll soon have a situation here right enough." Timmins had been made head of the Bowerstone Guards shortly after the devastating attack of the Nightcrawler upon Albion. With his brusque but professional, thoughtful manner he had won a place in the king's affections as well as his esteem. He wasn't Sir Walter Beck. No one could be. Walter was irreplaceable. But Timmins was turning into a true and loyal friend as well as a shrewd military advisor.

The monarch barely had time to acknowledge Timmins when Sabine came trundling through the door, looking as furious as the king had ever seen him. With him was of course Boulder, and a young man—though not the Dweller messenger who had called Sabine away from the ceremony. This boy, who couldn't be much older than twenty, if that, appeared different from anyone the king had ever seen. He was clad in Dweller clothes, but they were ill fitting and clearly not his own. His skin was the same shade as Laylah's, but his brown eyes had a slight slant.

Those eyes looked almost vacant, and the boy seemed to be sleepwalking. The king winced in sympathy. He knew the look of one who had borne witness to horrors no one should ever see.

"This young fellow managed to survive crossing the Blade Mountains chain in the dead of winter," Sabine began.

"From Samarkand?" The king looked with renewed interest at the boy. No wonder he looked exotic. The monarch had never personally met anyone from Samarkand before, though of course he had heard stories of the place. The king's father, a Hero himself, had traveled with a Samarkandian known as Garth as well as the disliked Reaver. The king recalled his father's speaking of Garth as one of the most powerful Will users he had ever heard of.

"No, from Brightwall," said Sabine, his voice dripping with sarcasm. "Yes, of *course* from Samarkand. Now, go on, boy. Tell these good people what you told me. It's all right."

The youth lifted his haunted eyes to the king and said simply, "They are coming."

"Who is—" began Kalin, then fell silent. Laylah locked eyes with her, both of them clearly fearing the worst. Everyone else stared at the floor. No one wanted to speak, to give a concrete reality to what was now simply a horrible fear.

Sabine nodded miserably, reading their expressions. "It's as bad as you think. It took those who found him several days to get that much out of the poor lad. It seems that portentous statement is a direct quote. They spared him so we would know."

"Why?" asked Timmins. "Why warn us?"

"To make us fear, Timmins," the king said quietly.

"They came from nowhere." All eyes turned to the Samarkandian. He spoke in a hollow, empty voice. "We don't know what happened. The roads were blocked against the attack, and all the gates in the wall around Zahadar were lowered. It was like—like . . ."

"Being locked in a prison in your own city," Laylah said quietly. The boy's gaze jerked to her, and he stared at her raptly. "Under siege by shadows and whispers. Not a darkness like that of the sky at night, filled with comforting stars. An absence of everything—and a presence of hate and fear and a delight in torment." She strode over to the boy. He permitted her to take his hands though they remained limp in hers. "They told you things as they took all you loved. No rest, no respite."

He nodded slowly. His throat worked for a moment, then he continued. "No one ever got inside Zahadar. Anyone who attempted it would have been slaughtered."

"The ships we sent last year," Kalin said to the king and Laylah. The king nodded, pressing his lips together. Samarkand and Aurora had traded with one another sporadically through the years. With the defeat of the darkness—at least they had all believed it to be defeated, he thought bitterly—and the new prosperity the alliance with Albion had brought to that desert land, the Auroran fleet had once again opened trade routes. No fewer than eight fully loaded ships had been sent to Samarkand and were never heard from again. It had been ill luck indeed, and a sore blow to the economy of Aurora, but no one had thought it more than that. It seemed they had been dreadfully wrong.

"Some of us could bear it no longer." The boy was speaking as if a dam had burst inside him, and his hands closed so tightly on Laylah's that she winced slightly but did not let go. "We fled. Over forty of us started out. We even had protectors. Those were the ones they picked off first. We kept them at bay at night. They called the beasts in from the wilds to attack us during the day, and the winds—the winds . . ." His voice trailed off.

"That's more than he's ever said before," Sabine said.

"He knows Aurorans," said Kalin. "We are familiar to him in a way the rest of you are not."

"Let him rest," ordered the king. "Sabine, I imagine your

messenger brought him as soon as he showed up in your encampment. I do not discount your hospitality, but I think some rest and food here in the castle will help him."

"Agreed," said Sabine. "He might tell us more afterward."

The king opened the door and beckoned the butler, Barrows, in. "Take this young fellow to one of the guest chambers. See that he has plenty of food and water on hand. And stay close—let me know if he awakens."

The boy's eyes suddenly widened, and he clutched Sabine. "It's all right," said Sabine. "Go along with this fellow, then. You're safe here."

The look in the youth's eyes as he followed Barrows told the king that he didn't feel safe anywhere. The monarch couldn't blame him.

"We must hope he can indeed tell us more," said Kalin. "Information is our greatest weapon."

"Well then," said Timmins, getting to the heart of the matter as was his wont, "where do we go from here? Literally and figuratively."

"Samarkand," said Ben. "Isn't that right?" He looked as distressed of any of them, but on some level, the king knew, Ben was itching for action. He was not a man who accepted peace comfortably.

"Your Majesty," said Kalin, "you have ever been honorable in your dealings with my people. You have kept your word at every turn. It is because of you that the darkness is no more in Aurora and that we have a fortress filled with soldiers experienced in fighting it. Our ships are many and powerful, and we have some familiarity with Samarkand, more than Your Majesty does at least."

The king's heart was sinking. Albion had known almost ten

years of relative peace, and he supposed he should be grateful for it. But the darkness, again? Hadn't they sacrificed enough to defeat it already? Melancholy settled on him. He wondered if the darkness was something that was eternal, if it would ever be defeated, and if his whole life and that of his descendants would be devoted to doing battle with it and keeping it on the edges of the world.

It was not exactly the most cheerful of thoughts. He felt a cool, moist nose nudging at his hand, and caressed Rex's silky ears.

"One thing we have learned," he said quietly, "is that delay only gives the darkness time to gather strength. But Kalin is right. We must learn everything we can and first make sure we are as safe here in Albion as possible. Sabine, do you feel your borders are safe?"

"Safe?" Sabine was practically jumping up and down. "With everything that lad has said, and more to come? Take the cotton out of your ears and listen! They let him live to brag about themselves! Surely things darker than a teenage boy can cross the mountains!"

The king nodded. "Agreed. Timmins, round up some of the veterans from the first war against the darkness and send them back to Mistpeak with Sabine. Sabine, you will be my eyes and ears here when we depart. Kalin, we'll discuss the Auroran navy's role in this and start reassembling an army here. Ben, you'll come with me to Samarkand."

"Not a chance I'd be anywhere else," Ben replied.

"Page, I'll need whatever information your network can supply." She nodded.

"And what of me?"

The question was asked in a quiet voice, but it froze the king in place for a minute. He looked at his new wife and realized to his shame that he had completely left her out of the planning. What of Laylah, indeed?

"I can't take you with me." That much, at least, he knew.

Her raven brows lifted. "Why not? I am an Auroran. I know firsthand of the darkness."

"Begging your pardon, my lady," said Timmins, "everyone here does as well. And everyone else here has taken arms against it."

Laylah colored. "Instead of sitting and cowering in our homes, you mean."

It was Timmins's turn to flush. "I didn't mean that at all, my lady!"

"Timmins here can be a bit rough," Ben said quickly, giving the mortified Timmins a sharp look. "But what's true is that you are a civilian. We're not. Besides, it's obvious our good ruler is so smitten with his new queen he'd be too distracted worrying about you."

"Do not be embarrassed," Kalin said gently. "We Aurorans know more of the darkness than they, for we have known it longer and more intimately. But they are right. This is war, my child."

"And Albion needs a leader," the king said. "With me gone, you shall represent the crown. The people will feel safer with their queen here. Page will stay with you." Page started to open her mouth to protest but closed it again. She nodded, seeing the wisdom in what he was doing although she did not much care for it.

"You—would trust me to lead the kingdom?"

"Well, who else?" said Ben. "Jasper's a fine fellow, but if we left him in charge, and the darkness came here, we'd all be fighting it with the proper silverware."

The unexpected joke broke the tension. First Laylah groaned, then they were all giggling. It was nervous laughter, but it felt good, and the king's head was clearer when it died down.

"Then it's settled. We'll meet again for a detailed strategy-planning session. But until then"—and he extended his arm to Laylah—"I am a newly married man, and I have a reception to attend. As do all of you. Let's not keep poor Jasper waiting."

"Too bad horrors beyond the imagination had to ruin the king's wedding parade," Finn said as he tipped back a second ale.

"They look happy," Page observed. The king and queen were dancing together, and Finn had to admit that yes, despite the dire news that had come on them so unexpectedly, the couple did indeed look disgustingly happy.

"For the moment," he agreed. "Sorry you have to miss all the fun and babysit a new queen instead."

He had expected her to fire back with a sharp remark, but instead she looked somber. "Have you really forgotten what it was like to fight those things? How they got into your head?" She shook her head. "I haven't. And she's not a child, she just needs to learn."

Ben regarded Laylah. "She's lovely, I'll give her that, and she's got a sharp brain in that head. But this is a pretty rotten time for on-the-job training."

"And who better to teach her than I?" Page sipped her own ale, relaxing a little.

"You raise an excellent point, ma'am." He clinked their glasses—glasses, not tankards—together. Right enough, here in the castle you didn't sip ale from pewter like you might at some third-rate tavern.

"Page is right," came Kalin's voice behind them. Ben started and splashed the very excellent brew on the tablecloth. "Laylah is stronger than one might think."

"Does *everyone* have to come sneaking up behind me today?" Ben muttered and dabbed at the spill with a napkin, belatedly realizing that all he'd done was dirty *two* linens that now needed to be washed. As he put the napkin down, he saw Jasper interrupt the dance. The king looked over the crowd, and his gaze landed on Ben. "And there's our cue," he said, fairly leaping up to follow as the king indicated.

They weaved through the crowd and were joined by Timmins. "The boy's awoken," the king said without preamble. "And Sabine says he is ready to tell us everything he knows."

Chapter Three

Sabine sat on the boy's bed. The youth was propped up on several pillows. A few hours of sleep had helped him. He no longer looked blank and stunned but merely frightened and exhausted. He was eating roasted chicken as if he hadn't seen food in days. Maybe he hadn't.

"His name is Shan," Sabine said. "He's got holes in his memory, he says, but he can tell us some things at least."

Shan's dark eyes flitted to the door. He relaxed a little as Kalin and Laylah entered the room.

"I'm glad to see you're feeling better," the king said. "You're a very brave young fellow, Shan."

The boy's dark gaze slid away. "I do not think so, Your Majesty."

"Well, Sabine and I do, and so does everyone else in this room. And if two kings agree on it, it must be so, mustn't it?"

"Ha!" cackled Sabine. "True, true, eh?"

Rex trotted in and went straight to the boy, plopping his forepaws on the bed. He panted cheerfully, then licked the youth's cheek. The monarch was relieved to see a ghost of a smile curve Shan's lips. Then it faded.

"You—you won't send me back?" he asked.

"Sire," said Timmins, "this boy's a native of Samarkand. He knows its history, its geography, far better than we could hope to. He's seen firsthand what we'll be up against. His presence could mean the difference between success and failure."

Laylah gave Timmins an unhappy look. Timmins shrugged. "Begging your pardon, Your Majesty," he said to the new queen, "but I speak the truth. Your husband knows it."

The king looked at his friends, then back at Shan. "I will be honest with you, because courage deserves honesty. My friend Jack does speak the truth. I am planning on going to Samarkand, to fight this darkness of which you speak. Your help, indeed, would be invaluable. But I also know what you've seen. You've already endured more than most strong men could and survived to warn us. If you don't wish to go, then no one will force you. You have my word as King of Albion."

The boy's eyes searched his, suspicious. The king had heard that Samarkand was a place of wonders, of magic, of beauty and peril. It would seem also that it was a place where trust did not come easily. But Shan was still petting Rex.

"I believe you," he said at last, and relief relaxed his taut face. "I will tell you all I know, I swear."

They listened raptly as Shan spoke of a realm in which knowledge and beauty and art were honored as well as wealth and power. A place with an old, old civilization, a reputation for birthing Heroes such as Garth, and a history that was as much myth as fact. He spoke of his own life, of an infant brother, two sisters, one older, one younger, of a mother and father. His parents served the Emperor as all did, not directly, but with their good citizenship, devotion, and skills. In return, few in Samarkand knew hardship. The Garden of Pleasures—a title which had Ben Finn sniggering and subsequently being elbowed by Page—was open to the public. Fruits and flowers were freely harvested. "No one took more than his share, so that others could enjoy all the pleasures of the Garden."

Ben sounded like he might choke.

"I was little then, but I remember. It was a good life," said Shan. "A happy life. There was a saying in my land: No honor is greater, no joy sweeter, than being a child of Samarkand."

"So it sounds," said Laylah. "Yet you seem to think otherwise."

"That was before *she* came," said Shan, his voice dropping so low they strained to hear.

"Who?" asked Kalin.

"The Empress," he said, the word infused with such fear that the very air in the room suddenly felt cold. "Almost ten years ago, our Emperor, Zarak, went with one of our trading ships. To meet the king of a distant land, it was said. He returned after almost a year, with a wife. No one ever learned her name. It was said that her beauty was so great that all who looked upon her went mad with desire, so that she had to hide her face from the eyes of all but her husband."

"So no one ever knew what she actually looked like," said Timmins, rolling the words over as if he were sifting through them for information. "Interesting . . . and convenient."

"She probably looked like a horse," said Ben. Page elbowed him again. "What? I bet it's the truth."

"That, or she didn't want her appearance to become common knowledge," said Timmins. "Perhaps so she could pass unnoticed in the city . . . if she chose."

"The Emperor was never the same," said Shan. "He began to hide himself away. He started enacting laws that seemed cruel simply for the sake of it. All but a select few were barred from the Garden. He commissioned a wall to be built around Zahadar—Zahadar! The jewel of Samarkand! When he did appear to the people, those who beheld him whispered that there was nothing behind his eyes." He fell silent for a long moment.

"You said 'was never the same,'" prompted the king.

Shan started, then nodded. "He did not live long after bringing her home. And after he died, she became ruler in his stead. And the cruel laws that Emperor Zarak had enacted in his last year suddenly looked like acts of benevolence. The Empress ruled from behind the closed doors of the great palace. There was still trade with other countries, but it was limited."

Kalin's eyes went wide. "I do remember that—my father once lamented that trade had slowed down. He said nothing about an evil Empress."

"You were his daughter," Page pointed out. "It was likely he did not want to disparage women to you—especially if the Empress's reputation was based on rumor."

"It wasn't," said Shan, with a bitterness incongruent with his young age. "I do not know what your father knew, but it could not be worse than the truth."

"Sounds like you were very young when she came to power," Timmins observed. "And you certainly weren't part of the inner circle. Even what you are telling us is hearsay."

The king lifted a hand. Timmins had a sharp brain and a skeptical bent that had served the monarch well, but now was not the time for it. "While that might be true, what is *not* hearsay is what Shan underwent. We all know, firsthand, about the darkness."

"Of course, Your Majesty."

The king turned back to Shan. "When did the Shadows come?"

Shan cringed at the word, then took a deep breath. "About three years ago. Slowly, at first. Rumors of dark things lurking in the mountains, in the deserts, in the old ruins. At the edges of the world. Then—I remember my father speaking to my mother of something he had found on the outskirts of the city. The body of a jackal."

"A jackal?" asked Ben.

"It is a sort of . . . dog of the desert. A scavenger."

"I know what a jackal is, son," Ben said kindly. "I'm just wondering why finding its body was worth mentioning."

The boy fixed him with his brown eyes. "It was not a jackal any longer."

Realization hit them all simultaneously. Ben let out a low whistle. "Balverine," he said. At the boy's look of puzzlement, he elaborated, "half wolf, which is our version of a jackal, and half man. And all nasty."

"Yes!" the boy said. "That is it exactly! And things—things long forgotten, out of stories, out of nightmares—they started hunting anyone who went out at night. It is said that she calls them, when she is braiding her hair at night, singing a song and weaving a spell as she weaves the braid."

"Now that's definitely got to be a story," scoffed Timmins.

"How do you know?" asked Laylah, glaring at him. "Perhaps that is the way her magic works."

"Madame," said Timmins, with a hint of exasperation, "I do not think Shan is lying. I've no doubt that a cruel woman sits on the throne of Samarkand. She probably murdered her husband to get there. And clearly she's in league with dark forces—things that all of us here are too wise to dismiss as fables. But if we're to defeat her, we must separate fact from fiction!"

Shan's eyes were drooping again.

"What we must do now is permit Shan to rest," the king said. "Sabine, he will return to Mistpeak with you when he is well enough to travel, will he not?"

"Oh yes, we'll gladly take care of the brave boy," Sabine said.

"Until then, Shan, as you recover, I'd appreciate your telling us all you can."

The boy nodded, almost asleep already. Quietly the adults rose and made their way out. The king didn't notice that Rex lingered behind until the dog whined. Halting at the door, the king glanced back to see boy and dog curled up together. He smiled a little. Rex knew when someone needed cheering up, and frankly . . . well . . . the king would be just as glad to be completely alone with his bride tonight. He inhaled a breath to blow out the light.

"Your Majesty?"

"Yes, Shan?"

". . . please . . . can you leave the candle burning?"

The king looked at the shadows in the corners of the room and understood. "Of course. Sleep well. You too, Rex."

Rex whuffed.

The king closed the door behind him and faced his friends. "What do you think?" he asked bluntly. "Is this true, or is this child being used by the darkness?"

Ben looked uncomfortable. "If Sir Walter could be, so could Shan," he said. It was an unhappy thought. Walter, the most loyal man in the world, had in the end become a tool of the darkness. He had been infected in Aurora and supposedly healed of its taint by the Auroran priestess, Mara, she who had joined the king and Laylah just this day. Walter had fooled them all for over a year. The king never knew if Walter had truly returned then, only to have the darkness overtake him later, or if the darkness had remained in Walter during the last several months of preparation for war. That uncertainty had haunted the king since Walter's death—by the king's own sword.

And now, they were considering believing someone he didn't even know—someone who was not from Albion, and who had a strangely convenient story about—

"No," said Kalin, breaking the uncomfortable silence. "This was how the darkness worked. Poisoning one's mind to arouse fear and suspicion."

"That's true enough, but what happened with Walter is also true," Ben said. "What if we go haring off after the darkness over in Samarkand, and it's actually waiting to jump on Albion?"

"And what if the boy is right?" said Sabine, thumping his staff. "How nice of the darkness to let us know it had sent the poor lad as a messenger. It already told us it's contacted him! It's probably hoping we'll get all afraid and kill the child!"

"I don't like any of this, Majesty," Timmins said. "It's too suspicious. We could send a small scouting party to Samarkand to check out Shan's story before committing resources."

The king looked at his friends, then made his decision. "That would be wisdom, Jack, if I did not feel in my bones that time is truly of the essence. I agree with Sabine and Kalin. Turning us against one another—killing the messenger—is exactly what it would want. I'm not my brother. We have laws in Albion. Someone is innocent until proven guilty. If Shan betrays us, or if we find proof that there is darkness within him, rest assured that I will deal with him."

Both Ben and Timmins looked unhappy but nodded. He was the king, after all.

"Sounds like we've got our work cut out for us, then," Ben said.

"Indeed we do," the king said. "But no more work tonight. I can hear that the celebration is still in full swing downstairs. My lovely bride and I, however, will be retiring."

"Of course," Ben said with a straight face. "Our rulers need their rest."

"Absolutely," said the king. "A great deal of rest. Very, er, *restful* rest. And lots of it."

Laylah blushed, but she was smiling. Ben clapped his friend on the back, bowed to the new queen, and headed downstairs. The others followed, Page pausing to hug Laylah quickly before departing.

The king turned to his new queen. "I'm so sorry," he said.

"For what? For immediately responding to a threat to innocent people? For doing what you need to do to protect your kingdom?" She shook her head. "No, beloved. It is clear where you need to be and what you need to be doing."

He pulled her into his arms. "Later, yes. But for now, this is all I need to be doing." He kissed her, sweetly but passionately. She slipped her arms around his neck, her lips soft and yielding. They were both breathing quickly when she pulled back.

"No," she said. Surprised, he looked at her.

"No?"

"No," she repeated, then added, her voice soft and low, "That is most definitely not *all* you need to be doing."

For answer, he swept her up in his arms and went with all due haste to their bedchamber.

Chapter Four

"Love, wake up."

Laylah blinked sleepily, for a moment uncertain where she was. Memory of the night before rushed back to her and she smiled, turning over to look up at her husband's face.

"It is still dark outside," she murmured, stroking his cheek. "There is plenty of time for more . . . rest."

He kissed her hand. "Actually, it's the middle of the night. We will have some more time to, er, rest later. But first . . . there's something I need to show you. And it's best done at this hour. Get dressed and follow me."

Laylah was confused but obeyed, slipping into a simple dress and stepping into a pair of boots. He placed a cloak around her shoulders. "It's cold outside," he said.

". . . Outside?"

"Outside. Come on!" Shaking her head in confusion, Laylah took her husband's hand as he led her past the dying fire to the wide double doors at the far end of his chambers. She was glad of the cloak at once; the skies were clear, and moonlight shone on the snow-covered gardens. "It's lovely in the summer though

Jasper always said it was sinister out here at night. Of course," he added, "he only saw it at night the one time, I believe."

"When was that?" Laylah pulled the cloak more tightly around her. They walked past the area where King Logan's statue once stood, and she didn't think Jasper's assessment was altogether wrong.

"The night he, Walter, and I escaped," he said. "I'm going to take you where they took me. It's a place I never knew about. Only a very few are aware of its existence even today, and only two of us know how to get there." He smiled down at her. "Three, after tonight."

"What a great mystery!" she teased, and his smile faded a little bit.

"Not so much a mystery—a secret. An important one." They passed topiaries with snow for hats and headed toward a large, stone structure. It led down into the earth.

"Where are we going?"

"I'm taking you to meet my parents . . . sort of," he said, and Laylah realized that this was the royal family catacombs. And suddenly, she was frightened. At once, she banished the feeling— did she not trust her husband completely? Nonetheless, Laylah would much have preferred to be nestled in a warm bed with him rather than visiting his parents' tombs at midnight.

He touched a panel, and the doors creaked open. "I am surprised it isn't locked," she said. She was relieved to see that candles were lit.

"No one would desecrate the tomb of the Hero of the Spire," said the king. "As you can see by the candles, it's tended regularly."

The place was beautiful, in its fashion, thought Laylah. Her people, too, were buried underground, but she had never seen anything so lavish and ornate. Her eyes widened as they approached the tombs, and she gazed up at the larger-than-life statue of a hooded, winged figure that appeared to be weeping into its hands.

"I am sorry they didn't live to meet you," the king said, indicating the stone tombs. "They would have loved you as much as I do."

"You miss them," she said quietly.

"I do. I always will. But their lineage will continue with our children." He smiled warmly at her. "Let me show you something."

He took her to the right side of the winged, weeping statue and knelt. Placing his hand on one of the stones, he pushed. With a grinding sound, the stone retracted.

Laylah gasped. The statue was coming to life! It lowered its hands and—

She realized an instant later that it was merely a mechanical movement, that the hands were connected to a chain. She let out a nervous laugh. "What is it holding?" she asked, recovering herself.

The object in the carved hands was circular, intertwining hues of gold and blue in loops and swirls. It looked like a small shield. "That's the Guild Seal. It belonged to my father, and now to me. And, in a way, to you."

"I don't understand."

"Well, as Walter described it to me, it chooses those who have the power inside them. Who have the potential to become legends." He picked it up, holding it respectfully. "The first time I touched this, it sent me on quite a journey." He smiled fondly, remembering. "I want you to be part of this."

"Part of what, my love?"

He took her hand and placed it on the Seal. The simple gold band that united them as husband and wife glinted. He placed his own hand over it and closed his eyes.

She heard . . . no, the words were not uttered, they were inside her head, and she felt a faint prickling of fear and wonder combined as her husband "spoke" without speaking.

The Seal is my lineage. She who touches it now is my wife, heart of my heart. Grant her the gifts you grant to me.

There was a bright flash of light. Energy crackled around Laylah, alarming but somehow comforting too, in a strange way. When Laylah could see again, she was standing in a brightly lit chamber.

"Ah, greetings, Your Majesties," said a familiar, cheery voice.

"J-Jasper?" She blinked and turned, seeing the ramrod-straight, elderly butler. Jasper bowed.

"Of course, Madame. Welcome to the Sanctuary!"

"Sanctuary?" Laylah repeated, stunned, and she realized what had happened. Her husband had used his Will, what some people called magic, to bring her here. She knew, of course, that he was a Hero, and she had heard the stories, but this was the first time she had ever actually seen him use his Will. Did this place truly even exist, or was it somehow real and unreal at once? She swayed, and he caught her—his hand strong and gentle on her arm.

Laylah looked up at him, and he gave her a reassuring smile. "You're completely safe here," he said, and she knew she was. If this place was connected to her beloved, how could she be anything but safe? She tried to take it all in—the white-and-black squares on the floor; the alcoves ringing the round chamber in which statues, bearing weapons or clothing, struck various poses; on the table a giant map that looked like Albion in miniature.

"Only you, Jasper, and I know about the Sanctuary," the king was saying, and she turned her full attention to him. "Walter did, too. He helped me find the Seal, and came with me on my first visit. He'd heard my father talking about the Sanctuary but had never been here before. I think Ben and Page have an inkling that such a place exists. But even they don't know how to reach it, nor could they—or anyone—if they tried. The Guild Seal is the only way in or out."

Laylah looked down at the Seal, then at Jasper. "Jasper has sworn fealty to me," the king continued. "He has my full trust, and I his. It's a powerful oath. You, my love, agreed to marry me. Thus, my Seal obeys the two of you. I removed a small piece of it to give to Jasper, so that he may come and go as he pleases."

Jasper held up a hand. A small ring with a blue gem winked in the light.

"What . . . is this place for?" Laylah asked.

The king grinned at Jasper. "Please enlighten her."

Jasper beamed. He proceeded to explain to the queen that this site was not only a refuge for the king should he require it in the event of a siege, but a place where weapons, outfits, and other memorabilia from his adventuresome past would always be protected and ready for use, if needed. There was also a book here on how to be a Hero that had proven to be "utterly indispensable," crowed Jasper.

"I am no Hero," said Laylah.

"Nor am I, my Lady," said Jasper, "but we can nonetheless be of great service to this young king whom we love." He coughed. "In a perfectly class-appropriate, avuncular manner, of course."

"When we return I will replace the seal," the king said. "It is safer there than in our chambers, or indeed anywhere in the palace. The catacombs are seldom visited, and it is not far for you to get to. All you need to do is hold the seal and think of the

Sanctuary. And to return, select a place on this map and do the same thing."

"I don't understand . . . how does it . . ."

He stroked her hair gently. "It is all part of what is inherent in my bloodline . . . inherent in being a Hero. Even Jasper doesn't know exactly how it works . . . only that it does. In this, your will is my Will, as it were."

She swallowed hard. "You should take the Seal with you," she said. "If you are in danger—"

He frowned. "My soldiers deserve a king who will lead them, not flee from battle. No, my love. It is hard enough for me to leave you behind. Give me the comfort of knowing you are safe in case anything happens here, and I will better be able to do what I must."

Laylah nodded. It was bitter, but she understood. The last thing her love needed was to be distracted with worry over her. "I have fine advisors. I am sure all will be well in your absence."

"If I have anything to do with it, not a hair on Her Majesty's crowned head will be harmed," Jasper declared.

Laylah smiled fondly at him. "Well then," she said, "surely no harm will befall me."

"At least not your hair," said the king, then grinned. "Thank you Jasper. I know you'll look after her."

"With my life, Your Majesty. Now, if I am not mistaken, there was a wedding at the castle earlier today, was there not? And usually after a wedding day falls a wedding night. I am not so old that I don't know what that means. So, with the utmost respect: Shoo, the both of you."

Chapter Five

Despite the direness of their mission here, Ben found himself smiling as he and Timmins rode up to the huge double doors that served as the gates to the town of Blackholm. It was midday, and the doors were wide open. The only tracks in the freshly fallen snow were foot- and hoof-prints leading in and out. No trampled or bloody snow to warn of anything untoward.

"You seem to think we'll receive a warm welcome," Timmins observed.

"For once, I believe so, yes. I've rather fond memories of my time here."

"I've read your account," said Timmins.

That surprised Ben. "Really?"

"Mmm," said Timmins. "I must be fair and say I suspected a tad bit of embellishment."

"Well," said Finn cheerfully, "perhaps a tad. But if I'd *really* been embellishing, I'd have gotten the girl."

"The 'girl' would have handed your arse to you on a platter if you'd tried anything," said Timmins.

Since the "girl" in question was Page, Finn was forced to agree.

Word had obviously been sent of their coming, for curious onlookers started to gather at the gates. Ben took off his hat, exposing his gold hair, and waved. A cheer went up, and cries of *Finn! Finn! Finn!* filled the air. It was, Ben mused, a damned shame that he didn't get this sort of reception everywhere.

Standing waiting to greet them was Russell, the son of the late "Old Henry" and the Lord Mayor of the town. Beside him was Captain Thorpe, a powerfully built man with a bristly red beard that was just starting to show silver threads of gray. Finn remembered them both. Russell had been a timid fellow and a poor shot when they had first met, but the years and the tragedy he had endured had made a fine man out of him. Thorpe had once been with His Majesty's guards, but had left due to disagreements on policy. Finn had been here six years prior, to help defend the city twice against attacks from hideous Half-breeds, part man and part beast, designed to serve Reaver. Ben's brother William had been among the Half-breeds, retaining enough of his humanity to kill himself and his increasingly mindless "pack" in order to save the inhabitants of Blackholm.

And his brother.

Ben chased away the sorrow. It had not been the outcome he had wanted, but he knew that William had found peace. The years had been good to Blackholm, it seemed, with Russell their mayor and Thorpe, back on the right side of the law, as their protector.

"The Hero of Blackholm," said Russell, grinning, pumping Ben's arm so hard the older man feared it might fall off. "Come back to take up my offer as deputy mayor, I hope?"

"No such luck, I fear," Ben said. "Allow me to introduce Captain Jack Timmins. He's head of His Majesty's guards."

Thorpe saluted smartly, and Timmins returned it. "We know

one another," Timmins said. He grinned and extended a hand. "Good to hear you've rejoined us, Thorpe. We'll need good soldiers like yourself."

"Knew I wouldn't be seeing you otherwise, Timmins," said Thorpe. Ben raised a blond eyebrow and shrugged.

"Well," he said, "since we're all such jolly pals, shall we discuss this over a drink?"

The small tavern that serviced the town was much cheerier and less riddled with bullet holes than Ben remembered it. They were served tankards of frothy ale "on the house" from the barkeep Ben last remembered as holding a sword in his hand and hacking at the Half-breeds. They clinked their mugs, raised a toast to "soldiers and all who value them," and took a drink.

Ben got right down to business. All four of them had looked horrors right in the eye as they fought them. There was no need for softening. Russell and Thorpe listened gravely as Ben explained what Shan had told them and what the plan was.

"So you're looking for recruits," said Thorpe finally.

"Aye, as many as you can spare," said Timmins. "Ben tells me you all stood together to defend your town."

"That's because it was our town," said Russell. Ben was surprised. The anxious-to-please youth he remembered was no more. Russell was still amiable, but he certainly had grown up. "And if threat comes to it, we'll defend it."

"Russell," said Ben, "by the time anything nasty gets to Blackholm, you might not be *able* to defend against it."

"Who says anything will even come here?" asked Thorpe. "All I've heard is the ravings of a young Samarkandian boy. He might have imagined it all."

"Then he must have read my memoirs," snapped Ben, "because he certainly manages to accurately describe something I've fought firsthand!"

"Something we both have done," said Timmins.

Ben had had enough of this. He leaned forward. "Look. Are you in or are you out?"

They were silent for a moment. Then Russell said slowly, "Ben, you came and helped defend our town when you had absolutely no stake in doing so. I can't rightfully say that now, when you're asking our help, we won't give it to you. Thorpe?"

Thorpe nodded slowly. "Just so as we're clear—we're not sending every strong-limbed youth in the village to Samarkand."

"That was never the idea," said Timmins. "Certainly, some need to stay behind in case the darkness encroaches here. But," he added, "the greater the force that can be brought to bear where the darkness is strong, the more chance to prevent anything from happening in Albion at all."

Thorpe grunted. "We'll send as many as we can spare," he said grudgingly. "Though your young monarch better be right about this."

Ben had no response to that, so he simply drank.

The king was proud of his people. Once recruitment got under way, they came to Bowerstone for their assignments on horse, in cart or caravan, or on foot. Some of them had weapons to contribute, or food stores. Others had nothing but the clothes on their backs, a few coppers in their purses, and a willingness to serve.

The monarch kept expecting Reaver to show up any minute now, offering some new spit-polished weaponry in exchange for something degrading and cruel. But he didn't, though Reaver Industries—sans child labor these days—was going great guns, as the turn of phrase went.

Both the King and Queen of Albion were no strangers to the

men and women willing to fight. They moved regularly among the tent cities that sprang up around Bowerstone proper, making sure the recruits were as comfortable as possible and keeping up their spirits. Ben undertook training the most raw of them, while Timmins worked on getting an entire army up, running, and on Kalin's ships.

Sabine had departed for home but left Boulder behind to escort young Shan back to Mistpeak when the boy was ready to leave. Shan had agreed to stay on, to give the king as much information as he could about his homeland. He kept to himself at first, but eventually became a fixture in the castle. The servants felt very protective of him; everyone knew what he had undergone. Shan moved at the king's side at meetings, and even went with him to help recruit more soldiers. Laylah especially had taken him under her wing. With her kindness, the king's appreciation, and the quiet acceptance of his presence, Shan had begun to come out of his shell.

And six weeks after Shan had stood trembling before the King of Albion warning of the darkness that had infiltrated Samarkand, the fleet was ready to sail.

The mood was somber at the last meal before the dawn departure of the fleet. The king had invited his friends to dine with him at the royal table. The food was delicious, but as he chewed and swallowed, washing the bite of roast pheasant down with wine, the king realized he wasn't really tasting it. Which was quite a shame; the rations they would be forced to eat at sea and likely upon their arrival in Samarkand wouldn't be nearly so tasty.

There was idle conversation, about weather, popular theater, and fashion; and finally the king put down his knife and fork.

"We're all dancing around the fact that the fleet departs on the morrow. This is our last chance to be together. If anyone has any doubts, or comments, or ideas, or incredibly brilliant last-minute plans on how to whip the darkness good and proper and be home before spring, now's the time, ladies and gentlemen."

"My men are ready," said Timmins. "I daresay a few of them will be nursing headaches tomorrow, but they'll be there. We've got plenty of equipment, ammunition, and stout hearts."

The king glanced at Ben and realized from Finn's expression that he, too, was thinking of the terrifying shadows they had fought. "I'd say when it comes right down to it, the last one's the most important," the king said.

"I would agree," said Ben. "I've been drilling them daily. They know what they're doing. And they know why they're doing it."

"Page?"

"I stand ready to help Her Majesty manage the kingdom in your absence," said Page. "And I have eyes and ears in many places. We'll hear quickly if there's any disturbance in Albion while you're gone."

He nodded and squeezed his wife's hand. She was, not unexpectedly, taking this harder than any of them. But he was proud of how well she was bearing up. To his surprise, she cleared her throat.

"I will be coordinating with Jasper, Page, and Captain Timmins, and getting regular updates from them," she said. "Page and Captain Timmins have also offered to help train me to defend myself, should the need arise. Our allies such as Sabine and others in distant places are to send me reports once every two weeks. I intend to continue to make myself visible to the public, to keep up morale. And if there are any hints of threats to Albion, I will act on them swiftly."

He smiled at her. "Well," he said, "it sounds like my kingdom won't even notice I'm gone."

"*I* will," she said for his ears only, and he kissed her hand.

"The ships stand ready," said Kalin. "The Auroran people are eager to repay Albion for its aid. You will have many who know this enemy and are more than willing to die to see it brought down."

"There will be loss of life," said the king. "But I pray it will be kept to a minimum."

"Sire? May I speak?" The king turned to Shan, surprised.

"Of course, please, go right ahead."

The young man swallowed hard. "I lost my family to the Shadows and the darkness. I have no wish for my whole country to fall—or yours. If you truly believe my presence can make a difference . . . I will come with you."

The king was deeply moved. "Shan—you are the only one among us who knows your country. We are all operating on legends, folktales, and accounts in history books older than Jasper is. What do you think?"

He smiled resignedly. "I think I could be of help."

"Good lad. Now, let's all finish this dessert because we certainly won't be getting berry pies where we're going."

The King and Queen of Albion sat astride beautiful white horses. Rex, an expert at evading horses' hooves, trotted along beside them, tongue lolling and tail wagging. The king wore his regalia, the cut and style of the tunic and trousers marking them as a military ensemble. The queen, in honor of the name of her homeland, wore a gown in shades of rose, gold, and light blue. The day was cold, but clear and bright, and the winter sunlight caught the glitter of their golden crowns.

The crowds thronged the streets of Bowerstone, cheering, tossing confetti and flowers, their faces shining with hope and devotion to their leader. The king returned their smiles, exuding an air of confidence he did not quite feel.

Behind the royal couple rode Ben, Page, Timmins, and Shan. They, too, were greeted with adulation and approval. Finn seemed to revel in the attention, catching the odd thrown rose now and then, inhaling, and smiling at the lady who had tossed it to him. Page and Timmins, however, did not seem quite as comfortable with being, quite literally, on parade; indeed, Page's horse seemed uncomfortable with her on his back as well.

They rode to the docks and dismounted. The horses were led onto the waiting ships while the king, Rex following, moved to a dais and podium that had been set up the previous night. He waved for the cheering to die down, then began to address his subjects.

"For seven years, I have striven to bring peace and prosperity to Albion," he said, his clear tenor voice carrying. "To an extent, I have succeeded—thanks to the hard work and faith of you, my people. Now, a threat looms, both perhaps in Albion and in a far-distant land. Benjamin Finn and thousands of trained soldiers, along with engines of war and weapons aplenty, will be sailing to Samarkand to meet the enemy in its own lair. Know that I have the utmost faith in my lady wife, Queen Laylah, to lead you as well as I should. She will be advised by Page, whom many of you know as a woman whose passion for justice and equality helped make our revolution successful, and Captain Jack Timmins, whose military expertise is without peer and whose loyalty and insight is beyond question. You may do better with these three than you did under my solo rule!"

Friendly laughter rippled through the crowd. The king let it linger for a moment, then sobered.

"I will do everything in my power to stop this evil, and to protect Albion and all those who dwell here. With your support, we embark today on the noblest of crusades. And we will return victorious!"

Enthusiastic cheering went up. He waved and stepped back, then glanced down at Rex. His gut twisted when he realized that he couldn't take his old friend—literally, *old* friend. He had been warned that Samarkand had freezing nights and scalding days. Rex was over a decade old, of an age where he liked warm fires and soft pillows. To take him into so harsh an environment would be wrong. Rex had earned a comfortable retirement.

"I'm sorry," the king said. "You'll have to stay behind."

Rex lifted his black ears, his brown eyes soulful, and whimpered. The king patted his head.

"Stay, Rex. Stay with me," came a soft voice. It belonged to Laylah. The king rose and regarded her. She looked every inch a true queen, calm and confident, but he saw tears she refused to shed filling her eyes. Impulsively he swept her into his arms and gave her a deep, loving kiss. He heard Timmins clearing his throat, Ben saying, "Yes!" and the crowd going wild. The exotic love affair of their king and the beautiful maiden of Aurora had been very popular, and it seemed that they would willingly support being ruled by Queen Laylah. Reluctantly he let her go.

"Look after Rex, and he'll look after you," he said.

"I know. We'll take care of one another."

Softly, he whispered, "My only regret is not being with you."

"As is mine, my husband and king," she replied quietly. "But all will be well, and we will be together soon."

He tore himself away from her, waved to the crowd, and trotted up the gangplank. He did not look back; he was too afraid that if he did, he wouldn't be able to leave.

To the dark-skinned Captain Samur, he said, "Let us set sail. The sooner we depart, the sooner we can return."

"Aye-aye, Your Majesty."

Behind him on the dock, Rex let out a long, mournful howl.

On the pier, standing by the podium, Queen Laylah watched the fleet depart. She placed her left hand on her heart and folded the right one over it, feeling the reassuring hardness of her wedding ring.

Beloved . . . I will do my best to prove your faith in me. Only . . . come home. Please come home.

Chapter Six

"A few m-more days like the last six and I'll be so w-wet I'll be able to *live* in the water," muttered Ben.

The king said nothing, but he shared his friend's sentiment. The first storm had come upon them barely a few hours into the journey, and storms had been virtually unceasing since then. The swells had been so intense that the ships' cooks feared to prepare meals with fire, and so for the last four days, no one—not even the king—had had anything hot, not even so much as a cup of tea. Then again, with all the pitching of the ships, no one had had much of an appetite. Even the king had found himself in the undignified position of hanging over the railing with a stomach rolling as violently as the ship itself. More than once.

"I thought you l-liked adventure," the king said. It was not particularly cold in the dank, fetid hold, but being constantly wet made one constantly chilled.

"Adventure? Certainly. T-torture? Not quite so much," said Ben.

They and a few others were huddled belowdecks, staying only marginally drier than the crew who were bombarded by crashing waves and pouring rain. The only one who seemed completely stoic under the adverse conditions was young Shan. Considering that the young man had already faced his greatest fear—returning to Samarkand—to aid them, the monarch supposed that anything else might seem a stroll in the gardens to him. The phrase made him think of the Gardens of Pleasure that had once been open to all citizens of Samarkand. He turned to Shan.

"Looks like we're stuck here for a while," he said. "I keep thinking the weather will clear, but it seems to like it all dark and thundery. Perhaps this would be as good a time as any to talk about our plans."

Shan nodded. "As you wish, Your Majesty." Shan got to his feet, unhooked one of the swaying lanterns from the ceiling, and made his unsteady way to a table in the center of the room. The king and Ben joined him. Ben lifted the lantern and shone it over the map, everyone being mindful both of the fire and the dampness. The king saw other soldiers sitting in various corners.

"Come forward," he said. "I may be the general of this army, but it's you who'll be fighting alongside me."

He saw awkward but pleased smiles as a few of them moved to sit on the benches and peer at the map.

It was simple, as such things went. Shan had informed them some time ago that their "classic" maps in the Bowerstone Castle library were terribly inaccurate and had drawn them a new one. It lacked the artfulness displayed by the professional mapmakers, but to the king, it was much more valuable.

"Over here, to the west, is your Dweller town of Mistpeak," Shan said. "These are the Blade Mountains that . . . that I crossed." A shadow passed over his face for a moment, but he continued. "The mountains embrace Samarkand on three sides—west, north, and east. The south is the shoreline of our country. We will make landfall at Fairwinds, a very wealthy port, then follow the main trade route as directly as possible to Zahadar, which is here." He tapped the northeast corner of the map. The king saw the Great Trade Road begin at the center of the shoreline, then arc away to the west before swinging back to the northeast.

"That's a pretty roundabout way to go," said one of the men, then added quickly, "Your Majesty."

"So I said as well," the king replied. "But we'll never be able to get engines of war, or horses, or so many soldiers to Zahadar without a decent road. Or water," he added, "or places to stop for resupplying."

"Over here, and here," said Shan, "is only desert. Here is Sweetwater Trees, the first oasis village we will come to. We can rest here and resupply. Close by, there once was a great city. In the course of three days and nights, it was completely covered by a sandstorm. Very few people escaped. Its name is no longer spoken. We call it, 'Asur-keh-la,' which in our ancient tongue means 'The Place From Which No Living Thing Returns.'"

"*That* will help tourism," said Ben.

"Well, er, we'll make sure we steer well clear of it," the king said.

Shan nodded, not noticing Ben's sarcasm. "Elsewhere along the Great Trade Road, there are a few other small villages and places where we can find water. But one place we should be sure we go to is this. It is the 'Cave of a Thousand Guardians.' I was only there once, as a child, but it was very beautiful. The statues of all of Samarkand's Heroes are there, and it is a serene and healing place. Plus, there is an underground spring that has never run dry." His brown eyes regarded the king solemnly. "You will notice, Majesty, that our path is based largely on where we can find water."

The king nodded. "Go on."

"These spots are where we can find oasis towns. And all along the road, if we are lucky, we will encounter nomads who will be able to sell us food and other necessities."

"Well," said Ben, "this doesn't sound as bad as I feared."

Shan turned to him. "Mr. Finn, what I tell you, I tell you from memory. From before the Empress rose to power and the darkness came. This," he said, indicating a place on the map close to the Blade Mountains, "is my village, Sammah. This, I know recently. The rest of Samarkand . . ." He shook his head. "Majesty, I cannot tell you if any nomads are left to walk the roads. I cannot tell you if the oasis towns have not been swallowed by the black storms of the desert. I cannot tell you that the Empress's army won't be waiting for us right on the shore."

"Then what bloody use are you to us?" The bellow came from one of the soldiers, who had been growing increasingly distressed by Shan's words. He reached across the table and grabbed Shan by the shirt. "We've heard the stories . . . how you claim to have been 'released' by the Shadows to come warn us. Well, maybe you are one of them!"

"Let him go!" ordered the king. The soldier did so, reluctantly. Shan's face had gone pale. "Do you think this had not occurred to me? This boy is under my protection. And if I hear that any harm befalls him, or there are any disrespectful words or actions directed at him, rest assured I will deal with that. Do I make myself clear?"

The man nodded, chastised.

"Now," said the king, "what's that mark, over there?

The sword glittered as it descended. Swiftly, clumsily, Laylah brought her own sword up just in time. The blades clashed, sending a shower of sparks. Her arm trembling, sweat dotting her brow, Laylah leaped back, then made a desperate feint to the left. Her opponent anticipated the move and easily blocked the queen's blow. With a swift, almost lazy movement, the blade twisted. Laylah's sword flew out of her hand, clattering to the floor. As her opponent's sword descended in a merciless arc, Laylah screamed and squeezed her eyes shut.

"Laylah," said Page's voice, calm and slightly annoyed, "we agreed that screaming was not the right thing to do."

"Actually," Laylah said, her voice quivering slightly as she opened her eyes and picked up her dropped weapon, "when you think about it, it would be a fine thing to do."

"No, we discussed this," Page reminded her, grinning a little. "Scream at the *start* if someone attacks you, and you'd like help. Then fight your enemy off until help arrives." She went to the sideboard and poured water from a crystal pitcher for herself and her friend.

Laylah took a few gulps, then said, "You're right, of course. I panicked. I'm sorry."

"I'm glad you recognized it," said Page, squeezing Laylah's arm warmly. "That's why we're doing this. The more you practice and get familiar with coming under 'attack,' the more you will become used to the idea. If something ever does happen, then you won't be paralyzed by fear."

The two women were dressed in shirts, trousers, and boots. Page had said it was easier to learn the movements without the encumbrance of skirts. "Although once I had to fight in a formal costume," she said. "That was interesting."

"Oh?" asked Laylah. "Against whom?"

Page made a sour face. "Your husband and I were pitted against a variety of opponents by one Mr. Reaver."

Laylah was startled. "What? He never told me. I knew that

Mr. Reaver wasn't very popular because of his cruelness to his workers, but . . . he tried to kill the king?"

"He did," said Page. "He has entertainment rooms in all of his houses, where he and his twisted toadies can watch as some hapless prisoner is pitted against balverines, sand furies, and . . . other things."

It was clear that Page didn't want to talk about it, so Laylah let the subject drop. For now. The revelation had deeply distressed Laylah, and she wondered how many other things her husband had kept from her.

"Well," said Laylah, "at some point, I probably should try to fight in a dress. I mean" — and she tried to lighten the moment — "someone trying to kill me isn't going to wait until I change into trousers and tie my hair out of the way."

"An astute observation, Your Majesty." The two women turned to see Captain Timmins entering, giving his hat and walking stick to Barrows. "Mind if I see for myself how Page's tutoring is going?"

"Not at all," said Laylah, though in truth she was uncomfortable with the idea of sparring with Timmins. He nodded, shrugged out of his coat, and handed that, too, to Barrows. He strode to the row of weapons hanging on the wall, examining them carefully. Laylah looked down at her scimitar. Thus far, it was the only weapon she had practiced with.

"Ah, here we are," said Timmins. He turned around and Laylah saw that he had a dagger in one hand and a short sword in the other.

"*Two* weapons?" she asked.

"Why not?" said Timmins, as if it was the most obvious thing in the world. "You may well be the target of an assassination, Your Majesty. You do realize that, don't you?"

"Of course she does," said Page before Laylah could answer.

"You can't content yourself with simple swordsmanship," Timmins continued. His voice was hard. "You need to be prepared to defend yourself with a pistol on the bedstand, the knife you use to slice cheese for a snack, a figurine you can break and use to gouge out eyes, even your own body. Do you understand this?"

Laylah, taken aback by the flurry of words and the seemingly angry tone, nodded.

"Then have at me!" Timmins cried, and charged.

Laylah had thought sparring with Page had been difficult and challenging. She realized now that Page had been going easy on her. Timmins attacked with lightning speed and strength, shouting words at her she was too overwhelmed to even understand. A scant few seconds later she was unarmed and on the floor, staring up at a man who had both a dagger and a sword respectively pressed to her throat and belly.

Timmins grunted and stepped back. Page hastened over to Laylah and helped her up. Laylah was shaking violently but did her best to hide it, folding her arms tightly across her chest. Timmins clearly thought little of her; she had no desire for him to think less.

"What are you doing?" Page snapped at Timmins. "We've only been practicing for a couple of weeks!"

"That's all some of the recruits had to train, and they're on ships sailing to fight a terrible and terrifying darkness," Timmins said. "The king—"

"Was trained by Sir Walter Beck from childhood how to fight," Page said. "Laylah didn't have that luxury."

"No one has the luxury now to let others down—or get themselves foolishly and senselessly killed," Timmins said. "Least of all the queen who's currently ruling Albion." He put away the weapons and rang for Barrows. As he shrugged into his coat and took his hat and cane, he said, "Step up the sparring, Page. I'll come work with her again once she's got the basics down." He bowed deeply, and, it seemed to Laylah, with genuine courtesy, which confused her. "Your Majesty."

He turned and strode out. Page squeezed Laylah's arm. "I'm going to talk to him. I'll be right back, I promise."

Laylah nodded, endeavoring to look relaxed and composed. As soon as Page had gone, she forced herself to calmly put away her weapons properly, then rang for Barrows.

"Have a chambermaid draw me a bath, please," she said.

"Right away, Your Majesty." Barrows bowed and withdrew.

Alone in the sparring room, Laylah finally unfolded her arms. Blood was wet and sticky on her right hand, where she had clamped down on the thin slice across her left bicep. The shirt was damaged beyond repair, and indeed, Laylah had no desire for anyone to see it. The cut would heal quickly once it was cleaned and bandaged for a day or two.

Was she so terrible at defending herself that even a master swordsman like Jack Timmins couldn't stop himself from injuring her?

Or was this Timmins's way of teaching her a lesson?

Page hastened through the castle, racing down the stairs until she caught up with Timmins. He didn't slow his long-legged stride but did glance down at her.

"Was that really necessary?" asked Page.

"Yes, it was."

"There are other ways to teach rather than shouting at someone and making her feel useless."

"There are," Timmins agreed, "and I'd prefer it if this was simply teaching Queen Laylah how to fight in order to keep her figure trim. But it's not. I appreciate that she's suddenly been hurled into the deep end of the ocean, but she either sinks or swims. And I know you understand that."

Page sighed. "I do," she admitted.

He softened a little. "She's got to rule so that this country believes in her as much as they do her husband. And she's got to be able to defend herself in case no one's around to do it for her. She can't keep quailing like a doe every time someone raises their voice or approaches her with a weapon. Do you think I want to hear the hue and cry and find her dead on the floor one night?" He looked stricken at the thought. "She's one of the kindest people I've ever met. It's no wonder the king loves her so much. But she's got to help us help *her* to stay safe!"

"I know, I know," said Page. "But—give her a little time. I'll step up the training, I promise. You need to understand she still gets sore from simply holding a sword."

He did come to a halt now and looked at her. "You treat her how you wish, Page," he said. "But I intend to do everything necessary to make sure that she's strong enough to inspire her people and to defend herself if some bloody assassin sneaks past the guards and into her room one night. That's what I pledged to do when I swore fealty to her and the king—to devote myself to serving them and protecting them. I couldn't bear to let them down."

"I understand," said Page, and she did. The trick was, how to make Laylah understand.

Chapter Seven

After two weeks during which the idea of dry land that was actually both A) dry and B) land became everyone's wildest dream, the shore was finally sighted. The joyful cry of "Land ho!" from the first ship to behold it was caught up and echoed with cheers from ship to ship. Right now, it was only a speck against the horizon, but in a few hours, they would all have to get their land legs again. Everyone was pleased at the prospect. Everyone, it seemed, except Kalin, who stepped beside the king and turned her aquiline face to the brownish smudge on the horizon.

"The sun is already sinking," she said.

"It is," said the king. "It will be full-on night before we can make landing. Not only would it be unwise to attempt to unload such massive weaponry in the darkness, but—"

"But there is the darkness itself to fear," said Kalin. "We will have to wait until dawn."

The king agreed and issued the orders. No one overtly complained—the logic was too sound—but no one was happy about it, either.

"At least we can have a hot meal tonight," said the *Queen*

Laylah's cook, and that seemed to brighten a few spirits. As night fell, everyone came up on deck to enjoy the clear, calm evening. The sunset was beautiful, and the hot meal, a simple beef stew and hard tack to go with it, tasted like the finest meal the king had ever had.

"Look!" said Finn. He held up a spoonful of stew, and the king could see steam wafting off of it. The king laughed. Someone broke out a lute and began to regale them with lively tunes. Many voices joined in, and some brave folks even got up to dance.

The cold set in once the sun finally set. Even so, most seemed to prefer settling in for the night on deck, where there was fresh, if cool, air, and no rain for a change. The king stood and leaned up against the railing. He peered down but could see nothing in the darkness as the ship peacefully rocked at anchor. He looked up, to the north, the shore of Samarkand no longer visible.

But something was.

He rubbed his eyes, making sure they weren't playing tricks on him. No—they were lights, bobbing gently, pinpricks in the darkness but closing.

Lights from the lanterns of approaching vessels.

"All hands on deck!" cried the king. "Battle stations!" So the bastards weren't even waiting for them to land before attacking. They—

A hand fell on his arm. "Your Majesty, these are not Samarkandian vessels. They are the trading ships from Aurora! Look at the colors of the lights—we tint our lantern glass that particular hue of red!"

Relief washed through him. "Belay that order!" he cried. "These are *our* ships!" The bustle of a crew about to engage in attack muted to shaky laughter then cheers.

"This is a good sign," said Kalin, beaming. "The ships are greatly overdue, but they are intact and free to sail to greet us."

"But why were they delayed at all?" the king asked.

"We will ask the crews and find out," said Kalin. "I'm sure they will have much to tell us." The ships were drawing closer now, and the king could faintly make out the distinctive Auroran design. He could even see faint shapes moving about on the deck. He narrowed his eyes. There was something he couldn't put his finger on—something about the way they were moving, in a halting, jerky sort of manner, and there were little lights, barely visible, where their eyes—

"They're hollow men!" he cried. "It's a trick! Battle stations, everyone!"

The captain took over shouting orders while the king began loading his rifle. Beside him, Kalin looked stricken. "Get below and take Shan with you!" he shouted to her. "You're a leader, not a fighter. Let us handle this!"

"I am no Hero," said Kalin, "but I have learned how to handle a rifle. Give one to the boy as well. Thank goodness there are only the eight ships."

The ships were drawing closer. There was no time to argue, so he merely nodded.

Finn, not surprisingly, was already in position. His rifle, dubbed "Vanessa," cracked with what seemed like lightning speed, and the king saw a shape drop with every shot.

The enemy vessels were converging on the flagship *Queen Laylah*. Only eight they might be, but it was still a terrible sight—eight tall ships manned by the dead. Their eyes shone with an eerie red glow, mimicking the deceptive lanterns that had gulled the king's navy into thinking the approaching ships were allies.

"Fire!" came a shout. The ship's timbers shivered as the port cannons roared, striking one of the Auroran ships full on.

"What are they?" Shan cradled a rifle at his shoulder and

fired. He was nowhere near as good as Ben or the king, but he had clearly used a rifle before.

"They were once men," the king answered. He steadied the rifle, held his breath, then exhaled as he pulled the trigger. It struck in the center of a hollow man's chest, and the walking corpse dropped. "They should have a peaceful rest. Instead, their bodies are inhabited by angry spirits, who would live on at any cost. Most of them are mindless, but not all. Aim for the center of mass. Some of them survive losing arms"—he fired— "legs"—he fired again—"even heads."

Shan nodded, reloading. "I have heard of such things," he said. "But I only ever saw the Shadows and the beast-men—the jakala."

Click. Click. Out of ammunition.

The air was pierced by screaming—not the angry, take-that-you-rotter shout of one person attacking another, but the scream of someone utterly in terror.

The king swung around just in time to see four hollow men crawling over the railing. Soldiers were hacking at them wildly, their wits and skill returning. Two of the undead, cut literally to pieces, splashed—multiple times—into the ocean below. The other two made it onto the deck and began fighting, each carrying two pitted but lethal swords.

The king unsheathed his own sword. Blue-white runes danced along its edges as he swung in a wide arc, cleaving through one of the leathery, skeletal, undead creatures. The red light in its eyes went out. Six more were clambering up the sides.

"Crossbows!" he cried. "Dip them in pitch and set them aflame! Aim for the sails!"

He swung again and again, cutting a swath through the lurching things that once were men. A huge boom sounded, and the ship shivered again. *Good. Keep firing.* Some would surely be trapped by the sinking ship, and he and the crew could take those that survived as they tried to climb aboard.

And then suddenly there was another boom, and the king was knocked off his feet as the ship lurched violently to starboard.

These hollow men were clearly not all mindless.

The king scrambled to his feet. Other ships in his navy were firing on the hollow men's ships as well. One of them was almost completely blown to timbers, while another one was halfway sunk. Hollow men were crawling off it like the proverbial rats, heading straight for the *Queen Laylah.*

"We're taking on water!" the captain cried. "Your Majesty—what should we do?"

Panting, the king swiftly assessed the situation. The hollow men seemed exclusively focused on the flagship—and his soldiers were hampered, as they dared not fire their cannons too close to their king.

"It's the *Queen Laylah,* and me, they're after," he said. "Tell everyone to abandon ship. Have them head for the nearest friendly vessel or else strike out for shore. We're not that far. Give everyone a few moments to get clear, then have every single ship still afloat target both us and the remaining two enemy vessels."

The Auroran captain nodded. The monarch was impressed by his calmness. "Aye, sir," he said, and began to shout the orders. The *Queen Laylah* was sinking quickly, and staying upright was becoming nearly impossible.

"We're not going to leave you!" Ben shouted. He, Kalin, and Shan hurried up to their king.

"No, you're not," said the king. "Because we're all going to swim for it. The shore is due north! Come on!"

And with that, he grabbed Kalin and Shan and leaped overboard.

The water was freezing and black as pitch. The sinking flagship threatened to pull them down to the briny depths with it, and the king kicked and pulled furiously to escape. He sank for what seemed like forever, then his head broke the surface and he gasped for breath. Beside him, Ben, Shan, and Kalin surfaced.

The ploy seemed to have worked. The flagship was partly submerged by now and was crawling with hollow men. "Go, go!" the king urged, setting action to word and striking out with all his strength toward a gap between two ships. If the *Queen Laylah*'s captain had made it to another vessel and relayed the king's orders, they didn't have much time.

They had barely gone twenty feet when it seemed like chaos itself was unleashed. The nearly deafening sound of several cannons firing at once made the king wince and he dove, letting the water muffle the sound. He went as far as he could, his lungs burning for air, and when he surfaced he looked back.

The *Queen Laylah* was nothing more than a pile of burning flotsam. So were most of the hollow men who had been on it. The cannons kept roaring as the royal naval ships slowly swung about to target the rest of the enemy.

The king sucked in air, relieved, and was even more pleased when he saw so many survivors. He waved his arm, and gasped, "To shore!"

A few minutes later, they drew close—and Ben swore. Quite colorfully.

Not all the hollow men had been on the ships.

Ben let out a yell and charged, wielding the soaked and useless Vanessa like a club. Running at full tilt, the king unsheathed his sword. The wet hilt was slippery in his hands, but the blows he struck were true. He grasped the weapon and swung mightily, turning the hollow men into just so many body parts. Out of the corner of his eye the king saw Shan fighting desperately, and even Kalin, unfamiliar with swords, was doing the best she could. Several yards out to sea, the skies were lit with red and orange, against which rose plumes of smoke.

They kept fighting. The sound of gunshots erupted behind the king, and he realized that some of the soldiers had made it to shore in small boats. More and more came, firing guns and charging with swords, until at last it seemed that they were finally outnumbering the enemy.

The king continued to fight. Finally, the sounds of gunfire slowed, then ceased. A cautious cheer went up.

"That should teach those buggers," Finn said cheerfully. He picked up Vanessa, tilted the rifle muzzle down, and sighed as water poured out. Vanessa would be usable again, but not without some tender loving care.

The king looked back over the ocean. The fighting was over there, too. The ships were approaching, and he realized sickly that there were several fewer of them. One of the men strode up to him.

"Sir," he said, touching his forelock, "we lost four other ships."

"Which ones?"

"*Sea Lady, Good Boy Rex*, the *Sir Walter Beck*, and the *Tide-runner*," the man said somberly. "Seems like many of the crew and passengers survived, but all the cargo's at the bottom of the ocean."

"No," breathed Kalin, who had stepped beside the king. She folded her arms closer to her chest, shivering.

"Please don't tell me those were carrying ballistae and catapults and other very handy siege weapons," said Ben. "Or food supplies and ammu . . ." When silence from the king and Kalin was the answer, he grimaced and turned away. "How is that possible? They're bloody walking corpses!"

"Remember the scarecrow when we first fought together, Ben," the king said grimly, and Ben grew pale. Ben and the king had met at Mourningwood Fort, where the first indication that the hollow men were coming was when one of them disguised itself as a scarecrow—that came to terrifying life. Or undeath, as the case may be.

"What about . . . scarecrows?" asked Kalin, unfamiliar with the term.

"Let's just say that both Ben and I have run across some hollow men who seemed to know exactly what they were doing," the king said grimly. "At least some of them had enough of a mind left to steer the ships and direct the attack." He sighed. "Come on. Let's get a fire going—we don't want to be surprised by anything else tonight. Once it's light, we'll assess our situation."

Few slept that night even though the fires offered warmth and comfort. Morning arrived early, with a heat that was at first welcomed but hinted at a scorching day to come.

The news was not as good as they had hoped, but not quite as bad as they had feared. Over two hundred soldiers and crew were lost, but considering only five ships were sunk, the loss of life was small. Ben was cheered after locating his friends Russell and Thorpe alive and well, if a bit waterlogged. A few heavy weapons still survived, and enough horses and oxen to move them. And best of all, they had sufficient rations for the time being, including precious fresh water. The morning was spent unloading and inventorying, and the day grew ever hotter.

The animals—horses, donkeys, and oxen—were led onto land and given water and food. What ammunition, weaponry, and supplies had survived last night's attack had been prepped for travel on wagons, which would be drawn by the oxen. Shan sought out the king and showed him where they were on the map.

"We came ashore too far to the west," he said. "The main port city, Fairwinds, is about seven miles east."

The king stroked his chin, thinking. "I rather think we should avoid Fairwinds if we can. Those ships crewed with hollow men most likely sailed from there."

Ben and Kalin had come up while they were talking and listened attentively. "Agreed," said Kalin firmly. "My people only have sketchy maps, but that is the closest port—and the main one. It is likely that it is under the Empress's control—or else everyone there is dead."

"Either way, sounds like a highlight to miss," said Ben. "What about it, Shan? Can we pick up the Great Trade Road a bit farther north?"

Shan looked uncomfortable. "It will require a detour of about twenty miles through difficult terrain," he said. "I do not know if the siege weapons can cross it."

"Lovely," said Ben. "Towns ruled by an evil Empress or dying in the desert."

"We will not die," said Kalin. "But we may need to leave weapons behind if they cannot cross."

"Well, I don't like either choice," the king said. "But I think the one that gives us the best chance is the desert crossing. I've no desire to become a hollow man myself."

Everyone was forced to concede he had a valid point. There were several horses that had been intended for riding; now the noble beasts would be pressed into service as mere pack animals, and all of the would-be riders, including the king—he would not ask of his soldiers what he himself would be unwilling to do—would have to walk. At least until they hit the Great Trade Road.

The king made a point of shaking the hand of every captain and thanking him or her personally for aid rendered. "Sail for Aurora as soon as you can. When you arrive, get word to Albion that we have arrived safely," the king said. "I have faith in our victory, but it won't be for at least several months. Return for us in four. Hopefully, we'll all be sitting here, playing Keystone while we wait for you." There were a few chuckles and smiles at the image. He grinned reassuringly. "I will be able to send up some magical activity that you can spot a fair distance from the shore."

He hesitated. He disliked what he needed to say next—not out of fear for himself but because he knew even mentioning the possibility would dampen morale. Still—the words had to be spoken. "If for some reason I am not able to be present, we have a few flare guns. And if we're pathetic enough that we don't even have *that* . . . look for a large fire on the beach."

This time, the smiles were forced. The king, however, kept up his own good cheer. "Off with you lot, then."

He clapped Captain Samur on the back, then deliberately turned from the departing ships to his troops. His snow-white horse, Winter, bearing not the ruler of a land but instead several sacks of dried beans, gave the king an annoyed look and whickered.

"I know, it's a terrible indignity," the king said, and stroked the horse's pink muzzle. Privately, the king had misgivings about bringing the animal. Shan had confirmed that horses, donkeys, and oxen were not uncommon in Samarkand. Some of them even survived the desert, he said, in an effort to sound encouraging. Better would be the exotic-sounding desert pack animals Shan called "camels," which, they all hoped, could be purchased along the way.

The ships were already the size of toy boats against the horizon. Soon, they would be out of sight altogether. The king looked northeast, where the nearly white hue of sand gave way to the gray and brown smudges that indicated rocks. He felt he should be saying or doing something of great portent—delivering a rousing speech while galloping among his men, Winter's mane flying. But Winter was essentially little more than a pack mule, the king on, literally, equal footing with the lowest-ranking foot soldier, and his voice wouldn't carry if he just walked.

Actions, then. "Right," he said, squaring his shoulders. "Let's go."

Chapter Eight

Page was in a sour mood. She sat in a corner of the Cock in the Crown tavern, morosely downing an ale. The king had only been gone a month, and it seemed to her that his queen and his captain of guards were at each other's throats on a regular basis.

It had been a lot to put on an inexperienced young girl. Even Timmins acknowledged that. And honestly, other than the nearly constant clashing between a queen and a captain who both had extremely strong personalities, Queen Laylah had been doing an admirable job. The populace was loyal to their king, and cheerfully so—but they adored Laylah; if he had their respect, she had their love. Unlike the king, Laylah was not of royal blood—she was one of them, and the few who had expressed doubts about her being a "foreigner" seemed to have changed their tune. Laylah had a knack for striking the perfect balance between accessible and majestic. Perhaps it was that she was always willing to give a petitioner her ear in the throne room, and her manner of settling disputes probably produced better results even than her husband's. Perhaps it was that she paid visits to some of the smaller towns and hamlets, ready to exclaim over their local improvements and snuggle their babies.

The very things that so endeared her to her people seemed to drive the captain of her guards mad. Of course, it was a security nightmare, and the queen—despite rigorous training with both Page and Timmins—was still barely able to parry four out of five blows.

A soft nudge at her knee snapped Page to attention. She peered beneath the table, ready to punch whoever was trying to get under her skirts, then chuckled as she saw warm brown eyes, a lolling tongue, and a furry black-and-white face.

"Hallo, Rex," she said fondly, scratching behind his ears. "Your mistress sent you to fetch me, eh?"

At one point, Page had left a glove behind at Bowerstone Castle. In the king's absence, Laylah had trained Rex to find Page whenever the queen desired her company by giving Rex Page's scent from her forgotten glove. Page didn't mind—it was much more practical than taking a guard off duty to find her, and much faster. She also knew that there was no point in ignoring the canine summons. Rex, it seemed, had endless patience. She plunked down some coins and headed for the castle.

She found the queen in the weapons room. Looking wan and tired, Laylah turned and smiled as Barrows announced Page.

"Not sleeping well?" Page asked, concerned.

"Is it that obvious?"

"To someone who knows you, yes," Page said.

"It's funny," Laylah said. "We were not some old married couple, but—I find it odd now not to awaken next to him."

"I wouldn't know about that," Page said. It was true, in a way—she had not let anyone get close enough to her for the innocent intimacy of growing accustomed to waking beside him. But there was someone she, too, missed.

"And—I have troubling dreams," Laylah admitted. She turned away from Page, making a show of selecting a weapon.

"That's not unexpected either," Page said. "Your husband's gone off to war to fight the thing that terrorized your youth. Naturally you're going to worry."

Laylah turned large brown eyes to her. "Then . . . dreaming about the Shadows is normal?"

"We can have Timmins step up inspections of various towns if you like, but yes, I believe it is in your situation." She went to her friend and placed her hands on Laylah's shoulders. "The king has a great army and has fought this darkness and triumphed before."

The queen smiled tremulously. "Yes, of course. It was he who banished it from my own homeland. It's just my silly fears."

"There, you see? Nothing to worry about. Besides, you have Rex here to protect you." The dog, hearing his name, whuffed happily.

"A single bullet will dispose of Rex," came a voice. The queen flinched. "And of you, Your Majesty, far more efficiently than any Shadow that might make its way into your bedchamber at four in the morning."

A hardness replaced the unhappiness in Laylah's eyes. "You know, Captain," she said—he was always "Captain" now, never "Jack" or "Timmins"—"I believe you enjoy frightening me."

"I wonder that myself," said Page.

"Fear is an excellent motivator," said Timmins, "if properly utilized. It is not my intent to terrify you out of your wits, Madame, but to incite you to face your fears head-on. Jasper can help you with knowledge; the fellow has a vast store in his head and in that Sanctuary, wherever it is. Page and I can train you to fight more substantial foes. How is your shooting coming?"

"Very well, actually," Laylah said. She lifted her chin almost defiantly.

"I'd be happy to see that," said Timmins. "Come, let's ride to the training-quarter area and you can show me."

The queen had wanted to train where the soldiers did, near the barracks. Both Page and Timmins had refused. "It would destroy morale for those left behind to see how poor a shot their queen is," had been Timmins's exact words.

The comment had wounded Laylah, and even Page had given Timmins a dirty look. He had meant nothing by it—it was a simple fact as far as he was concerned. He disliked "coddling" Laylah, as he termed it.

"It's not so much coddling as it is . . . gentle guidance," Page had said. "She improves by leaps and bounds when I spar with her. You make her nervous."

A special training area outside Bowerstone had been constructed. The area had been enclosed with timber and no one was allowed to approach within a certain radius without clearance, and never when actual practice was going on. There, Laylah was able to fire as erratically as she needed to, striking only dummy targets made of straw.

Laylah was taciturn as they made their way there, and continued not to speak even when Page and Timmins addressed comments or questions to her. Growing annoyed with her silence, Timmins said, "Right then. Choose your weapon and ammunition." Laylah selected a pistol, not elegant but one that shot true, and gathered the lead ball, small powder sack, and a few of the cut pieces of cloth that were placed beside it on a bench. She turned to Timmins, still not speaking.

"As always, you have five minutes." He withdrew a gold pocket watch, flipped it open, and waited.

"Begin."

Swiftly and efficiently, Laylah cocked the hammer halfway. She poured a small amount of gunpowder down the barrel, wrapped the bullet in the piece of cloth, and using the small ramrod attached to the pistol, pushed it firmly in place. She filled the pan with powder, snapped the frizzen in place, fully cocked the hammer, and pulled the trigger.

She hit the dummy in the shoulder.

With impressive speed she repeated the motions. Each time, her shots were better. The last one was dead in the dummy's chest.

"Time."

Laylah lowered the smoking pistol. "Well?" she said, breaking her silence.

"You got off thirteen shots in five minutes," said Timmins. "Better than a raw recruit, but not as fast as your husband."

"Perhaps when I have trained with a pistol for fifteen years, I too shall be able to fire twenty shots a minute," Laylah said icily.

"Your aim's getting better," said Timmins, as he if hadn't heard her. "But this weapon doesn't have much range. Work on your speed rather than your accuracy. If you can fire and reload fast enough, you'll be close enough to drop someone regardless. Now, show me what you can do with the rifle."

Page wanted to smack both of them. Why couldn't Laylah understand that the reason Timmins kept pushing her so hard was because he wanted to make sure she stayed safe? And why did Timmins have to treat an inexperienced young woman like he did his soldiers? Page held her tongue until shooting practice was over, then as Timmins was about to make his final acerbic comments, she interrupted him.

"Timmins, thank you. Laylah, it's a nice clear day—we haven't had one for a while. Shall we take one of our little walks? And yes, Timmins, I've my own pistol," she added, forestalling Timmins's protest.

"Madame?" Timmins turned to Laylah.

"Er, yes, that sounds lovely," said Laylah, drawing her fur cloak about her. Timmins bowed, nodded curtly to Page, and strode off.

They headed back toward Bowerstone Castle, walking through softly fallen snow and enjoying the rare sight of blue sky above. "We should see if any of the villages need more blankets," said Laylah, mindful of how her own comfortable boots sank in the snow.

"You have a big heart, Laylah,"

"I simply know what suffering can do," said Laylah. "I would ease it where I can."

"And . . . you know that's rather how Captain Timmins feels, don't you?"

Laylah stared at Page as if her friend had just suggested that she grow wings and flap about. "*What?*"

"You don't like seeing people suffer because you don't want any harm to come to them. Timmins doesn't like seeing you not able to defend yourself because he's worried he won't have taught you the skills you need if something bad happens to you."

"I see. So he's afraid it will reflect badly on him if the queen dies during his watch."

"It's not like that," Page replied. "He likes you. Everyone does. Your being comfortable with weapons—it's his way of giving you a blanket against the cold."

Laylah laughed, but it was not a pleasant sound. "He certainly has a strange way of showing it. I know you're always sticking up for him, but to be honest with you, if we were not at war, I'd dismiss him from his position."

Page stopped in her tracks. "You can't be serious."

"Very. You know I do not put on airs, Page. But he does not speak to me as one should his queen. He speaks to me like — like —"

"A recruit," said Page.

"Yes!"

"Why does that surprise you? His whole family was military. He's rough, but then so am I."

"Oh no, Page, you are warm and kind!"

"If Ben were here, he'd dispute that," said Page. "Just . . . look. We'll work extra hard. The more he sees you improving, the more reassured he'll be."

"I care not about 'reassuring' Captain Jack Timmins," said Laylah, "but the idea of his finally ceasing to badger me is most appealing."

Page didn't mention Timmins any more after that, but she was deeply troubled. She herself didn't have to personally like someone in order to work with them, and she feared Laylah was taking this far too personally. One day, if they couldn't find a way to cooperate, they would clash, and one of them would want to be the winner.

And that would mean that Albion would be the loser.

"I hate this place," said Ben. Despite precautions — Shan had advised them all to cover their heads and faces as much as possible — Ben's fair skin had burned and peeled twice now. He took a long drink of tepid water as he walked. "No offense there, Shan," he added quickly, realizing how the youth might take the comment. "But I'm not well suited to this sort of climate."

"Do not worry, Mr. Finn," Shan said. "No one is suited to *this*, not even native Samarkandians. That's why no one lives here."

Ben grinned. "Lad's got a point," he said, and toasted Shan with his waterskin.

The "long cut," as the king called it, that avoided Fairwinds Port had cost them dearly. None of the larger siege engines had made it, even when a dozen oxen strained to pull them over the rough terrain. Four horses broke their legs and had to be mercifully put down. The going was so slow that they went through their water supply much quicker than they had planned. But now, at last, they were on the Great Trade Road and making better progress.

Of course, they were sitting ducks, traveling on the only, and quite exposed, road. "Before the Empress came," Shan had said, "the Emperor had soldiers patrolling the road to protect against sand furies and other brigands."

"And now," Kalin said, "any such officials would mean trouble, not aid, for us." The king sent scouts ahead and also had some bring up the rear, just in case of an ambush. Thus far, nothing had happened.

"We will need to make a detour," Shan said. "The water supply is getting low."

"We've still got several days' worth," the king said. The sun beat down mercilessly. He tried to ignore it and think cool thoughts. "Can't we make it to the major oasis town, what was it—Tree something?" It was the first oasis town they would come to along the Great Trade Road.

Shan looked uneasy. "Speak freely, child," Kalin said kindly. "His Majesty would rather hear bad news ahead of time than be surprised by it later."

"I don't shoot messengers," the king said, "especially not when one's our guide."

Shan nodded. "Then—speaking freely—I do not think it is worth the risk to go all the way to Sweetwater Trees without stopping. We have lost more days than we bargained for already." They halted while he unrolled the map. "To the west, this road will take us to Sky Blue Lake. It is the dry season, so it will not be full, but we should be able to water and rest the horses and oxen and refill our supplies. The lake is also a stop for the nomads who wander this area, and we could negotiate with them for their horses and sheep. It is only a day out of our way."

The king looked around at his army, making an unbiased assessment. They were already severely rationing the water. Progress had slowed due to weariness and thirst—of animals and the men. He made his decision.

"We will divert to Sky Blue Lake," he said. "We will take an extra day to rest both man and beast."

"I knew there was a reason I liked you," Ben said. "Good call. Also, not to put too fine a point on it, but everyone stinks."

Not surprisingly, they made better progress once word of the detour had spread. Cheered by the thought of a full day of rest, all one could drink, and a swim, the pace was happily picked up, and spirits were raised.

The detour road was steep but still easily passable, even for the remaining heavy weaponry. The sand turned to earth and stone, then to dried grasses, then finally to green. Up ahead the king glimpsed the shimmer of water. "I do hope that's really the lake and not a trick of the eye," he said, mindful of the mirages that could befall thirsty, weary travelers in a desert.

Shan smiled. "No, my lord, it is Sky Blue Lake."

The king returned the grin. "Break formation, all! Don't drink too much all at once or you'll get sick!" In the happy rush that followed, Ben doubted that many obeyed that second order. But it didn't matter. Several men, heedless of who saw them, shucked armor, clothes, and weapons and dove, whooping, into the luscious blue water.

Ben could take it no longer. "I'm for it, too," he said. "Kalin, you might want to look away for a moment."

She chuckled. "You have nothing I have not seen before, Mr. Finn. Enjoy your swim."

Oddly for Ben, her frankness made him blush a little, so he kept his trousers on as he plunged into the cool, sweet water. He opened his mouth and took a huge swallow. It tasted wonderful, sweet and clean. He took another few gulps, then dove deep.

She was the most beautiful thing he had ever seen.

She swam a few yards below him, her black hair floating out behind her like ink, her skin blue as the sky that reflected on the water. Her lips curved in a smile, and she crooked a finger, beckoning him deeper. Eagerly, he obeyed the silent summons, except he realized that the water, which usually muffled sounds, was now full of singing.

He reached her and she was cool, cool as the water, and she floated into Ben's arms, wrapping legs and arms around him and pressing her cool blue lips to his. The kiss was like drinking fine wine, and Ben lost himself in it, closing his eyes as her naked body pressed against his and her mouth devoured his hungrily.

"What's wrong, Shan?" asked Kalin, as they approached the lake in a more leisurely fashion than the more enthusiastic among them.

"The nomads," said Shan, looking around. "Their tents are here, but I don't see them. Or their animals."

"Interesting winds up here," the king said, stepping up beside them. "Sounds almost like singing."

Shan whirled, eyes enormous. "What?"

"Singing. Can't you hear it? It sounds like women singing."

"No," breathed Shan. "Majesty! Call your men back! *Now!*"

"What's going on?" the king asked. "Why do you—"

Suddenly the water was churning, white froth disturbing the calm blue surface. Eight or ten men were already well out into the lake, and another dozen or so followed. Not just followed, they were racing eagerly toward the water, vanishing almost at once.

The king cupped his hands around his mouth and cried, "Stay back! Retreat from the lake! Retreat! *Retreat!*"

Something grabbed Ben's arm. His eyes snapped open wide as he was tugged out of the woman's embrace. Her mouth was open, and he saw with horror that she had sharp teeth, and all at once, he saw thin red ribbons of blood drifting from his own lips.

Ben gasped, inhaling water, and struggled against the strong hand that hauled him inexorably to the surface, the horrible, bright surface with its aching heat and sunlight—

"Breathe, dammit, Ben!" shouted a voice. Ben began to cough, expelling water and heaving as he gulped in air. He was being pulled toward the shore, but he didn't want to go. The song, the sweet, pure, beautiful song, was calling him back, to his home in the water with the—

"They're sirens!" came the male voice again. "Don't listen to them!"

Come to me, come to me,
In the depths is where we'll be
Cool and calming, clean and sweet,
In the water we shall meet.

Soothing waves shall ease your care,
Singing of the joys found there,
In the waters, we shall be,
Stay with me, oh, stay with me . . .

Ben wanted to. He struggled, but he was weak, so weak, and the farther he got from the water, the more his heart ached.

A sleek head broke the surface, and he realized she was coming after him, calling out to him, *stay, stay with me.* Ben cried out, his heart breaking within him, salty tears filling his eyes as he reached back to her.

He was thrown on the ground, a knee wedged firmly in his back. Hands were clasped over his ears, hard. He couldn't hear the song anymore, and he wept for that.

They're sirens.

Ben blinked the tears out of his eyes. "Bloody hell," he muttered. "Sirens?"

The pressure was gone from his back. "Sirens," the king repeated firmly, "and you were almost theirs."

Ben gave an unsteady laugh. "First time I've ever been completely seduced by a woman's charms," he said. The king helped him to his feet, steadying him. Ben looked back toward the lake. He could still hear the song, but it was distant enough now to be merely heartbreaking, not the unbearably devastating loss to his soul it had been a moment earlier.

"How many?" he asked grimly, to keep reminding himself of what had nearly borne him down forever into the depths.

"About twenty or so." Twenty or so good men lost—to those . . . things. "I'm very glad you weren't one of them."

"That makes two of us," Ben said. "How did you stop them?"

"Shan noticed that the nomads' tents were here but neither they nor their livestock were. And I heard the singing. They may be legends or folktales to us, but they're obviously real enough here. Once I understood what was going on, I was able to use my Will to quiet their song long enough to help rescue the survivors. Including one very lucky Ben Finn."

Ben smiled weakly. "One very *grateful* Ben Finn. I guess this means no water."

"No water, no purchasing of sheep for mutton dinners or hardy horses for traveling," said Kalin grimly.

"So in other words, we wasted a day and lost twenty-odd lives," said Ben morosely. The king nodded mutely.

There was nothing more to say. In silence, the men who had survived a brush with a seductive but watery death dressed, rounded up the horses and oxen that had paused to graze, and fell in line to march back the way they had come.

Nothing, not one thing, had gone as planned, and the king had to fight back a sinking sense of impending disaster.

Chapter Nine

Three more horses died, all of them simply collapsing and refusing to get up, the only moisture in them seeming to be the froth on their muzzles. Even one of the oxen succumbed to the killing thirst. It was an ugly fact that with the death of twenty-three men, the water rations went further. It made the king so sick to think about it he sometimes skipped his own rations till Ben caught him at it and chewed his ear off. *What were you thinking? You're the bloody king! We can lose anyone else in this army except for you, don't you know that? Without you, we're all buzzard food! So drink your damned water!*

Normally even Ben wouldn't speak to him in that manner. But Ben confronted his friend and liege privately, and the king saw how parched Ben's mouth was, and how he barely had moisture enough to form the words. And, frankly, Finn was right. So the king began drinking his proper share of water. His body felt better, but his heart was heavy.

After what seemed like an eternity but was in actuality only four days, they caught a glimmer of green to the east of the road. This time, the king sent someone ahead to scout it out. The young soldier returned chewing on roast mutton impaled on a stick and carrying a bulging waterskin. With his mouth full, he said, "The good people of Sweetwater Trees welcome His Majesty the King of Albion and his people!"

A cheer went up, and they all moved toward the oasis with a lighter heart. Sweetwater Trees was a sizable place. As was indicated by the village's name, there were acres of waving trees laden with exotic fruit and what looked to be fertile fields, irrigated by channels of water diverted from a river that flowed from the nearby small cluster of mountains. Small homes made of stone and dried mud, shored up with timbers from the local trees, dotted the landscape. The village's leader met them on the outskirts of the village. He was small and wizened, reminding the king a great deal of Sabine, but without that ruler's hyperactivity. He spoke slowly, in a grave voice.

"I am Pahket, leader of Sweetwater Tree village. We welcome Your Majesty with open arms. If you are to continue along the Great Trade Road, you will need supplies. We will sell them to you at a fair price and invite you to share a meal with us this evening."

"You are most gracious, and your offer is most welcome. This is my friend and trusted comrade-in-arms, Benjamin Finn. And this is Kalin, leader of Aurora, and Shan, a Samarkandian who has agreed to be our guide. We will recompense you fairly for what we purchase, and if my soldiers may camp close by, I promise they will cause no trouble in your village."

"Of course, of course! We are familiar with hosting travelers though not usually so large a party! Welcome to Finn and especially Kalin, whose people we have traded with happily in the past."

After the horrors of the night attack by the hollow-men-crewed ships and the seductive sirens, the normalcy and peace of the place offered balm to the spirit as well as the body. "The oasis offers ample water, so all your men and beasts may drink their fill as well as refresh your supplies," Pahket said as they walked. "We cannot cook enough in time to feed you all this evening, but we will supplement your soldier's rations with fresh meat and milk and cheese from our sheep."

"You are very generous, Pahket," said the king. "I confess, I am a little stunned by our reception here."

The dark eyes went hard for a moment. "What makes you say that?"

The king had been wondering how to broach the subject, and now seemed as good a time as any. "Because we have heard of a great darkness that has come to plague the good people of Samarkand," he said.

Pahket looked away. "You mean the Empress," he said in an unhappy voice. "Indeed, since she captivated our beloved Emperor, dark times have befallen us. We host few visitors these days. Aurora is too afraid to trade with us, and the road is very dangerous. So this is why you travel with an army and great weapons, not caravans."

"It is our hope to confront the Empress and put an end to this evil," said the king, encouraged by Pahket's words.

"That would be a great blessing to this troubled land," said Pahket, though he looked as if he suddenly bore a heavy burden. The king understood. Bad as things were, people sometimes were more afraid of change.

"The king of Albion has no desire to rule in the Empress's stead," said Kalin, whose mind was clearly going down the same path. "He helped my people throw off the darkness from Aurora, and the only 'disruption' to our society has been the saving of lives and the reintroduction of peace and prosperity."

"I have no reason to doubt Aurora's leader," Pahket said.

Which, the king noted, was not quite the same thing as saying, *I believe you.*

"The darkness that troubled Aurora spread to my land as well," the monarch continued. "There is a chance the same thing will happen here, and I must defend my own realm by helping yours. But trust me, ruling one kingdom is quite enough!"

Pahket laughed at that though it sounded a trifle forced, and the king wished there was something more he could do to convince the village's leader. The lingering shadow of the conversation was dispelled once they reached the village. Many people had gathered to greet the king and his friends, their eyes wide seeing so many visitors. They bowed as he approached; clearly word that they were hosting royalty had spread.

The afternoon passed in a most pleasant fashion. Everyone drank water that was clean, fresh, and cool for the first time in weeks, and enjoyed a swim to wash out the sand and sweat of travel. Even as the king stood waist deep in the flowing water, looking back at the village, he saw cartloads of supplies—large water gourds, sacks of quick-cooking grains and dried meats, and baskets of fresh fruit—being pulled by donkeys heading off toward the northern area of the oasis, where the soldiers were camped. Men and women both led the donkeys.

"I have to say," said Ben, "I wonder how far Samarkandian hospitality goes." His eyes were not on the carts but on the women.

"Careful, Ben," warned the king. "We really don't want to cause an international incident so early in our journey."

"Ah, where's the fun in that?" Ben shot back, then splashed him. A water fight began, which eventually left both men laughing and choking in equal amounts.

Cooled and clean, they dressed for the feast as best they could. The king had brought a single set of formal clothing, including his crown, in the happy chance that the confrontation with the Empress would take the form of negotiations rather than war. Something told him not to bring it out on this occasion, though. These were simple people, already in awe of him; he contented himself with wearing clean, if wrinkled, traveling clothing and opted not to put on his crown.

He, Ben, Shan, and Kalin were given places of honor next to Pahket. The feast began at dusk, starting with fresh-cut melons and other fruits passed around on a platter. After weeks of rations, the flavor was intoxicating. And the food kept coming: spiced mutton carved fresh from the roasting spit, root vegetables, delicate greens, tangy milk and cheeses. It was simple fare compared to any meal the king had eaten at Bowerstone Castle, but no meal had ever tasted so delicious. They ate and ate, licking their fingers clean of the dripping juices. After there was no more room for another bite, what remained was borne away to be shared with the soldiers, and the entertainment began.

Several men bearing unusual instruments took seats by the fire while women dressed in lovely, flowing silk garments stood in a row. The night air was filled with songs that, to the Albion ear, initially sounded almost disharmonious but strangely beautiful. The women took no such getting used to. They were slender but strong, no doubt a testament to their difficult lives. Their skin was dark brown, darker even than the Aurorans, and their long hair black as night. The dancing was lovely and graceful as they performed for their honored guests. Ben had a rather stupid grin on his face, and the lead performer gave him a wink without missing a beat.

"Interesting," said Kalin. "The music and the dancing are very similar to our own traditional songs and dances. We are closer to the Samarkandians than I had thought."

Shan was smiling. "It is good to hear the old songs again," he said. "I . . . I have missed my home."

The king squeezed his shoulder. "We're here to bring your home back to its people. So that traditions like this can continue."

"I like *this* tradition," Ben said as the lead dancer whirled and bowed low in front of him, affording him an excellent view.

"International incident," the king reminded him, and Ben sighed.

All too soon, the evening wound to a close. His stomach comfortably full for the first time in what seemed like ages, his mouth no longer parched, the king was more than ready to trundle off to his tent, fall down on the sleeping mat, and be dead to the world.

A few hours later, he wondered if he might be dead, period.

A hand covered his mouth. The king surged upright. He shot one hand out to choke the intruder and closed the other on the dagger that he kept constantly at his side. A strangled "Dammit, it's me! Ben!" reached his ears just in time to stay the blade.

"Ben? What the bloody—"

The king released him at once, and saw that Ben had not come alone. With him was the lovely young lead dancer. She looked scared, and Ben looked furious.

"I've been—er, talking with Shalia here. She's old Pahket's daughter. She told me that we're all in danger. We need to go now."

"What? What's going on?"

"I am ashamed," Shalia said. "Two years ago, the sand furies came to us. They threatened to murder the whole town unless we tricked all those who came to trade or buy. We would sell them goods and—"

"We were going to be killed in our sleep," said Ben.

"Sounds like this has been going on for a while," the king said. "What made you change your mind and try to save our lives, Shalia?"

She glanced down, and even in the dim lantern light he could see her blushing furiously. Few actresses were accomplished enough to do that at will, and the king realized that Ben Finn's charms had entranced yet another young female.

"Well, thank goodness for your sex appeal, Ben," the king said, getting to his feet. He threw on his clothes and grabbed his sword. "Thank you, Shalia," he said. "Go wake Kalin and Shan. But be quiet. We don't want them to know that we're on to—"

Howls rent the night, ululating cries that raised the hairs on the back of the king's arms. The noise was closely followed by that of gunfire.

"Too late," Ben said, and they charged out of the tent.

The fires had died down, and the only light was moonlight. Even so, it was enough to see what was going on. The king's men were engaged in hand-to-hand combat with several of the villagers. Many of both had fallen, some of them writhing in pain, others too still.

Dark forms could vaguely be seen, like something glimpsed out of the corner of one's eye. Sand furies—bandits of the desert. The king knew them well. Their dark clothing served them even better at night, but the king's army was well trained. There were only a hundred or so villagers, and the army numbered in the thousands. Even with an entire tribe of sand furies thrown into the mix, the fight would go to the king.

He and Ben sprang into the fray. The king wielded his sword with devastating speed, the blade clashing against the scimitar of one sand fury. He shoved hard and the bandit staggered back. Two others charged him. With the skill and strength of a true Hero, the king whirled in a circle, lopping off the head of one attacker, slicing a furrow through a second, and completing the move to impale the first who had charged him.

He caught his breath, looking around. His gaze fell on the supply carts. He saw movement, and realized that one of the villagers was stealing water gourds. The king raced toward the thief, quickly ascertaining that the man had no weapon. He lifted his sword and brought the hilt down on the back of the man's head. The robber fell silently, the gourds tumbling down next to him. Sensing a presence behind him, the king turned, bringing the sword around quickly in a blur. It caught the attacker, his sword raised to cleave the king in two, across the midsection. The sand fury fell to the ground, blood spurting. In a mercy blow, the king lifted the sword, drove it straight down into the man's heart, and looked around for more foes. There were only a few left fighting; apparently the sand furies and the villagers realized how badly they were outnumbered and had fled. Even as the king hurried up to offer his aid, the last of the combatants turned and slipped into the night.

"That's got 'em!" said Ben. "So, how bad was it?"

The king looked around. Most of the bodies stiffening on the ground were clad in either the long white desert robes of the villagers or the black tunic and trousers of the sand furies. "Looks like there are only a few of our own people slain. And most of the wounded seemed to have only minor injuries. I think a better question is, why in the world did they even attack us at all? They had to know they'd lose."

He grabbed a torch burning next to one of the tents and jumped up into one of the carts, the better to see and be seen. Most of the male villagers were nowhere to be found, but plenty of the women and children clustered together, looking up at him fearfully. The king realized now, as he hadn't truly done before, how sharp their cheekbones were against their skin. The villagers had been utterly desperate, to attack as they had done. They were more afraid of the sand furies than of death. He felt sorrow for their plight, but it could not excuse their actions.

"Listen up, troops!" he shouted, holding aloft the torch. "Tonight hospitality has turned to betrayal. Most of those who attacked us have fled, leaving behind those who raised no weapon against us. We will not seek vengeance," he stated firmly, looking at a group of women holding their children close. "But we will recover what we have honestly paid for and depart. If anyone seeks to hinder us, then we will attack to defend ourselves."

Anger was still running high, and there was some muttering, but the men turned to begin reloading the carts rather than seeking out the lingering villagers. The king nodded. Good. He jumped down and began helping.

The villagers stayed well clear during the process. Shan and Kalin had survived, and set to assisting as eagerly as the king. At one point, the monarch noticed that Ben was looking around for the lovely Shalia, who had so bravely come to warn them, doubtless at the risk of her own life. He hoped she had not been forced to pay with it.

In record time, everything was packed and the army was ready again to move. Shan had advised against traveling at night, citing the shadows and other dangers. Thus far, however, the only enemies they had encountered were hollow men, who could attack day or night; the sirens, who were confined to their body of water; and the treachery of men. Given the incidents of tonight, everyone, including the king himself, was eager to put distance between them and the traitorous village of Sweetwater Trees.

Several torches were lit, so that they could navigate the road safely. The oxen seemed refreshed by their few hours of rest and ample watering, and appeared almost as eager as their masters to be under way again. As the army marched, Ben fell into step beside the king.

"Shalia vanished," Ben said.

"You . . . didn't see her among . . ." the king said, trying to be gentle.

"The bodies of those bastards?" Ben replied bluntly. "Fortunately, no. But that means that in the end she was just as much a traitor as the rest of them."

"You don't know that for certain. And she did warn us."

"Yeah, about a minute before we would have found out on our own."

"It doesn't make sense, Ben. She didn't have to do anything at all."

"Yes it does. We were, uh, together in my tent. She knew if I found out about it I'd—"

"Kill her? You wouldn't kill an unarmed woman out of anger, Ben."

"No," he admitted, "but *she* didn't know that."

The king had no argument to that and so fell silent. They walked on for a time, and then the monarch said, "Well . . . at least we're alive, and we have our goods back."

"Majesty!" It was one of the scouts who had moved on ahead. He had not had a torch; he had moved quietly, in the moonlight, and now was racing back. "The road ahead . . . is blocked," he said, gasping for breath from his sprint. "Looks like . . . it has been for some time. Manned by . . . sand furies. Dozens of them!

"*What?*" exclaimed the king.

"No doubt part of the pact between the villagers and the bandits," said Kalin. "If anyone such as we managed to escape the initial trap, they would ensure that we would go no farther."

"Your Majesty!" came another voice, this time from the rear of the caravan. "Looks like we got ourselves a spy!"

The king turned to see Shalia, her hands tied with ropes, being all but dragged toward him. Ben's lips thinned, but he said nothing.

"I am no spy!" the girl was saying as she struggled. She looked more angry than fearful. "Your Majesty! I was trying to come warn you!"

It was possible, the king admitted to himself. Ben opened his mouth for a sharp retort, but the king silenced him. "If that's true, why did you flee with the rest of the villagers?"

"Do you not remember that Pahket is my father?" she said. "I was forced to accompany him. I have only just managed to get free. There is a—"

"Blockade ahead, we know," said Ben. "That's twice now your warning hasn't really come in time."

"This one will," she said quietly. The king nodded to the men to release her. They cut her bond, and she straightened, rubbing her wrists and trying to gather composure. "The road is blocked at a critical juncture. The path is narrow, and tall cliffs rise on both sides. The sand furies have had years to perfect their strategy. They have the advantage of higher ground and familiarity with the terrain. Should you try to force your way through, they will send boulders crashing down on you while picking you off from above. You will never make it through."

"Well that's nice and cheery," Ben said.

"I presume you have a suggestion," the king said.

"There is . . . a detour," Shalia said. "Through the mountains. It will emerge beyond the blockade. You will not be able to take any of your larger weapons through it, and it is a route almost as dangerous as fighting the sand-fury blockade. But at least with this route, there is a possibility you will survive."

"What makes this place so dangerous?" Kalin wanted to know.

"It is called, Asur-keh-la."

The words were familiar, but the king couldn't recall exactly what they meant—until Shan spoke quietly.

"It is the place I spoke of on the ship," he said. "Asur-keh-la . . . The Place From Which No Living Thing Returns."

Chapter Ten

"Oh, this is just bloody lovely," snapped Ben. "Our choices are death by boulders or death by a cursed, buried city. Wonderful."

Privately the king was thinking the same thing, but he couldn't let anyone know it. "Tell me more about the specific dangers," he said.

"We . . . do not know," said Shalia. "It is, as Ben says, a cursed city. The sandstorm that devoured it came so suddenly that hundreds, perhaps thousands, of innocent people died in a few hours. No one has ventured there in centuries. It is said that the spirits of those who died are angry and will bring any living thing into their doom with them."

"So," said the king, "it might just be nothing more than sand-covered ruins, as far as you know. This could all be legend and superstition."

"Legends like sirens?" Ben said archly.

"Shan, what do you think? You grew up with the stories about this place."

Shan looked as if he were about three seconds from sheer

panic. Kalin placed a motherly arm around him. "I . . . Majesty, please do not ask me to advise you on this!"

"I will make my own decision, Shan. I merely want to know what you know."

His eyes fixed on Shalia, he said, "She is right. It is a terrible place, filled with pain and torment. And why not? How would you feel, dying in a sandstorm, your mouth and nose and lungs choking on sand, your body imprisoned by it after it had scoured the skin from your bones?"

"Maybe we don't need quite so colorful an account," the king suggested.

"You must decide, Majesty. I would never have taken this route, never in a thousand years. But . . ."

The king smiled sadly. "But it seems the only chance we have is certain death or possible death. I for one will always choose the latter."

"If you're directing us into another trap, girl," Ben began. The king knew why Ben was being so uncharacteristically nasty. Finn liked Shalia and had trusted her.

"The only trap is the one that lies directly ahead on the road. The underground passageway will open out onto Asur-keh-la. From there, we can find the Great Trade road again."

"Do you think the passageway itself will present difficulties?"

She smiled a little. "The passageway to the city of the dead? Not even the sand furies dare hide there. It should be safe enough, I think."

"And you say we'll have to leave the siege engines behind," the king confirmed.

Shalia nodded. "I know how all this sounds," she said. "But if it is any reassurance—I am willing to go with you. I will be putting my own life at risk alongside yours."

"Not if your buddies are waiting to ambush us," muttered Ben, but even he sounded less certain.

The king made his decision. "We go through Asur-keh-la. If nothing else, we shall deny the sand furies the pleasure of killing us."

"We will just be handing them these weapons, along with the oxen pulling them," Ben said.

"And where," said the king, amused, "are they going to take them? They themselves have blocked the road!"

"Oh. I hadn't thought of it that way," said Ben, brightening. "Right then."

The king couldn't help but wonder how much he would wish, later, that they hadn't been forced to leave the large, cumbersome weaponry behind. But there was no help for it. The oxen and the horses, at least, would be salvable, along with all their precious supplies. The king had dealt with things unliving before. And there was a chance that, in the end, this would prove to be nothing but an old folktale, and they'd all have a jolly good laugh at how scared they'd been.

Not a good one, but a chance.

"Our scout reported that the ambush is over a mile down the road. Shalia, how far ahead is the detour to Asur-keh-la?"

"There is a bend a few yards ahead. It is at that junction that an old road goes off through the mountain pass to the left. That is the pass to The Place From Which No Living Thing Returns."

"Let's just call it Asur-keh-la, shall we?" said Ben.

"All right. We'll have to be careful. They clearly know we'll be heading in their direction." The king frowned, thinking. "They won't be expecting the heavy weaponry to go fast, and that's what's going to be the most noticeable. If we do this right, we should be able to get the foot soldiers and the smaller carts well into the passageway without the sand furies realizing anything's amiss. It will take them at least a few minutes after we come to a full halt for them to suspect what we're doing. Spread the word up and down the ranks. Once we hit that bend in the road, we'll peel off a few at a time. Tell the oxen drivers to go slowly but steadily."

Ben, Kalin, and Shan nodded. Shalia watched him go, then turned stoically to the king. "I will show you where the entrance is when we approach," she said quietly.

"Give Ben a little time. You must understand how he feels."

She nodded. "You likely will not understand, but . . . these are hard times, Your Majesty. Frightening times for those not strong enough to defend themselves. My father did what he thought best to ensure the safety of his people. He reasoned, better to sacrifice the lives and property of strangers than our own."

"I can understand how that would be a difficult decision," the king said. "I have had to make such no-win choices myself. It isn't easy."

She gave him a relieved smile. "I am glad you understand why he did this."

"I said I understood," the king said. "I didn't say I approved— or that I would have done the same thing."

"He had no choice!" Shalia insisted.

"There is always a choice," the king replied. "As you well know—you chose to warn us, and now you choose to face the danger with us. Some would say, you had no choice but to obey your father. Things are usually much grayer than they appear to be, Shalia. Now—let's move, and you can show me this path to the Place From Which—er, Asur-keh-la."

Slowly, they rounded the bend. While the moonlight was fairly bright, the king would never have seen the darker smudge against the cliff sides if Shalia had not pointed it out. Two or three at a time, the donkey- and horse-drawn carts laden with precious food, water, small weapons, and ammunition drifted over to the aperture. The torchlights they had with which to see seemed very feeble against that darkness. The king thought with a pang of Sir Walter, and his dislike of dark, enclosed spaces. Despite Shalia's logical reassurances, the king made sure several men armed with weapons went first, just in case.

He watched the first seven small carts enter. When there was no sound of gunfire or anything else signaling danger, the king directed a few more inside.

"I think we're going to be able to pull this off," Ben said.

"I do too," the king said. "But I've got a plan in case we don't."

"Oh?"

The king told him.

The oxen steadfastly pulling the heavy weaponry were only too happy to move slowly. More and more light carts and men dropped out of the caravan, slipping away unseen into the darkness of the tunnel through the living rock. Finally, the last dozen or so slowed and turned aside, leaving only the enormous engines of war being pulled along by plodding oxen. And at last their drivers, as well, gave the beasts farewell pats and headed for the cave.

"Go, go," the king urged them. He had already sent Kalin and Shan in earlier. The only ones lingering near the entrance were himself, Ben, and about six of the king's best sharpshooters armed with rifles. They waited, expectantly.

For several long, taut minutes, nothing happened. Then they started to see vague shadows slipping around the siege engines. The sand furies had now learned that their quarry had eluded them, and they were, apparently, quite baffled as to what had become of an entire army.

"Stand fast, but be quiet," the king hissed. "They may not figure it out."

The shadows ran past, moving with almost inhuman litheness. The king fought the urge to hold his breath and was suddenly foolishly certain that the bandits could hear their very heartbeats.

Just as he had the thought, one of them paused. Slowly, he turned his masked head and gazed right at the entrance. All at once, several bright blades caught the gleam of moonlight, and the sand furies descended upon the tunnel.

"Run!" roared the king. Everyone turned on his heels and raced into the tunnel. Those who had gone before them had a single torch burning, so they wouldn't stumble blindly. They reached the torch.

"Halt! About-face, weapons up!"

There was just enough light to see down the short length of the tunnel. The king prayed that the stretch would be long enough. Brandishing the weapons, the sand furies charged.

"Fire!"

The rifles cracked as the men fired—not at the approaching sand furies, but at the keg of gunpowder seated at the entrance.

The tunnel exploded in a flash of light and sound like captured thunder. Tons of rock came tumbling down, crushing the sand furies unfortunate enough to be in the tunnel, and sealing out those still left outside. The earth trembled, then subsided.

As dust from the fallen stones rose, the king coughed and helped a few of the others who had fallen to the ground.

"It held," Ben said to the king. "Just like you said it would."

The king merely nodded. He didn't see the point in telling

Ben—or anyone—that he had been as nervous as the rest of them. He'd felt fairly sure the tunnel would hold . . . but there had been no way to be certain.

They had prevented their enemy from following them—but at a cost. There was, quite literally, no turning back now. The only way out was through.

"I don't understand him," Laylah said. She and Page were in the drawing room. They had just finished another sparring session, and Laylah was in a temper. "I fought well today. You saw!"

"Yes you did," Page readily agreed. "You nearly got Timmins three times."

"But he never said a word, not one word!"

"I noticed your improvement, and so did he. That's just the way Timmins is, Laylah. He's brusque, a bit grumpy, and probably the best instructor you could possibly have. Has it ever occurred to you that the reason you're making the excellent progress that you are might be because he's pushing you so hard?"

"I don't mind being pushed," said Laylah. She held a cup of tea, and her hand was trembling—not from exhaustion but from anger. "You know that. You push me. He's just—I feel like why should I bother? He'll never think I'm good enough. I'm worried, Page. My beloved is off leading an army to fight the darkness. I've been away from him longer than I've been *with* him! I don't know what's going on, I'm trying to keep morale up and support the people, I'm learning how to be a warrior and a queen when I've been neither before in my life, and I can't even get a 'good job' out of Timmins!"

Page squeezed her hand. "I've talked with him, and believe me, he has nothing but respect for you. He just wants you to be safe."

"I know, I know, there could be an assassin hiding in the chamber pot, Your Majesty, and then what would you do, blah blah blah," she said. Her anger was subsiding now, and she was feeling more wounded than furious. "I feel like I have enough to worry about. I need him on my side."

"He is, Your Majesty."

"He's on the king's side. I daresay he could do without *me* just fine." Page had no response to that, and the queen realized what she had said in a moment of self-pity was true. *Who is loyal to me? Who sees me for who I am, not just as the wife of a king?*

Does Page truly see me, or is she like Timmins?

"Majesty? What is it?"

Laylah realized that her thoughts had been reflected on her face, and she shook her head quickly and forced a smile. "It's nothing," she said. "Pay me no heed. I think I'll go for a walk in the garden to clear my head for a bit."

"It's cold out, but pleasant," said Page. "That sounds like a good idea. We could both use it. I'll let Barrows know." She reached for her cloak.

"No," the queen said, almost as surprised as Page to hear the words escaping her lips. "I think I'd just like some time to myself."

Page nodded. "Of course, Your Majesty." She smiled. "You can always send Rex if you wish my company."

"I shall," Laylah said.

"And of course you'll take your pistol," Page said. Anger again flashed through the queen, but she nodded. She had promised both Page and Timmins that she would never be alone anywhere without a way to defend herself. They didn't need to remind her as if she were a child.

"Of course."

Page bowed courteously and left quietly. Laylah wasn't sure if she had offended the other woman. Page often—what was the phrase? "Kept her cards close to the vest," that was it. Laylah had seen her do so before with others, but never before with her.

She had initially used the gardens as an excuse, but now a walk in the chill, moist air to clear her head did sound like a good idea. She put on her cloak, grimaced a little as she fastened the pistol about her waist, and as she stepped out the door, she said to Barrows, "I'll be in the garden."

"Very good, Your Majesty."

Laylah's boots sank deep into the snow. By her own order, the gardens were now open to the public during daylight hours, but only a very hardy few availed themselves of the privilege. In contrast to the often clear days they had seen recently, today the air was thick with mist. She recalled Jasper's dislike of the gardens at night and decided she didn't like them on foggy wintry days, either. She wouldn't encounter anyone in this kind of weather, and the thought kept her outside despite her discomfort. She walked for a bit, looking at the skeletons of rosebushes and trees as they appeared and disappeared in the mist, then found a bench piled with snow. She cleared a space with her gloved hands and sat down.

She could see her breath, and while the cloak and boots kept her warm, her face felt cold. Cold was something she had yet to grow accustomed to here in this strange land of Albion, and she privately marveled at the Mistpeak Dwellers, eking out a life in so harsh a land, and at young Shan's hardiness in crossing the hitherto impassable Blade Mountains.

It was a bad thought. It led to her recalling the night—her wedding night—when Shan had arrived, and told them the horrors of the approaching darkness. She wanted her love back safely, wanted to wake up beside him. Laylah had understood that life as a queen would be far different from the ordinary life she had always expected to lead, and had accepted that. But to have him ripped away from her so very soon, perhaps never to come back—

It overwhelmed her. She was so very miserable. Her husband was gone, Timmins hounded her daily, and even Page didn't seem to be quite the friend Laylah had thought. She had no one. She felt alone in a way nobody could imagine.

She bowed her head, and, alone, let the tears flow, hot down her cold cheeks. *My love, my love, I miss you . . .*

"Dear, dear," came an aristocratic voice. "How terribly distressing to happen upon so lovely a young lady in such a sorrowful state. Here, please do take my handkerchief."

Laylah turned, her hand on her pistol. There was no one there! Her heart sped up for a moment until a tall, elegant, dark-haired man materialized as if birthed by the fog. While he wore a cloak against the weather, the stranger also sported a top hat with goggles perched on the brim. His clothes were elegant and bespoke considerable wealth. He handed her a white handkerchief.

"Thank you," Laylah said, gathering what dignity she had left around her even as she pulled the cloak more tightly about her slim frame. The stranger carefully swept off the snow on the bench with a gloved hand and, uninvited, sat down beside her.

"You are most welcome, Your Majesty," he said. "Now, pray tell me, what troubles you, and how can I best serve my lovely liege?"

So, even though she was simply dressed and her cloak was far less elaborate than his, he had recognized her. As she looked at him, she realized that he powdered his face slightly, and his thin lips were very red, but not from the cold of the day. There was a sharpness to him, a precise crispness that reminded her of the cold. She noticed that he had a small heart tattoo on one cheek.

"You are most kind, sir, but I fear there is nothing you can do. I am just being a silly girl who misses her husband. No doubt I have tarnished your image of a queen, and I apologize."

"Not at all, Your Majesty," he said heartily. "It is heartening to know that one's rulers are people, just like oneself. And I think that perhaps I can be of help to you. A very great help indeed."

She smiled at his assurance despite herself and handed him his handkerchief, which had the letter "R" embroidered on it. "And who might you be, Mr. Very Great Help Indeed?"

He put a hand over his heart, mindful of the extravagant cravat. "Perhaps you have heard of me. My name, dear lady," he said, "is Reaver."

Chapter Eleven

"Reaver?" gasped Laylah, her eyes widening. Her heart had only just slowed from the start he had given her; now it began to pound again. She had heard stories, all right; stories about his charm and his brutality, his selfishness and ego. The king had established a détente with the man, but Page loathed him. And now, here he was, manifesting like something out of a fairy tale.

He gave her a rueful smile. "I see that those who would slander me have already done so to your ears."

"My husband does not slander," she snapped, getting to her feet. Beneath the cloak, her trembling hand clasped the pistol. "He and Page have both told me of your schemes and your greed!"

His elegantly plucked brows lifted. "Schemes? Greed?" He gave her a wounded look.

"You even—" She could barely get the words out. "You made sport of their lives! Pitting them against all sorts of enemies in some kind of, of gladiatorial combat to entertain your guests?"

"That was a long, long time ago," he said, "and surely the evidence that all has been made right can be found in the fact that His Majesty did adopt some of my proposals shortly after his coronation."

"And rejected many more," Laylah said. She shouldn't even be speaking to this man. She turned to call one of the guards. Swift as a cat, Reaver was on his feet, standing close to her.

"Page is an impractical idealist, and that stuffed shirt of a military mannequin Captain Jack Timmins is insufferable. Your husband is someone I respect and can work with. But he has left you with terribly poor advisors," Reaver said. "I admit I have flaws. Though poor fashion isn't one." He gave her a playful little smile. "Your husband and I found a way to work together for the good of the kingdom. Granted, we didn't always see eye to eye on everything. Such strong personalities are bound to clash from time to time. But I tell you this: My fate and my fortune, which is considerable, is tied in with that of the kingdom. And therefore, I want to see this realm as safe and prosperous as anyone in this world—including the King of Albion."

Before he had had an impish, almost mocking air. But now he looked deadly serious to Laylah, and she knew in her bones that he was not lying. She swallowed, still wondering if she ought to call the guards.

"I have more experience in how to manage people than either Page or Timmins. And now that your husband, the lone voice of reason crying in the wilderness that is Albion politics, has departed for the noble cause of aiding one country while protecting his own, people who have absolutely *no* head for business are trying to run Albion in his absence."

"What exactly is it you want?" asked Laylah cautiously. She was still deeply skeptical of this man, who, by all accounts, was not to be trusted—and who, perversely, was also known to have his own peculiar code of honor.

"Want, or want to do for you?"

"Either. Both."

"Well, I see no reason to feign Page's pitiable idealism. I want to continue to expand my businesses and increase my profits, naturally."

"Naturally."

"And I want to provide you with the experience of many years spent being a Hero myself. I've traveled all around this world and learned more things than you can imagine."

That, Laylah thought, was also likely very true.

"If you would merely admit me to your circle of advisors, all my wisdom and experience are yours to command." He executed a perfect bow.

Laylah considered. She might be inexperienced, but she wasn't a fool. She had been warned how dangerous and slippery this man could be. But Reaver raised several good points. It would be foolish not to avail herself of what he offered. It was just advice, which she could take or leave. He would have no real position of power, and as he had quite frankly pointed out, his own greed would ensure his loyalty.

"I will consider your request," she said.

The passageway through the cliff side blocked the sun and stayed at a steady temperature, which was a welcome relief. It also had clearly once been used with great frequency, though not for some time. There were cobwebs aplenty, but the route was large and open and the stones over which they traveled well-worn. Compared to trying to heave siege weaponry across soft, shifting sand or hard, nearly impassable rocks, this was almost a pleasant stroll. Shalia had told them that long ago, trade between Sweetwater Trees village and Asur-keh-la had been frequent and beneficial.

"Until the Black Storm came," she said in a low voice as she walked beside Ben and the king. They were at the forefront of the caravan, and the sounds of booted footfalls, carts, and horses' hooves echoed behind them.

"Samarkandians are hardy people," the king said. "To us, your land is exotic and full of wonder. And yet you face such perils as sandstorms or drought regularly. That, to me, is most wondrous of all."

"You are kind, Your Majesty," she said. "And yes, we have always had to deal with such things. This, we accept." Her face grew hard in the light of the torch she carried. "It is what the Empress has brought upon us that will destroy us. I love my home, Your Majesty. I took no joy in betraying my family and friends, and truly, they took no joy in betraying others. My father saw it as the only way the village could survive. If you triumph, and the Empress is defeated, that can only help my people."

"It must have been a terrible choice for you," the king said sympathetically.

She looked up at him, her dark eyes serene. "It was no choice at all. We were losing who we were."

The king thought about Shalia and Shan. As with the Aurorans, they had been strangers in a most alien fashion. And yet, as he had with the Aurorans, he was finding he liked and respected their courage and their rich culture. Even though his army had already suffered many setbacks, he was even more certain now that coming here had been the right thing to do. For Albion, and for this land of proud, hardy people.

The way seemed to be lightening subtly. At first the king thought his eyes were playing tricks on him, but no—it was definitely growing brighter. "Halt," he ordered, and as the message was passed back he heard the echoing sounds cease.

He nodded to a pair of scouts, who hastened ahead. They reported back a few moments later.

"Sir," one of them said, "We . . . see nothing. Just a stretch of sand."

"That is all that is left of a great city," said Shalia. "The Black Storm has swallowed it all."

While the king did not wish to pooh-pooh the strong conviction that both Shan and Shalia seemed to have that the city was a horrible place, he thought their concern unwarranted. It was the site of a great tragedy, true, but seemed to be nothing more.

"Let us be about crossing it then," he said.

The army moved out of the tunnel, the light growing stronger with each step until they were once more in the familiar, nearly blinding whiteness and heat of sun on sand. The scouts had been completely accurate. Nothing was left to indicate that this place had ever been anything other than simply another stretch of desert wasteland. It loomed ahead of them, shocking blue sky and nearly white sand, a daunting path. He debated waiting for the coolness of nightfall but did not want to risk getting lost. Better to press on in the daylight.

It was slow going. The carts sank into the sand, and the oxen and donkeys struggled to pull them. The army had to stop often to rest. The sun beat down mercilessly, and their sweat dried instantly on their skins.

The sun began to sink, and both Shan and Shalia looked agitated. "We still have far to go," Shalia warned.

"Maybe," said Ben, "but it'd be safer to make camp here. I don't much fancy getting lost in this place."

"No, please!" Shalia insisted. The sun touched the horizon. And the sand began to shift under their very feet.

The king suddenly realized the true depth of the danger they were in, and why the city was rumored to be cursed. They did not only have to worry about the sand covering the city of Asur-keh-la, or the hot sun that beat down upon it.

They were facing the citizens of The Place From Which No Living Thing Returns.

Hundreds of hollow men burst forth, clawing their way up from the sand that had buried them so long ago—that had filled their lungs as they cried out in terror. Some were nothing more than bleached skeletons whose remains had only been recently covered by the shifting sands of the cruel desert. Others had been buried deep over centuries, preserved and desiccated, their faces like leather masks, bodies nearly intact though thin as rails. But they were all identical in their rage and hatred as they charged at the living. Some carried swords, some rocks or fragments of pottery as ancient as themselves. Others were armed only with their bony hands, which were peril enough. The numbers were staggering—it seemed the entire population of the once-thriving city had lain dormant here, to be awakened by the approach of the living.

More than swords and rifles were called for here if the army was to survive. As others charged into the fray with blades and bullets, the king held back, took a deep breath, and summoned the third skill that was the birthright of Heroes: Will.

Focusing on the strength of his intention and the power of his mind, he moved his hands in a pattern in the air. He called to him a power more than physical. And that power obeyed the call.

Chains of blue lightning sprang forward from his hands, and the king set the captured magic loose on six shambling corpses. The dried bones were pulverized into dust, but the mummified hollow men continued on. Keeping his concentration sharp, he conjured a ball of fire and hurled it at them, and their dried flesh curled as it slowly burned.

He turned, assessing where best he could attack. Something closed like a vise around his ankle and pulled hard. The king fell face-first onto the sand, and felt himself being dragged downward into the sinkhole to keep the dead men company. He struggled, but he could find nothing to grasp onto, nor could he even see his opponent. Merciless sand filled his mouth as he tried to call out for aid, then something lightly struck the back of his head.

"Hold on!" came Kalin's voice. The king grasped at what had been tossed to him, realizing as his flailing, blind hands grabbed it that it was the reins of a horse. He was buried up to his chest now. Coughing violently, he wrapped the reins around his hands.

"Hah! Hah!" Kalin shouted to the horse, and the beast surged forward. His belly scraping along the sand, the king and his undead enemy were dragged forward. Twisting around so that he was on his back, the king managed to grasp his sword and brought it down, hacking at his foe. The undead hand was severed at the wrist and the king scrambled backwards, struggling to his feet as the owner of the arm rose from the sand.

In its remaining hand, it clutched a scimitar, which slashed down at the monarch with shocking speed. The king was barely able to parry, his body quivering with the strain while his left hand summoned energy. He blasted the hollow man at close range with a whirling ball of fire.

"Thank you," he said to Kalin. She sat atop Winter, nodding briefly as she reloaded her rifle.

The fight raged around them. Their enemy was not only the ghoulish undead creatures but the sand itself, shifting each time a new enemy erupted. Men were dying as the king had nearly died, choking as the original denizens of this place had choked — buried alive.

That was it.

"Kalin," he said. "Find Shan and Ben. Tell them to press on as fast as they can. They're not to stop to fight unless they have to."

She looked around at the sand that seemed to be a living thing, realized what he intended to do, and clapped heels to Winter's sides. The noble beast hastened off.

While the army would be retreating north, to catch up to the main road, the king turned to the south. He ran as fast as he could, skirting the fighting clusters of living and dead and aiming for solid ground—at least as solid as sand could be. Once the tide began to shift from hand-to-hand fighting to retreat, the king put his plan into action. He scanned the area, searching for a roiling patch of sand that presaged the emergence of another cluster of hollow men. Racing toward it, he dropped to his knees, pressed his hands down onto the hot surface, and sent a blast of magical energy down toward the ruins of the buried city. The shock wave rippled through the ground, then the area was still, save for pockets where the sand began to sink as it adjusted to encase what had been disturbed beneath. The king got to his feet, rifle at the ready, but no skeletal creature clawed its way to the surface.

He worked his way north, reburying the ancient city, sending its unnatural inhabitants back to another few centuries of slumber until the presence of living things once again roused their envy. He followed his embattled army, closing the distance until at last the only hollow men that remained were those on the surface. He unslung his rifle and joined in the fray, dropping the foe with shot after perfect shot, reloading so quickly his hands were a blur. Once his men realized they did not need to fear wave after wave of hollow men, they made short work of the mere few dozen that remained.

Silence fell, punctuated by one or two more random shots as the last stragglers of The Place From Which No Living Thing Returns were destroyed. Then the cheering started. The king took Winter's reins from a weary but smiling Kalin and began to ride among the troops, congratulating them and calling their attention back to him.

"Today," he said, "we put an end to a legend which has struck fear into the hearts of the Samarkandians for centuries. I grieve for the terror that the inhabitants of Asur-keh-la must have felt when their city was swallowed by the sand. But we have faced hollow men before, and may well do so again. Unnatural they may be, and well might we call them cursed after such tragic deaths. But invincible, they are not. This is no longer a place from which no living thing returns. Not for the army of Albion!"

"For Albion! For Albion!" came the cheer. The king held up his hand for silence, then, smiling at Shan, he shouted, "For Samarkand!"

"For Samarkand! For Samarkand!"

Shalia threw her arms around Ben and kissed him.

Chapter Twelve

P age met Timmins as they both entered Bowerstone Palace. Rex, who had once again fetched Page, wagged his tail and licked Timmins's hand as the captain of the guards petted him.

"Good dog," said Timmins, his normally reserved mien breaking into an affectionate smile. "Hello, Page. Do you know what all this is about? We don't usually meet with the queen this day of the week—for either a conference or training."

"I've no idea, I was hoping you might." Page was very fond of Laylah, but she had been right in the middle of meeting with her own people when Rex had scratched at the door, demanding admittance. She was beginning to resent being—well, "fetched" by a dog at Her Majesty's whim. But then again, Laylah *was* the queen of Albion. Page supposed she could fetch whomever she jolly well pleased.

"Not a clue," said Timmins. "I am sure we'll find out."

Barrows greeted them politely. "Follow me, please," he said. "They are waiting for you in the War Room."

Timmins and Page exchanged confused glances. They? Who were "they?" Page wondered if for some reason the queen had received a messenger from another part of the kingdom, and perhaps this was the reason for the unusual summons. Was the darkness already threatening Albion? Worry gnawed at her, and she quickened her pace.

Barrows opened the door and Page and Timmins stepped inside. Laylah was there, looking uneasy and fiddling with her hands. Page's concern increased. "Majesty, we came as soon as possible. What's wrong?"

"Actually," said a horribly familiar, self-satisfied voice, "everything could not be more right." Page whirled, her fists clenched.

"You!" Page snarled.

Reaver smirked and bowed so low it was a slap in the face, his hat sweeping the floor. "And a pleasure it is to see you again too, my dear Page. Ah, Captain Timmins. You're looking even more cross than usual."

"What are you doing here, Reaver?" snapped Timmins. His hand clutched his walking stick which, Page knew, sheathed an extremely sharp sword.

"I asked him here," came the completely unexpected answer from Laylah. Page turned and stared at her friend.

"I must be going mad," Page said, biting off the words. "I thought you said you asked him here."

"I did," said Laylah. She looked unsure of herself, and therefore spoke more firmly than usual.

"Laylah, may I have a word with you?" said Page. She stepped forward and started to take Laylah's arm and steer her into a quiet corner.

"I think," drawled Reaver, "that you should perhaps not take quite so familiar an attitude with your monarch."

Timmins snorted. "Since when do you give any real respect to anyone, even a queen?"

"Since Her Royal Majesty graciously welcomed me into her

inner circle of advisors," Reaver said, and the corners of his lips curled tightly at Timmins's expression. "Tut, tut. Both of you are severely lacking in manners."

Page's heart turned to ice in her chest. She turned to Laylah, incredulous. "Please," she said quietly, "please tell me he's full of—"

"Ah, ah, watch your tongue, dear Page! Just because one comes from the gutters doesn't mean one must speak with a sewer mouth," interrupted Reaver.

"Come with me, Page. Timmins." Laylah did not wait to see if they followed, but moved to a corner. Barrows moved to Reaver and, as if in a dream, Page followed, hearing the butler ask the single-most-despicable person in the world if he would like milk or lemon with his tea.

"I know you two have both had problems with Reaver in the past," Laylah began.

"Problems?" Timmins almost yelped the word. Laylah gave him an angry glance. "The word doesn't even begin to describe the run-ins we've had with this—this—"

"You know, it hadn't occurred to me until just now, but perhaps Reaver is right. You *are* lacking in manners, Captain. Mr. Reaver approached me in the gardens yesterday. I had heard the stories you, Mr. Finn, and my husband had told me about him, of course, and I was distressed to see him."

"You shouldn't have even spoken to him," Page said hotly. She wasn't looking at her friend. She didn't dare. She had the terrible feeling if she took her eyes off Reaver for even a moment, something disastrous would happen.

"And you, Page," said Laylah. "Look at me when I am speaking to you!"

Page dragged her eyes back to Laylah but couldn't help clenching her jaw. Every instinct, and every experience she'd ever had with the rat, screamed at her that Reaver's presence here was a bad idea.

"He pointed out that he, too, was a Hero, and a companion of the late king. He has experience and knowledge and economic assets of his own he has offered to contribute."

Timmins snorted. "If Reaver offers to help, it is only to help Reaver."

"Precisely," said Laylah, startling them both. "He made no bones about the fact that he wished to further his own self-interest. You may not like him—nor, frankly, do I—but he *does* have something to offer, and for now at least, a stable, prosperous, safe kingdom benefits him just as much as it does us." Her expression gentled somewhat, and she squeezed Page's arm. "His ego is enormous, and he made no attempt to hide it. Trust me, my friend, if he had come to me telling me he wished to do what was best for Albion for Albion's sake, I would not have believed him. I may not be as worldly as either of you, but I'm not a fool."

Page and Timmins looked at one another. Though the thought rankled, Page had to admit, it made sense. Reaver would never be called altruistic, but where his desires dovetailed with theirs, he could be a valuable asset.

"We don't need him," Timmins said bluntly. "We are currently peaceful and prosperous."

"My sources have reported no signs of unrest or unusual hardship," Page added. "I understand your reasoning, Your Majesty, but I see no reason to take the risk."

Laylah's lips pressed together, and Page realized with a horrible jolt that she had said exactly the wrong thing. "Risk? Do you truly think I would put my husband's kingdom at *risk*?"

"Of course not, Your Majesty. I'm just saying what Captain Timmins says—we don't need him. You're managing the kingdom just fine on your own! Any help this . . . person . . . offers will come at a price, believe me!"

"Captain Timmins doubts my ability to defend myself. I understood that. But you, Page—you doubt my ability to *think* for myself!"

"Majesty, you know that's not true! What I'm trying to tell you—"

"Trying to tell me? Because I am too simple to comprehend?"

Page gave Reaver a hate-filled stare. Infuriatingly, he merely lifted his cup of tea in mock salute. She stalked over to him and shoved her face up to his. "I don't know what your game is, Reaver, but I know you're up to something."

"The one thing you've never quite been able to get through your admittedly lovely head, dear Page, is that some of my ideas were actually good ones. If the king had listened solely to you close to a decade ago past, I doubt that any one of us would be alive to be having this present conversation. Well," he amended, "myself, perhaps."

Page flushed with fury. The worst thing about it was—Reaver was *right*, damn him. The kingdom had needed money in order to arm itself to defeat the darkness. Page had been so passionate about not letting the king descend to Reaver's level that she locked horns with the scum every time—even when his ideas, if not moral or admirable, had brutal practicality to them.

"Aha!" Reaver exclaimed at her expression, lifting a hand to his cravat-covered heart. "Dare I say that Page agrees with me? Let us trumpet the astounding news from the highest tower, for this truly is a day when we shall find pork in the treetops."

"Silence, all of you!"

Stunned by the outburst from the normally soft-spoken woman, everyone fell silent. Laylah stood before them, her fists clenched, her jaw set, her eyes snapping anger. "Reaver—it is no secret that you are in this for yourself, and aiding the kingdom is merely a happy side effect."

Reaver bowed.

"Timmins—I didn't expect you to approve. But I *did* expect you to at least honor my title as your queen. You have no right or authority to dismiss Reaver should I choose to ask his advice. And Page . . ."

Page's heart shrank within her at the hurt in Laylah's eyes. "I know you detest Reaver. I know you clash at every opportunity. How, then, could you think I would be taken in by him?"

"I didn't—" Page began, knowing even as she spoke that on some level, she had believed just such a thing.

"I said, silence!" Laylah lifted her hand imperiously, and for the first time since Page had known her, truly looked like a confident queen. "You are dismissed for now, Page. And you, Captain Timmins. I will not demote you from the positions my husband established for you. You will continue to serve as members of my council of advisors. But you will serve only as I require you."

Page had not had an easy life. She had grown up on the streets of the slums of Bowerstone, her only escape the rare luxury of reading. Poverty and brutality had not crushed her idealism, but it had made her keep her heart safer than anything that could be protected by a lock and key. Thrice she had dared grant entrance to her heart on any level: to His Majesty the King of Albion, as a true and loyal servant, to Ben Finn, as a companion and occasionally romantic friend, and to this girl, so lost and alone had she seemed in this brave new world of Albion. And now, Page felt the punishment of such relaxing of her heart's guardianship. She felt as if she had been kicked in the chest by a horse. Haltingly, she took a step forward, hand outstretched, trying to mend the damage.

"Laylah—"

"Your Majesty!" Laylah snapped. "Go, before I am forced to have you escorted out!"

Page didn't cry. She just didn't. So clearly she must have gotten some dust in her eyes as she turned and quickly left the august presence of Her Most Royal Majesty, Queen Laylah of Albion.

Laylah watched them go. Suddenly she surged forward, hand outstretched, lips forming around Page's name.

"I must say, I didn't expect you to have the backbone to properly chastise those upstarts," said Reaver.

Laylah halted in midstride, and let her hand fall. "It gave me no pleasure."

"I'm certain it did not," said Reaver. "As your husband discovered, ruling a kingdom properly does require that, from time to time, one must do unpleasant things. It's lovely to be popular, but it's better to be safe and wealthy. Then you can purchase popularity."

The queen turned to face him slowly. "You could not pay me enough to like you, Mr. Reaver."

He lifted a gloved hand in an appalled gesture. "Goodness, no! Not in coin, anyway. But I do have the ability to get you something you want, Your Majesty. A safe kingdom. And I think if I can assist you in obtaining that, you'll like me rather much."

Laylah swallowed hard, her eyes flitting back to the door through which Timmins and Page had exited. Right now, she hated Reaver more than she could ever imagine hating anyone.

Because he was right.

Chapter Thirteen

The days passed, long, hot, and astonishingly free from incident. The army had caught up with the main road again, and while everyone was on the alert as they traveled it, nothing untoward occurred. There were no attacks by sand furies, or hollow men, or shadows, but neither were there any convenient oases or friendly, wandering nomads. And thus that most boring of emergencies, dwindling rations, became the most serious threat.

"Well," Ben said as they roasted a sheep on a spit one night, "we'd best enjoy this. It's the last of the mutton."

"We still have plenty of basic rations," the king said, though privately he, too, would miss the fresh-roasted meat. And the sheep's milk. "How are the water levels holding up?"

"On the low side," Ben replied, taking another bite. "We're also out of the fresh fruits that provide additional moisture."

"Shan, Shalia, where's our next best place to find food and water?"

The two native Samarkandians spread the map out in front of them, and Shan repositioned a lantern so they could all see it more clearly. "I have not ventured beyond the sand-fury block in three years," Shalia warned them.

"And I have not been in this part of my country since I was very young," Shan put in.

"Terrific guides," Ben said, but a smile softened any edge the gibe might have had.

"We are fortunate to have any," the king reminded them all, "let alone two such courageous ones. Please—your best guess is going to be better than mine."

"I spoke earlier of the Cave of a Thousand Guardians, Your Majesty," Shan began. "It is a few days' east. This road here will veer off the Great Trade Road for several miles, and the cave is nestled at the base of the mountains."

"And there will be food and water in the cave?" Kalin asked.

"Water, yes," said Shan. "There is an underground spring that never goes dry. But more than that—it is believed to be a sacred place. It is called the Cave of a Thousand Guardians because of the beautiful statuary that was erected there long ago. It is said that each guardian statue represents a Hero from our country, and that their spirits still guide and protect those who enter the cave with respect in their hearts."

"And where were the Guardians when the darkness came into our land, Shan?" The king was surprised at the depth of bitterness in Shalia's voice. Then again, considering she had been forced to trick unwary travelers, rob them, and hand them over to sand furies if she was to survive, he supposed he shouldn't be so surprised after all.

"What did you expect, that they would come to life and rush to our aid?" Shan said. "It is a chamber of peace, yes, but evil can even enter such places. But there is water there, and it offers us a cool and well-defensible campsite before we press on to Zahadar."

"Your Majesty, I offer another suggestion. If we stay on the Great Trade Road past the turnoff Shan suggested, there is an area a bit farther on that will definitely provide water, if not food. Plenty of it, fresh . . . and cold."

"Ah!" said Kalin. "You speak of a kannat—a series of underground wells connected by a channel. We have such things in Aurora."

"Yes." Shalia nodded. "So which will it be, Your Majesty?"

The decision was not as clear-cut as either Shan or Shalia made it seem. The underground well system—the kannat, Kalin had called it—would indeed be the most direct route and the one most likely to still have water. But given his own history and that of his father, the king knew that so-called "sacred places" were, if not always truly holy, oftentimes wise places to visit. The faithful of ages past sometimes left behind tools or relics, precious items that deserved to be used again by ones who understood them.

But he had to think of his army first this time, not himself. Water was precious in this land, and that made it a target for the darkness. He thought of the lake crawling with sirens, and made his choice. If they kept up a steady pace, they would be able to reach the kannat by nightfall, and a place with water would be a very fine place to camp.

"Shan, I respect your desire to visit the Cave of a Thousand Guardians. But if it's water we're after, an underground spring is less likely to be contaminated than a single and rather famous body of water. We'll head for the kannat."

"As Your Majesty wishes," Shan said, but it was obvious he was unhappy with the choice. The king hoped he had not made a dreadful mistake.

The king walked among the army, encouraging them to press on with the promise of rest and fresh, cool water at the end of the journey. It was an inspirational thought, and even the beasts seemed to understand that there was a good reason for putting in extra effort.

The king called six scouts. "If there is water," he warned them, "there is likely to be danger. Be careful, go ahead, and report back without revealing your presence if possible."

They nodded. As they made ready to depart, the king added, "And if the way is clear—take some time to get the first drinks of that lovely cool liquid for yourselves. Take waterskins, but nothing larger—the extra weight will hamper you." They saluted him, grinning, then bowed and departed. They returned later that day, letting their washed faces and full waterskins announce the good news for them. Tired but happy cheers went up.

"All we encountered were the bleached bones of desert dogs," one of them said. "No signs that anyone other than beasts had been there recently. Majesty, here." And he offered his waterskin. "The water is cool and sweet."

The king shook his head. "Share it among the others," he said. "You have earned it. We have water left yet, and it sounds like there's plenty where we're going!"

The scout bowed respectfully, his smile broadening, and went to share with his fellows. "You know, *I'd* have liked some fresh water," said Ben, watching the scout wistfully.

"So would we all," said Kalin, "but look at them. The king has put their pleasure before his own, and they love him the more for it."

"They've earned it," the king said. "Besides, we have water!" He took a gulp from his waterskin, tasting the stale, tepid liquid, and said exaggeratedly, "Ahhhh!"

The successful scouting mission spurred the marching army on to even greater speeds, and the king arrived at the kannat as the sun was starting to sink. Several of the men were already hard at work, dropping the heavier containers down into the wells that were simple mounds of earth and pulling up water that spilled and splashed. The king smiled.

"I think it would be all right for us all to indulge now," he said. "There's plenty for everyone!"

As he spoke, the golden ball dropped below the horizon. And a strange sound went up.

It was not the familiar howl of a wolf. It was higher-pitched, more of a bark than a howl, a cry of something angry. Ben had Vanessa in hand before the king could even blink.

"It's likely the desert dogs," the scout who had offered the king water earlier said. "We told you we saw a lot of their bleached bones."

"But why theirs?" said Kalin abruptly. "I would expect to see bones of prey animals, not predators, at a watering hole. And if it is a well, then the jackals could not even reach the water."

Every instinct was shouting to the king that something was terribly wrong, but he couldn't piece the puzzle together. *When in doubt, defend.*

"On the well mounds, sharpshooters!" he cried. "Everyone else, press in tight! Sword wall!"

The cry went up swiftly, and the soldiers scrambled to obey. Those with long-range weapons hastened atop the dozen or so elevated mounds of earth, to get a better vantage point. The others pushed the carts in close, then unsheathed their swords and took up positions of defense. Against what, they didn't know. Neither did their king. But they would obey his orders without question.

Again the sharp bark-howls filled the air, lifting the hairs on the back of the king's neck. There was something . . . strange about them. And then, the memory of something Shan had said came crashing down on him.

I remember my father speaking to my mother of something he had found on the outskirts of the city. The body of a jackal . . . It is a sort of . . . dog of the desert. A scavenger . . . It was not a jackal any longer.

Jakala—a Samarkandian kind of balverine.

Just as the revelation struck him, one of the scouts who had first drunk the kannat water dropped his rifle and fell to his hands and knees. He started shrieking, as if in terrible pain. And so he had to be, as his very bones were elongating, twisting, shifting. His mouth and nose started to protrude, forming into a sharp-toothed muzzle. His chest broadened, ripping the leather jerkin, and golden fur erupted. His shriek changed, mutated into a singsong bark-howl as he called to his kin.

The king lifted his rifle, but there was a sharp sound, and the jakala dropped before he could fire.

Ben lowered his still-smoking rifle. "Let's get the rest," he said grimly, and the king nodded. The two men steeled their emotions and rapidly picked off the newly born jakala that had once been loyal soldiers as quickly and mercifully as possible. Everywhere they looked, a man seemed to be contorting, or had finished his transformation.

"How many of them do you think there are?" Ben asked. The air cracked with Vanessa's report.

Quickly, the king did the math, and his heart sank. The scouts, no doubt thinking they were showing kindness, had clearly shared their waterskins a gulp at a time among their fellows, and what should have been life-giving liquid was now instead transforming them into hideous, unnatural creatures. Six scouts. Twelve waterskins. Each waterskin could give fifteen men a solid gulp of water.

"Almost a hundred from the scouts' waterskins alone," he said. "And no way to tell who's drunk the water since we got here."

"Bloody hell," Ben muttered, reloading with determination. There was no time to warn the rest of the troops—the enemy suddenly was seeded among them. The king shoved away the thought of how close he and Ben had come to drinking the tainted water.

He glanced up after downing the ninth howling, contorting creature—barely making a dent in the number of the beasts— and saw a wave of swiftly running shapes approaching.

The rest of the pack. "To the southwest!" he shouted. "Fire at will!"

The clear desert air was filled with the sounds of firing rifles. The king even heard an enormous boom from one of the few cannons that had been small enough to navigate the passageway to Asur-keh-la. He calmed himself, focused, and summoned his Will. He splayed his hands hard. Balls of whirling energy mani- fested in his palms. He shoved his hands forward, hurling the missiles of pure, concentrated Will into the thick knot of the approaching pack. Several of the creatures flew into the air, landing limply, but their deaths did not deter their brethren.

"Just like at Blackholm," Ben said. The king had heard about that city's stand against the Half-breeds, as Reaver's depraved combinations of men and beasts were called, but Ben hadn't given him a lot of details. Page, who had also been present at the battle, had remained quiet as well. The king suspected that something profound had happened there but did not press the issue. Whatever it had been, it was clearly inspiring Ben Finn, who was always an excellent shot, to perform with almost super-human skill now.

Those with swords rushed forward to engage the pack, while others continue to fire. The king fired one more shot, then discarded his rifle and plunged into the fray himself. He splayed his hands hard, magical blue lightning zigzagging from one jakala to another. They froze, spasming, easy targets for sword or bullet.

There were dozens of them. The king suspected that the fouled water was a far swifter and more effective way of increasing the jakala population than the balverine method of biting. As they launched themselves at the soldiers, their frames bestial and powerful, it became harder and harder to separate the men from the beasts in the darkness. Others could handle hand-to-hand combat or were crack shots, like Ben. But only the king was a Hero who could kill many enemies at once. Sick about it, the king realized that to protect his people he would have to create casualties among them. It was a grim necessity.

On they fought, the brave soldiers of Albion and their king. More and more jakala appeared among their numbers, but gradually, the efforts of the humans won out over the beasts. Finally the last one uttered its high-pitched death cry and lay still. Whereas before when the army had won a victory, a cheer erupted, this night the king heard no celebrating. They had lost two, perhaps three hundred men, good ones, and not all of them had died *fighting* the jakala. Their trek hadn't even led them to potable water. This battle was not about a hard-won step to their final goal. It was a bitter and costly detour, and they would have to retrace their steps.

"I am sorry," said Shalia quietly as she, along with the king and others, moved among the fallen and gathered them for a proper burial. "I did not know."

"How could you?" said the king. "We're all moving in the dark. Even you and Shan." He paused. "The dark—the darkness. That's why they poisoned the kanat, not lakes or streams. The water would only briefly, if ever, be exposed to sunlight." Even he couldn't suppress a shudder at the calculated malice in so devious an act.

"I'm really starting to have a personal grudge against this darkness," Ben growled. He turned to Shalia. "His Majesty was right, Shalia. You gave us the facts as you knew them."

"I pray that Shan's memories of the cave are still accurate," said Shalia.

"After the misfortunes we have been forced to endure, we could certainly use a thousand guardians looking after us," said Kalin.

"We could use a thousand and one," said Ben. "So, yes—here's hoping."

Chapter Fourteen

They returned the way they had come, sending scouts ahead to make sure they did not miss the turnoff in the dark. Traveling in the dark was dangerous, but no one wanted to linger among the dead jakala and their poisoned wells. "I hope we don't walk right past it," said Ben. "The one Shalia led us through was barely visible. We'd have missed it for sure."

"I remember well where it is." Shan smiled. "And once the sun has risen, you will see it too, believe me. Keep heading straight east."

They continued marching. The sky started to lighten and the sun peeked over the rise of mountains. They looked expectantly, but saw nothing. Shan shifted his weight uneasily.

"Um . . . what . . . exactly were you expecting to see, Shan?" asked the king.

"There is a door," Shan said, his voice climbing high with worry. "A beautiful door, covered in gold. It has carvings on it . . . once the sun has risen it gleams, you cannot help but see it!"

The king, Ben, and Kalin exchanged glances.

"Gold, eh?" said Ben. "Bet the sand furies spirited that away right enough."

"We're not here for the door, we're here for the cave."

"Your Majesty," Ben began, "if it's been looted—"

"All right, hold up a moment," said the king. He drew Ben, Shan, Kalin, and Shalia aside and let the rest of the army trudge past them. "I realize that very little has gone as we had hoped," he said. Before Ben could speak, he amended, "All right, all right, *nothing's* gone as we had hoped. But we knew this land was troubled, and we knew we were poorly informed. We've come this far. Not everything can be corrupted, or turned, or poisoned by the darkness here. Look at Shan, and at Shalia. Shan came back with us when he didn't have to. Shalia has left her own people, out of a hope that she can perhaps truly save them. Those jakala who attacked us—they didn't want to be monsters any more than our own men who drank the water did. We've lost men. And machinery. But we've not let it stop us."

"The men can't take much more," Ben said quietly. "Setback after setback, horror after horror, watching their friends turn into those . . . things . . . well, it nearly broke some of them right on the spot. Something's got to go right, or else. . . ."

"Or else what?" asked Kalin quietly.

"Well, let me put it this way. There's been an overthrow of a king before in their lifetimes."

"You cannot be serious!" exclaimed Kalin.

"I certainly wish I weren't," said Ben.

"I can't say that I blame them," said the king. "It looks like I'm leading them to their doom."

"Oh come on," said Ben, "don't you go making their bleeding argument for them!"

"I'm not, really, I happen to like being their king. I'm just saying I can understand their unhappiness. Which means, ladies and gentlemen, that this Cave of a Thousand Guardians better pan out."

"No pressure, right, eh Shan?"

They continued marching. Eventually they were able to make out, if not a glorious, golden door, at least a boulder shoved up in such a way as to look like it was blocking an entrance. The king ordered the army to halt and made his way up to the front. Despite how unprepossessing it had looked from a distance, up close it was astonishing.

Someone might have stolen the golden door, but something else had survived unscathed. A huge section of the stone cliff side had been smoothed out. The boulder was lodged up against this. Dancing around the boulder were intricate, interconnected carvings of fanciful beasts and heroic-looking people.

"How many carvings are there, I wonder?" asked Kalin, craning her neck to look up at them.

"At a wild guess, I'd say . . . a thousand," drawled Ben. Shalia elbowed him. The king was briefly reminded of Page, and that reminded him of Laylah, and while that made him sad, it also steeled his resolve.

He strode toward the boulder and stepped to one side of it. Summoning his Will, he let the energy build up inside him, then thrust out his gauntleted arm.

The huge boulder rocked. A second time the king used his Will to shove the boulder, and this time it rolled away several yards. A cheer went up.

"That was the easy part. The way our luck's been running, I'm going to guess there's something unpleasant waiting in the cave for us," said the king in a falsely cheery voice. "Wouldn't want to break the record, now would we?"

"Oh, heavens no," said Ben.

"We will leave the heavy artillery behind and enough soldiers to use it if need be. The horses and oxen too. But those who can go on foot and swing a sword and fire a pistol—let's go. I want to be prepared for whatever we have to face. And if nothing's inside . . . we'll enjoy paying our respects to these thousand guardians."

"Agreed," said Ben. "Heaven forbid we should actually have an uneventful visit to someplace in this land." Shan looked downcast, and Ben's expression softened. "Hey now," he said to the boy, squeezing his shoulder. "You can't be thinking any of this is your fault?"

"I remember what they said on the ship, Mr. Finn," Shan said quietly. "That I might be already corrupted by the darkness. That I might be leading you all to your deaths. It certainly does look that way, doesn't it?" His voice was bitter and full of self-loathing.

"I'd say rather you had the bad luck to be living in a time when your whole country is running amok," said the king. "Nothing more sinister than that. You recognized the sirens before they got all of us."

"If anyone here has done anything wrong, it is I," said Shalia. "Your only crime, Shan, is ignorance of what has happened in parts of Samarkand. We are both doing the best we can." Her eyes flickered up to Ben's, seeking reassurance. He gave both Shalia and Shan a gentle smile.

"All right then," he said. "Let's see this spectacle you've spoken of, Shan."

The king, Ben, Shan, Shalia, and Kalin led the way. The entrance was narrow, only wide enough for two or three to walk abreast. Sconces filled with unlit torches lined the sides, which Kalin lit as they passed. The tunnel took a sharp left, and as Kalin lit the next torch, everyone gasped.

Until now, the walls had been carved smooth, but unadorned. Now, as the torches sprang to life, a beautiful tableau was illuminated. On every side, it seemed as though they had an army for company—Heroes, male and female, clad in colorful and exotic clothes, appeared to walk beside them. Some of them had beautiful faces, dark-skinned and tranquil, the very lines of their bodies radiating peace. Others bristled with weapons, their eyes hard and greedy, their powerful muscles clearly toned and strong, but their skins an angry reddish shade. Some of them even had horns and what appeared to be leathery wings fanning out from their shoulders. The noble Heroes bore large baskets of fruits and breads, sharing their wealth; the cruel ones bore not only bloody weapons, but sometimes the heads of those they had defeated.

"So beautiful," murmured Kalin, reaching out a hand as if to touch the brown face of a long-haired male Hero. "They seem almost alive."

"I am rather glad this one isn't," said Shalia, sticking close to Ben as she passed a sharp-toothed woman with bloody hands.

"This is called the Walk of the Heroes," Shan explained. "Each Hero is depicted here performing his most famous deed, be it for good or for ill."

"'Hero,'" said the king, "can mean a great many things. Garth was a great Hero of Samarkand, and worked with my father. And Reaver was a Hero as well."

"Takes all kinds, I suppose," said Ben airily, and gave his friend and ruler a grin. The beautiful paintings, their colors as fresh and vibrant as if the paint had only just dried, were reassuring, even if they did depict some of the nastier Heroes of Samarkand as well as the good and true ones. The king felt as if they had company, somehow. As if the darkness that seemed to have its tendrils woven into every part of the land they had yet seen had not quite reached here. As if the Heroes themselves held it at bay.

Shan seemed the happiest of them all, his face relaxed and smiling, his movements energetic and quick. The worry that had dogged him like a shadow thus far seemed to finally be falling away. *Maybe our luck has changed*, thought the king. *Maybe, finally, we're on the right path.*

"Up ahead," Shan said, sounding more like an excited teenage boy than he ever had before, "this pathway will open up into an enormous cavern. There will be statues there of every single Hero of Samarkand!"

"How many?" asked Ben, feigning innocence. By now, they were all relaxed, and everyone laughed.

"Forty-two, I think," said the king, and they laughed harder.

"No, no, it is said to be spectacular! And as I said, there is a fresh spring that never runs dry. It pours forth in a waterfall into a pool, and the Guardians stand watch over the pool and all who visit! It will be dark, of course, but there is a winding path down to the pool, and a large brazier there will illuminate the whole cavern. It is said that not only do they guard those who come here to pay their respects, but there is a great treasure for the next Hero of Samarkand to discover."

"That might be you, Shan," said the king. "Or you, Shalia?"

"Me?" she yelped. "Oh, I'm no Hero."

"My father was a street urchin," said the king. "You never know."

"Well, I for one would be bloody happy if it turns out I'm traveling with two or three Heroes," said Ben. "Especially such a brave and beautiful one."

Shalia ducked her head and smiled.

"Let's hurry!" said Shan. "I can't wait to see the cavern!"

They picked up their pace, as excited as Shan was to see the glorious cavern. Without any warning, the path suddenly widened. Cool air swirled about them, and though it was too dark to see anything, the king could sense that they had entered an enormous cavern. The single torch barely illuminated the path Shan had told them about, so they fell into single file as the king led the way.

"I can see them—sort of," Ben said. He pointed to the shadows beyond the dancing flame of the torch. Huge shapes loomed up in the darkness, but no one could make out details.

"And there's the pool, I can see the water glinting," said Kalin.

"There's the brazier, too, just like you said, Shan," said the king. It was laid and ready to be lit, the wood no doubt so well dried and seasoned that it should give more than enough light. He took a deep breath and touched the torch to the piled wood.

A sheet of flame sprang up, its heat almost scorching them, and they all took a step back, defensively shielding themselves. When the king lowered his arm and looked around, his eyes widened.

The sight was as enormous and commanding as Shan had described. The thousand statues of Samarkand's Heroes stood, each twenty feet tall, carved in such exquisite detail as to look like life writ large. The pool splashed and bubbled, liquid tumbling forth from the aperture in the side.

Except the liquid in the pool was black and viscous, and the Guardians had no heads.

Shan cried out in anguish at seeing the sacred place so defiled, and that sharp, pained sound shattered the paralysis that had frozen everyone in place. At that same moment, the thick liquid that had fouled the pool seemed to take on a life of its own. It formed what looked like a gigantic teardrop, falling *upward* in defiance of all natural law. Hundreds of smaller droplets splashed onto and oozed down the bodies of the statues, seeping into the porous stone.

And the king knew what to expect next.

Nearly ten years past, in a dark, best-forgotten place deep inside the desert of Aurora, he had watched a similar horror unfold—watched as the black, sludgy evil had animated empty suits of armor, which had turned into some of the most dangerous opponents the monarch had ever faced.

Galvanized to attention by Shan's wail of torment, he cried, "To arms! Stay out of the reach of the black fluid! Destroy the statues!"

Samarkand had certainly been full of dangers thus far. Sirens, jakala, sand furies, and treacherous villagers, all had attempted to halt or kill the king and his army. But this—here was their first true fight against a manifestation of the darkness they had come here to defeat, and to the king's surprise, he was eager for it.

There was a righteousness to this fray that had been lacking before, a sense that not just an enemy was now being directly faced but that if they won here, all that the enemy existed to do would be harmed. There was no latent guilt at taking a human life as in the case of the sand furies or jakala, no fraction of hesitation in dealing a death blow. No, this was pure evil, which needed only an animated stone statue of a dead Hero to use as its weapon.

His soldiers seemed to feel the same. They shouted their battle cries as they began hacking at the statues. A man could reach only to a statue's knee, but that knee was made of stone, and stone could be cracked and the statue would stumble. Bullets peppered the torsos of the headless Heroes, chipping relentlessly away until a huge section cracked and a chunk fell down. Black goo oozed out, and the king's men made certain to steer clear of the horrific splashes.

The king used his Will freely, sending fireballs directly into the chests of the stone monstrosities. They shattered into harmless shards, like pots dropped on a floor. He whirled, splaying both hands, striking two at a time. Another's motion was slowed so that the soldiers battling it could get in more blows. The king, his attention honed to razor sharpness, looked over at a cluster of statues descending on several of his men. Grunting, he thrust his hand out and the four statues stumbled backwards, falling and becoming easier prey.

The fight went on and on. Statues were defeated, but others trundled forward to take their places. Male, female, short, tall, slender, muscular, the images of the Heroes of old were perverted and used to fight for a darkness that all of them would have abhorred in life. The king was glad he could not see the carved faces.

Some of the soldiers, beaten back by the attack, fell into the pool. The darkness seized them, thrusting slender tendrils of slick black ooze into eyes, mouths, ears, and nostrils, then pulling them under. Others were slain by the oversized weapons the statues bore, their bodies lying broken on the stone floor.

Still the statues came, and still they were met with defiance. "We came to fight the darkness!" shouted the king. "Well, we're fighting it now, and we're winning! *We're winning!*"

He could tell they were, though it was at a bitter cost. Only a few dozen of the thousand guardians remained, fighting with the strength of the Heroes they were intended to honor, but with none of their wisdom or intelligence. The statues were dangerous, deadly—but defeatable.

More and more stone bodies toppled. A handful remained, now. The king was weary, but knowing they were so close to triumph revived him. He summoned every ounce of his Will, forcing his arms not to shake and blinking back sweat dripping into his eyes. One statue exploded from a ball of fire to the chest. Another fell to the onslaught of gunfire.

A final one remained, and as everyone turned attention on the armored figure with two swords, it fell almost at once, the echoing crash thunderous in the silence.

The king, exhausted, dropped to his knees. His body was shaking so badly it felt like the whole earth trembled beneath his hands and knees.

No—the ground really *was* trembling. The king forced himself to his feet just as something broke the surface of the black pool. The rising object was as black as the vile stuff that had kept it hidden from their view, but the thing itself was clean—the dark liquid did not cling to or sully it. Its hue was deep and compelling, and runes were etched on it in glowing blue light. Up, up it went, towering over the broken pieces of statuary, a base emerging now that provided a safe place to step. The dark fluid receded—almost recoiled, from the clean, chiseled beauty.

For a long moment, everyone stared. A soft blue glow jumped from the etched runes to slowly whirl around the obelisk, like a star dancing around it.

"What is it?" breathed Kalin.

"It's . . . for me," the king said, staring raptly. He knew, without knowing how, that this obelisk was intended for a Hero. The evil that had corrupted this very cavern dedicated to the most powerful Heroes of this land had been defeated. The darkness had retreated, scuttling away almost fearfully. And now, this humbling creation had appeared. He wasn't sure if it was a message, or a gift . . . but whichever it was, only he could receive it.

His eyes fastened almost without blinking on the huge black structure, he slowly ascended the steps until he stood before it. His skin seemed alive, jumping with anticipation, the hairs on the back of his neck standing up.

The glyphs on the obelisk hadn't changed, but somehow, he could read them now. Or at least, he knew what they said—he couldn't tell if the knowledge was before his eyes or in his own mind.

O Hero who hath need of me, release me, and I shall serve thee in the form that shall aid thee best.

The king blinked, the strange sort of spell broken. The form that would aid him best? What was this inscription all about? What did it mean, exactly? So many thoughts rushed into his head. The battle had reminded him, painfully so, of Walter Beck, who had been tortured and infused with the very essence of the evil while the king had frantically fought back the empty—yet not empty, not at all—suits of armor. What would Walter do if he were here? The king missed his friend terribly, missed his wise advice.

More than he realized, too, he missed dear old Jasper's acerbic but always helpful observations. He had gotten used to talking to the old fellow. To be able to speak to him now . . . He had friends, good friends, with him, and he had brought a fine and well-prepared army.

In the form that shall aid thee best.

He laughed suddenly. Well, that was pretty obvious, wasn't it? He needed something nearly impossible to defeat, that would be impervious to the harsh climate, that wouldn't have to be left behind because of poor terrain. Something that could fly over it all, and thrive in the heat like a snake or lizard did. Wouldn't it be wonderful to have a dragon out of the old fables obeying his commands! Who *wouldn't* follow him then, mounted on the back of so fearsome and powerful a beast!

But he needed to halt that flight of fancy. He needed to think seriously. What form would—

The voice in his head was like thunder.

The Hero hath chosen.

"No, wait!" he yelped. "I've not chosen anything, I'm still think—"

The obelisk paled from inky black to golden yellow, then crumbled into a pile.

The king stared at it, his mouth working, making little noises of utter confusion. All that for a pile of sand? Was this some kind of trick? He glanced back at his friends, but all of them looked as stunned and confused as he was.

Still reeling, the king knelt and placed his hand on the sand, for sand it indeed was.

And then the pile moved.

He leaped back, drawing his sword in one hand and summoning magic in the other. Some instinct made him hold back, though, and before his eyes, the billions of tiny grains began to swirl together, as though being tossed about by an unseen wind. Faster and faster they whirled, forming a solid, elongated shape far different from the obelisk. Four tendrils erupted, then two longer ones, and the shape became less nebulous.

The center mass sprouted leathery wings, the long extensions of moving sand taking on the more delicate imagery of a tail and a neck with a sharp-toothed head at the end. More sand trickled from the jaw and head, forming a sort of mane and whiskers. The form stamped each one of its massive, clawed feet, and the wings beat as though in joyful release. The tail thumped once, and sapphire-blue eyes blinked. They fastened on the king, and the head dropped level with the human Hero's.

"Crikey," he said, to the monarch's amazement, in Jasper's clipped, slightly supercilious tone. "Go to sleep for a few thousand years and look at the *mess* I wake up to. You Heroes always were a rather untidy lot."

Chapter Fifteen

The king stared. "Y-you're a dragon," he stammered.

The sand dragon rolled his eyes. "Brilliant deduction," he drawled. "Oh goodness me, look, I have *wings* too!" He sighed. "It appears that Heroes are not quite as perspicacious as they used to be."

The sarcasm penetrated the king's shock. "Wait—let me get this straight. You're my servant?"

"Alas, I fear so." The dragon sighed. A few grains of sand drifted down with the movement. "It certainly does appear you have need of assistance from *someone*."

"Why do you sound just like Jasper?" Ben demanded.

"I haven't the foggiest idea who Jasper is, but as for my appearance and personality, blame him, not me," the dragon said, nodding at the king.

And the king started to laugh. "Be careful what you ask for," he said, more to himself than anyone else. He'd been thinking of Walter, of Jasper, and of a dragon—and there he was, all three rolled into a sandy package. "I certainly hope there's some Walter Beck about you and not just snide comments," he said.

The dragon smiled, unexpectedly, and brought his head

down even with the king's. "Sir Walter was in your mind at the moment of my creation," Jasper's voice said gently. "I well know he is always in your heart. Seldom has any Hero I have served had such a good and loyal friend."

Unexpectedly and unwantedly, the king felt his eyes sting with tears. One hand reached up to touch the dragon's cheek. It was warm, and clearly made of sand, though it held its cohesion. "What are you, really?"

"I don't have to tell you that," the dragon said testily, pulling back and eyeing the king appraisingly. "I only have to help you, and that, I fully intend to do. I know why you have come to Samarkand. Others before you have fought to push back the darkness from gaining a foothold. Some of them succeeded. Some did not. You have already defeated a previous manifestation of the darkness before. You stand a halfway-decent chance of doing so again."

"Rip-roaring encouragement, that is," said Ben.

"It's truthful, and His Majesty doesn't need sugarcoated words, he needs facts. Knowledge. And the aid of someone I might be able to persuade to assist us."

"Dragon, I . . . what shall I call you?" asked the king.

That seemed to completely fluster the dragon. He flapped his wings agitatedly and looked about. "I . . . no Hero has ever asked me what I wanted to be named."

"Well, I'm asking you now. Pick a name, and I'll honor it. I promise."

The dragon settled back, lost in thought. At last he brightened. "Percival," he said, sounding extraordinarily pleased with himself.

". . . Percival?" echoed the king. "You're a mighty creature out of legend and you want to be called Percival?"

"Or Percy, if you like."

The king exerted every ounce of control and nodded imperiously. "So it shall be done—Percy," he said with great dignity.

The dragon beamed.

The king spread his arms. "You know what happened here," he said. "The darkness corrupted the pool and turned the very statues of Heroes past against us. You said you know of someone who might help."

The dragon—Percival—snapped back to attention. "Right-o," he said. "The Thousand Guardians that were represented here were all late heroes. But one of them still exists. He is the thousand and first Hero Samarkand has produced. I know where to find him. He might listen to you, given his history."

Sudden hope seized the king. "His history?"

"With your father," Percy said. "I speak of the Hero Garth."

The "council sessions," if such a civil word could be used to describe the tension-filled meetings of Laylah, Page, Timmins, and Reaver, had not gone well at all. There would be about five minutes of actual progress, then either Reaver would say something and Page and Timmins would come down all over him, or else Timmins and Page would make a suggestion and Reaver would disagree. The queen herself kept quiet, observing, making up her own mind about things.

Reaver was, without a doubt, arrogant, irritating, and utterly self-serving. But he also put forth ideas that seemed sound. What was wrong, for instance, with a curfew at least in Bowerstone, where unrest was most likely to foment? Page herself had led an underground resistance movement against the former king! Why in the world would she so vehemently oppose so simple a method? Who needed to be skulking about at night anyway, when the restaurants and inns were closed?

And the tax—Laylah had spent a great deal of time reviewing the royal ledgers of nine years past, when the darkness had come right into the very heart of Albion. While her husband had almost always chosen the kinder solution—the solution that Page had constantly pressed for—there were times when he had sided with Reaver. And it had been those decisions that had put money in the royal coffers. Laylah realized, with a heavy heart, that every choice her husband made that followed Reaver's advice had saved lives. Page had been so insistent on taking the higher moral ground that she was actually indirectly responsible for at least some of the death toll. While it was lovely, for instance, to preserve Bowerstone Lake as a scenic spot instead of mining it, or have Brightwall Academy admit anyone who wished to study there, were those two actions really worth nearly a million in gold? How much ammunition, how many weapons could have been created for that amount—and how many lives would those defenses have saved?

Laylah had never said anything to Page about this, of course. But she was beginning to feel that perhaps her husband had been a bit too kind. Laylah was entrusted with the safety of Albion, now. And she could not afford to let sentiment get in the way of protecting her people.

And Timmins—she had never liked Timmins, and she was growing to detest him, now. Why in the world would he, a military man, refuse to increase the patrols in the city? If he would agree to the raising of taxes, more people would be on the streets protecting the populace in nearly every city, not just Bowerstone.

And now they were at it again.

"Dear Page," Reaver was saying, "Your heart bleeds so profusely I confess a concern as to whether you have enough blood remaining to continue its beating."

"Whatever dark deal you made, Reaver, apparently it doesn't require you to have a heart at all!" Page snapped back.

Something broke inside Laylah, like the snapping of a dried twig. "Enough!" she shouted. "I cannot endure this any longer! You are so busy attacking one another that nothing is getting *done*! The country is suffering while the three of you figure out what—what the cleverest insult is!"

"They're always mine," said Reaver.

"This session is canceled. There's absolutely no point in continuing when the only thing you want to do is fight among yourselves, at Albion's expense. All of you are to leave, right now. I begin to think the only one I can rely upon is Rex!" They stared at her, stunned, achieving unanimity only in the shocked expressions on all three of their faces.

"Go!" cried Laylah.

They went. Laylah raced to her chamber. She closed the door and locked it. Barrows knocked, inquiring in a worried tone if perhaps she wanted some tea?

"No, thank you," she said, trying to make her voice sound calm. "And please, I will take care of myself tonight. Don't send any of the maids in. I don't want to be disturbed."

"As you wish, my lady."

Alone, she flung herself on the bed and sobbed herself to sleep.

It was in the early hours of the morning when she heard a knock on the door. Rex, instantly alert, lifted his head and growled. The queen smoothed her disheveled dress—she had fallen asleep fully clothed—and went to the door.

"Yes, what is it?"

"It's Barrows, ma'am. There's . . . someone here who insists on seeing you."

"Unless it's the king, send him away."

"I do wish it were His Majesty, but it's Mr. Reaver. He says it's urgent. The fate of the kingdom rests upon it."

"Tell him the fate of the kingdom can wait another few hours."

A pause. "Ma'am, he wrote a note for me to give you. I should be remiss in my duty if I didn't at least deliver it."

Laylah lifted a trembling hand to her forehead, pressing hard against the vein that throbbed in her temple. "Very well. Slide it under the door."

There was a slight scraping sound, and sure enough, a crisp piece of parchment marked with a red wax seal appeared. Laylah picked it up, then lit a lamp by the bedside. The seal, of course, was imprinted with a lavish "R." Taking a deep breath, she broke the wax and began to read the impossibly perfect handwriting.

My most noble Majesty, Queen Laylah,

It is with both a heavy heart and a sense of absolute duty that I disturb your slumber. I implore you to take a few moments to speak with me.

As I'm certain you know, my reach is far in this kingdom. Information has come my way that distresses me greatly, and is so very dire that I must needs come to you with it immediately, or else regret it to the end of my days, which will, of course, be some while.

The kingdom, and you yourself, Your Majesty, are in grave and immediate peril from those you think you can trust.

I do not say this idly. I have proof, which I am pre-

*pared to show to you. Please meet with me, or else I
cannot be held responsible for the tragedy that is about
to unfold.*

> *Yours in deep and respectful service,*
> *—R*

Part of her dismissed the letter as a histrionic attempt to gain her attention. The other part of her went icy with fear. Reaver did have a wide reach in the kingdom, and it was quite likely that any bad news would reach his ears before even the queen learned of it. She held the missive tight in one hand while petting Rex, who had jumped up on the bed to lean next to her comfortingly, with the other.

Laylah decided she would at least see what kind of "proof" Reaver had. If it was nonsense, she would let him know in no uncertain terms. But if it wasn't . . . she couldn't afford to take the chance.

She opened the door, suspecting that Barrows was waiting for a reply. He was. "Tell Mr. Reaver I shall meet him in a few moments."

He was waiting in the receiving room for her, leaning on the mantel and seemingly engrossed in the workings of an antique clock, and turned when Barrows announced her.

Usually, Reaver took an inordinate amount of pride in his appearance. Everything he wore was the cutting edge of fashion, and she had never seen either a wrinkle or a stain marring his clothing. Now, he had circles under his eyes, and his cravat was askew. His boots, too, were spattered with mud. And it was this change in appearance more than anything the letter had said that alarmed her.

"Thank you for seeing me, Your Majesty," he said.

She nodded mutely and indicated that they sit on the couch. "Let's get right to the point. You say you have evidence that there is danger afoot."

He hesitated and looked unhappy. Her unease increased a thousandfold. "Mr. Reaver, please!"

"Very well, I shall speak plainly. You have been betrayed, Your Majesty. All of Albion has been betrayed. By the two people you were led to trust the most."

Her eyes hardened. She well knew whom he meant. "This is beneath you, Mr. Reaver. Page and Timmins are completely loyal to me! I know the three of you have had disagreements—indeed, even I have had my problems with them from time to time—but betrayal!"

She expected him to defend himself, but instead the sorrow in his face increased. "I don't have to make the case," he said. "They have doomed themselves." He held out two packets of letters, each tied with a ribbon. "There are several people in this kingdom I keep a watch on," Reaver continued. "You will see that these letters are addressed to a few of them."

Laylah took the letters in a hand that trembled. She sat them on her lap, not moving to open them, knowing somehow that if she read them, her life would never be the same.

"I could tell you what's in them," he said, "But . . . hard as it will be, Your Grace, you need to see this for yourself. You would never believe me otherwise."

Laylah sat for a moment longer, then untied the first pack. The letters covered a period of several weeks. She did not know the names of those to whom they were addressed, but she knew the signatures. She knew the handwriting.

Plots. Deals with agents in Aurora—malcontents who wanted their own country back and were willing to help overthrow

Albion to get it. A secret buildup of weaponry in nearly every village in the country. All written in a bold but blunt hand, the messages within equally bold and blunt.

"Timmins," she whispered. She turned her eyes to Reaver. "He's been plotting to overthrow me!"

"We have witnesses who will testify to the veracity of these exchanges," he said. "And if Your Majesty wishes to travel to any of these cities, we know where the weapons caches are."

"This . . . this can't be true! He is a cross and irritable man, and quite impatient with me sometimes, but treason . . . !" Her eyes fell on the second pile of letters, and her stomach clenched hard.

"Don't make me read these," she whispered.

"You are the Queen of Albion, dear lady," Reaver said. "No one can make you do anything. But I do urge you to read them. Do you wish to live in ignorance, or in the light of truth?"

I just want to go back to my wedding day, Laylah thought, anguish ripping her heart. *I don't want to know any of this. I just want to be with my beloved, and be happy.*

But not even a queen could turn back time. And she owed it to her kingdom, her husband, and herself to know if there was any threat from a woman Laylah had come to think of as her dearest friend.

Her hands shook so badly she could barely read the first letter. As with the stack of missives from Captain Timmins, she did not recognize the name of the addressee, but she knew the handwriting.

> *. . . the situation has become intolerable. I am fond of the girl who now sits on the throne, but she is incapable of true leadership. With the king off in a foreign land, Albion is a certain target for the darkness. Our*

mutual friend J.T. has been corresponding with you,
and we should be prepared to strike sooner rather than
later. I insist no harm come to the girl; imprisonment
should suffice. L and I often go on walks together, just
the two of us, so I should easily be able to lead her di-
rectly into—

The letter fell from her nerveless hand. Darkness swam around the edges of her vision and she felt something press against her mouth. She drank, coughing at the strong whiskey, and her vision cleared slightly.

"My apologies for my forwardness, Your Majesty, but I feared you were about to faint. I understand—this must be quite a shock. Are you all right now?" Reaver inquired. He looked genuinely solicitous.

"P-Page," she murmured. "There has to be some mistake . . ."

"It's possible, I suppose. I imagine, for instance, if your walks together were common knowledge, then anyone could have . . . Oh dear," he said at the look on her face. The only one Laylah ever notified was Barrows, so that he would not be alarmed at her absence. No one else but she and Page knew about the walks. Page, and Timmins . . .

"The letters have details that no one else could have known," she said in a voice barely above a whisper.

"I see," Reaver said. "Then there is no doubt. They might just as well have scrawled on the castle walls 'We're going to topple the kingdom, hoorah!' and signed their names. And it pains me to say this, but there is but one punishment for treason— especially in such a difficult and delicate time."

Execution. Laylah knew it. She reached for the glass of whiskey Reaver still held and downed its contents in a gulp. This time, she welcomed the fiery burn down her throat and in her belly. It gave her the strength to do what had to be done. She turned to look at Reaver and, emboldened by the hard drink, said, "Isn't it strange, that the one man who truly proves trustworthy is the one who has been so dreadful to those I love in the past. And the ones to whom I have given my trust and my love have been wearing false faces."

"The old saying is at times true," Reaver replied, his smile rueful. "Politics does make strange bedfellows."

"Here is what I shall do," said Laylah.

Chapter Sixteen

"Garth?" echoed the king. "He's still alive?"

Percy rolled his eyes. "No, he's dead, and I'm taking you to his grave so you can weep bitter, bitter tears. Of course he's alive, though quite old by now. Your Majesty, I understand you're a bit taken aback by all this, but please cease talking like a vacuous idiot!"

"Idiot?" repeated the king. The dragon looked as if he were about to explode—and then he caught the smile on the king's face. "Ah, ah, you almost had me there, young sir," he said. "Bravo. I commend you. As I was saying before your jape interrupted me, yes, Garth is alive and well."

"Did you help him and my father? When they were traveling together?"

"No, but I can tell when a Hero still walks the earth, as I am bound to them after a fashion. I can even take you to him. I have no idea if he'd be interested in aiding us, but as he is with the warrior monks in the eastern mountains, it's an excellent place to start."

"We might find a whole slew of allies instead of just one even if the one happens to be a Hero," said Ben.

"I am sure the monks would joyfully offer their aid," said Shan.

"Providing the Empress hasn't wiped them all out," said Shalia.

"Oooh, such a cheerful lot you are," said Percy.

"We've seen enough recently to make us rather grumpy, I'm afraid," said the king. "But I am more than willing to go. How long will it take for the army to arrive?"

"The army?" said Percy. "Another few days, at least. You and I, however, should be able to travel there much more swiftly." He eyed the king and flexed his wings. "You didn't think these things were merely aesthetic, did you? Although now that I look at them, they *are* quite attractive," he amended.

The king couldn't believe this sudden turn in their fortune. They were still a long way from toppling a Empress and fighting back the darkness, of course, but a few moments ago he hadn't even conceived of stumbling across so valuable an ally. "Thank you," he said, "from the bottom of my heart."

Percy looked a trifle embarrassed. "Yes, yes, let's all sit around a campfire and sing life-affirming songs. But first, let's get you to the temple and Garth."

"That's the lot," said Captain Jack Timmins. He planted the shovel upright in the dirt and dusted his hands off with a handkerchief.

"That's a great deal," said Ed Wilkerson, who had been appointed Acting Mayor of Blackholm in Russell's absence. He, Timmins, and the man who owned the Black Horse Tavern had spent the better part of an hour secretly digging in the alehouse's cellar. The only witnesses to the activity were the casks of beer and rows of wine, and they would say nothing. "Guns, ammunition, nonperishable supplies—we should be able to give a good account of ourselves."

"Remember, say nothing of this cache," Timmins reminded them. "It could mean trouble if anyone else knows about it. It must remain a carefully guarded secret until such time as it's needed."

"And when might that be?"

The voice came from a man standing at the top of the stairs of the cellar. He was backlit so only his silhouette could be seen. A top hat, a cane, and an arrogant stance betrayed his identity as much as his distinctive voice.

"Reaver," snapped Timmins. "What are you doing here?"

Reaver stepped down the stairs, the dim light now revealing a self-satisfied smirk on his face. Behind him were three of Timmins's own guards, each of them leveling a pistol at their captain, Wilkerson, and the barkeep.

"Why, arresting the three of you for treason, of course," said Reaver. "You have most kindly enabled us to catch you in the very act."

Timmins stared at him. "What kind of farce is this?" he demanded. "Richards, Thompson, Jamison—you look ridiculous. Put those damned things away."

None of the guards moved.

"This is no farce," said Reaver, "although I confess, I do find it humorous." He waved his walking stick at the newly dug soil. "How clichéd, to bury your cache of weapons in a bar cellar."

"Look here," said Wilkerson, stepping forward. "Captain Timmins was giving us extra supplies in case we got unexpectedly attacked by the darkness. He asked us to keep it on the down-low so that some trigger-happy drunk didn't decide to steal the weapons and go shooting up the countryside."

Reaver cocked his head, as if considering. "That's very creative, and might even be plausible if it weren't for this stack of letters I have in my hand that proves your guilt beyond a doubt.

You have been conspiring with Page and many others to over-throw Queen Laylah."

His anger growing, Timmins tried to snatch the letters to see for himself what kind of nonsense Reaver had concocted. Before he even realized what had happened, there was sharp sting across his hand. His palm had been laid open and was dripping bright crimson on the cellar soil. Reaver's walking stick was also a swordstick, and its bloodied, nearly surgically sharp tip was but a few inches from Timmins's face.

"I also have a decree here from Her Royal Majesty Queen Laylah of Albion for your arrest and subsequent execution," Reaver continued in the same falsely pleasant tone of voice, though his dark brown eyes were cold and devoid of anything resembling mercy. "I could carry out the latter part of that sentence right now, if you wish. I'd prefer not to—it's always much more fun to have an audience for that sort of spectacle."

Timmins knew he would do it, too. "I'll have a trial, and I'll be able to prove my innocence," he said. "The queen and I may have our . . . disagreements, but she's no butcher." *Like you,* he thought but did not add.

"Your little friends here will, because they have a lesser charge. However, the queen seeks to make an example of you, considering that you were in her inner circle."

Timmins clenched his jaw. Trial or no, he would somehow prove his innocence.

Somehow.

Page stood in her own little world in the sewers of Bowerstone, more comfortable here than she was anywhere else. Timmins was traveling for a few days, helping shore up the defenses of the smaller hamlets against a darkness that might think this a prime time to infiltrate around the edges of Albion.

She had thought it a brilliant plan and urged him to start implementing it before the next council meeting.

"Because," she had said ruefully, "we don't know when Laylah will *have* the next council meeting."

"Or what Reaver would do with the information," Timmins had said darkly. "I'll never trust that fellow, no matter how much it appears his self-interest aligns with the kingdom's welfare."

"Nor will I," Page had said heartily.

Now she stood, her dark eyes on the spot on the map that proclaimed "Blackholm," and calculating how long it would be before Timmins returned.

A boy of about eight summers raced up to her, his small chest heaving with exertion. There was fear in his eyes.

"Miss Page!" he yelped. "You have to go! They're coming to arrest you!"

"Charlie, breathe," Page said soothingly. "No one's coming to arrest me. I'm working with the queen now. It's all right."

His hands grasped frantically at her arms. "No, no, they're coming! The guard, they're just a block away. I overheard them saying things!"

Charlie was almost too levelheaded for a child of his tender years, and Page suddenly felt a frisson of fear. "What exactly did you hear?"

Charlie gulped for air. "One of them said, 'it's about time that uppity sewer rat got what's coming to her,' and another one said, 'never much cared for her, but I never expected treason.'"

"Reaver," she breathed. Somehow he had to be behind all this. She would find a way to reach the queen and refute these mad charges against her, but the time wasn't now, not with a bunch of biased guards coming with a warrant for her arrest. "Let's go out one of the back ways," she said.

The guards were good. They were waiting for her as she and Charlie emerged, and Page froze when she heard the sound of several pistols being cocked.

"Page of Bowerstone," one of them intoned, reading from a scroll, "you are under arrest on the charges of high treason against Her Majesty. Because of the great love she bears you, despite the overwhelming evidence of your deceit and betrayal, she has decreed that you shall not face execution but rather live out your life in prison."

This couldn't be happening. Laylah, condemning her to life in prison? What the hell had Reaver done to convince her? She took a deep breath, doing her best not to give the guards the satisfaction of seeing her distress.

"I will go with you peacefully," she said, her gaze flickering over to young Charlie—who had risked so much to warn her but had failed to save her. Understanding the meaning of her glance, he began to step back, fading into the crowd. At least Laylah wouldn't be arresting a child. "I am certain that once I talk to Her Majesty, this will all be straightened out."

"You're lucky she spared you," one of them said. "Don't flatter yourself into thinking that the queen will visit a traitor in prison!"

Page said nothing, but she knew in her heart that Laylah would come. It was in her personality—Laylah needed to face someone she believed had done something so horrible to her. She would want to understand why. Laylah would come—and Page would be ready. She could convince Laylah that Reaver had played on the queen's insecurities and fears.

She had to.

They marched her down the streets of Bowerstone. Page

stood straight, but part of her was glad for the hooded cloak that concealed her face. She wanted desperately to inquire about Timmins, and the other members of her "underground," as it was no doubt starting to be labeled. Who else would they arrest? Reaver seemed to have Laylah well in hand, and this purging of those who opposed, or who might even possibly oppose whatever diabolical plan he had in mind, could have no limits.

Even as her mind raced with these thoughts, Page kept a sharp eye out for any opportunity to escape. There was none. All too soon, they arrived at Bowerstone Castle. Page looked sadly at the place where she had once been a welcome visitor as she was led around to another part of the castle, where there was an all-but-unseen door that opened onto a dank staircase.

"And here I thought I was going to Ravenscar Keep," she said, referring to the infamous prison where King Logan had kept prisoners he felt were particularly dangerous to him.

"You will," said one of the guards. "You're just going to be held here until your sentence is publicly pronounced."

Page hadn't even known these cells beneath the castle existed. As the guards led her down the stairs into a gloomy chamber with about two dozen individual cells, she tried to remind herself that she had been in worse situations. At the moment, though, she couldn't think of any. Her only chance of escape was here, while she was held at Bowerstone, before she was transferred. Only the king had ever been able to stage a breakout at Ravenscar Keep, and she was no Hero.

She immediately took notice of as much as possible in the few minutes it took to descend the stairs and be put in her cell. Yes, two dozen, twelve on each side down a long corridor lit with six lanterns. Someone, a man, was in one of the cells, but he lay on his cot with his back to her. There was a single door on the far side of the chamber. A guard sat at a desk, positioned so that he could see every cell and the stairs. He looked over-weight and bored—two good things for her. The keys hung on a hook on the wall behind him, and he was currently sitting with his feet up on the desk. He glanced over at the newcomer, and a lascivious smile split his face.

"Well, well," he drawled, "if it isn't the lovely Miss Page. I'll enjoy getting to know *you* better."

Her anger flared. "I'd kill you before you got within three feet of me," she snapped.

The man's small eyes narrowed, but the other guards laughed. "She's got you there," one of them said. "Besides, Queen's or-ders. She's to receive good care, not to be harmed."

"I wouldn't *hurt* her," Piggy Eyes complained.

"You know what we mean," the guard said. "You touch her, and the queen puts you in one of these lovely inn rooms."

"All right, all right," Piggy Eyes muttered. He trundled over to one of the cells, fiddled with the ring of keys, and unlocked the door. Page made careful note of which key it was.

"In you go," Piggy Eyes grunted. As the other guards turned away, Page extended an imploring hand to one of them—the youngest, who hadn't indulged in insulting her. She was good at reading people, and she could see the basic kindness in him.

"Please," she begged. "Please ask Her Majesty to come see me. We were friends once . . . I need to see her before I'm . . ." She let the words trail off. He made no answer, but she could see from the softening on his young face that her request would be delivered. That was the best she could hope for.

The guards left, ascending the stairs. The door boomed shut after them.

"Sorry they got you too, Page," came a familiar voice.

"Timmins?" Her heart sank. A cell separated them, but as they were only metal bars and not solid walls, she and Timmins could see one another. There was blood on his uniform and one eye was nearly swollen shut. A bandage had been wrapped around one hand. Page glanced over at the guard. He was watching her, his fat face ugly with dislike, but he was not forbidding them to talk.

Fine with her. He could eavesdrop all he wanted. Neither she nor Timmins would say anything of note.

"We've been set up," Page said.

"Of course we have," growled Timmins. "Reaver came across me laying the cache so those poor sods in the distant hamlets could defend themselves against the darkness."

"I don't even know what in the world he concocted to implicate me," Page said. "How long have you been here?"

"Not much longer than you," he said.

"How are the villagers holding up?"

"As well as can be expected," he said.

"Tell me about them," she said, sounding deeply sympathetic. "All those poor people." As she had hoped, Piggy Eyes rolled his . . . well . . . piggy eyes. The conversation was no longer interesting him. He reached underneath his desk, retrieved a bottle, and pulled the cork out with his teeth. As he took a deep swig, Page could barely conceal a smile.

They might get out of this after all.

She and Timmins made small talk until the guard's head nodded, finally thumping down on the desk. They heard soft snoring. Still, Page was cautious; it was only when she noticed a trail of drool puddling on the desk that she believed the man truly unconscious.

"I have a plan," she said, and told him.

"That . . . depends on a lot of things going exactly right," he said.

"Well, yes, it does," she admitted. "Have you got a better idea?"

". . . No."

"Then we'll just have to hope."

To her surprise, Page actually drifted into an uneasy slumber, snapping awake when she heard a door close. She sat upright, tense and wary, wondering if it was already time for her to be transferred to the Keep.

Instead, only Piggy Eyes and a tall, feminine figure in a cloak approached the door to her cell. The cloak's hood hid the woman's features, and both hands were inserted into a fur muff. The guard turned the heavy skeleton key, and the door opened with a groan.

The woman lifted a dark hand to her face and pulled back the cloak's fur-lined hood. Page gasped as she saw Laylah's face, haggard and full of sorrow.

"There you are, Your Majesty," Piggy Eyes said obsequiously. "I'll be right out here in case you need me."

"No, you will not," said the queen. Even her voice sounded broken, but with an underlying firmness Page wasn't used to hearing from her friend. "You will give us privacy."

"I can't possibly do that!" he exclaimed. "This woman is a hardened criminal! She's committed treason!"

Laylah reached into the fur muff and pulled out a pistol. "I am armed," she said. "And at this distance, even I couldn't miss. Isn't that right, Captain Timmins?" she added bitterly, raising her voice.

Timmins didn't reply, which Page thought was wise.

"But—the only place for me to wait would be the loo," protested Piggy Eyes.

"Then stay in the loo until I tell you to come out," Laylah said sharply. He bowed, muttered something, and opened the door behind his desk. He slipped inside and closed the door behind him. Page noticed he took his alcohol with him.

Laylah turned to Page. "I had to see you for myself," the queen said quietly. "To lay eyes on someone I trusted—someone I loved as a sister. Why did you do this, Page? What harm have I or my husband ever shown you?"

Even though she was completely innocent, the look on Laylah's face made Page feel guilty. "No harm, ever, Your Majesty, only love and kindness, and that is all I have ever shown you. I swear it."

Laylah's face twisted, and she threw down a stack of letters on the cot. "Even now, you lie to me! It's all there, Page, in your own handwriting!"

Page took the pile of letters and began to read them. "Oh, he's good," she murmured. "Very, very good."

Somehow, over the last several weeks while the king was gone, Reaver's minions had managed to intercept letters from Page to Timmins. He had used her own phrases, so that these falsified letters would truly sound like her, but had added to them and twisted them.

"Whoever he hired as a forger did a masterful job," Page said. She placed the letters down with a hand that trembled. "You have indeed been betrayed, Your Majesty—but not by me. Nor by Captain Timmins. Reaver has concocted this elaborate scheme to get us both out of the way because he knows that we and we alone have the courage to speak the truth to you!"

Something inside the queen broke. She strode up to Page and slapped her across the face, hard, but she was also sobbing.

"Reaver has made no secret of his greed, and all his plans are sound. It's you two who have made me doubt myself, you who have plotted against me, and even with the evidence right in front of you, you invent a story that . . ."

Laylah took a deep breath, regaining composure. She gathered up the letters. "I shouldn't have come. I won't come again. Good-bye, Page."

She turned around and filled her lungs to call out for the guard. She never got the chance. Page grabbed the tankard in which her stale water was served and brought it down at the base of Laylah's skull. The queen dropped like a stone. At that moment, Timmins started to protest, but Page silenced him with a finger to her lips. She bent and checked to make sure the queen was breathing. She was.

"I'm so sorry," Page said to Laylah, her heart breaking. "But I've got to be free if I'm to be of any help stopping the real traitor."

Working quickly, she stripped down to her undergarments and did the same to the queen. Page hadn't realized how difficult it was to undress an unconscious person, who was all deadweight, but she managed. In a few moments, Page was wearing the queen's garments, and Laylah was wearing Page's. Page wrangled Laylah onto the cot, pulling the cloak's hood down. While Page's skin was much browner than Laylah's, the hue was sufficiently similar so that no one would notice right away in the dark cell if they glimpsed a hand or a cheek. And the queen had been thoughtful enough to provide a muff . . . and a loaded pistol.

"Your turn," she said to Timmins. Page had noticed that Piggy Eyes had not locked her cell door when he admitted Laylah. He had left the key ring hanging on the hook, and Page searched until she found the one that unlocked Timmins's door. "Fortunately, you're still in your guard's uniform. At this hour, if we're glimpsed, it won't arouse suspicion."

"Just one moment," said Timmins. He stepped over to the guard's desk. Moving the chair over to the loo door, he lodged it firmly under the knob. "That'll keep him in there for a while."

"So will the booze." Page grinned. "Come on, let's go!"

Chapter Seventeen

lthough he was far from his home and beloved wife, had lost good men, and had met danger at nearly every turn, the king realized that right now, in this moment, he had never been happier.

He sat atop the broad, golden back of Percival the sand dragon, ally to Heroes, as the great beast's wings beat steadily. At this altitude, it was cool, and the desert below did not look the least bit dangerous. He realized that the experience of looking down from above was akin to viewing the magical, three-dimensional map in the Sanctuary. But the experience of flight itself—he had found nothing to compare to this.

After the revelation that Garth still lived, Percy had struck the stone wall of the chamber once with his powerful tail, creating a new spring of fresh, untainted water—more than enough to fill all their water gourds. "I fear I cannot help with food," he said, "but I would venture a guess that as you continue on, you will discover that creatures other than yourselves live in the desert."

The king assured him that they still had plenty of supplies if they needed them. Once rested, the army would be on the move . . . but with somewhat emotional farewells, the king left almost immediately.

On dragonback.

"We're going to win this," he said firmly.

"You have a crystal ball, have you?" said Percival. "I hate to burst your bubble, but every single Hero who's ever breathed thinks he can meet every challenge that is set before him. Many of them don't. I've seen it."

"Are you sure you're meant to help Heroes and not talk them out of things?" asked the king.

"That's helping—if talking them out of things is wisdom." This was said without an ounce of sarcasm, and while Percival's voice was that of Jasper, he could almost hear Walter saying the words. It *was* wisdom, sometimes.

"I care very much for my people," the king began. "And I'm learning to care very much for the Samarkandian. You've helped hundreds of Heroes before me. You have to have seen this darkness. I fought it twice before. Please—tell me what you know."

"Your wish is my command," said Percy.

"It's always your command," said the king, "but I don't want you to think of it that way."

"Majesty, I am bound to serve you, whether or not I like it. You are a Hero, and I am . . . what I am. Although I can comment on your decisions, and obviously I do, I cannot disobey them."

"Do you like serving me? Would you disobey if you could?"

There was a long, long pause. The golden wings beat slowly and steadily. Finally, Percy said, "I do not know yet."

"Fair enough," said the king. "At least you don't utterly despise me."

"I didn't say that," Percy amended, but craned his long neck to give the king a wink with one blue eye. "Now, as to your request, I know a very great deal about a great many things. You'd better narrow your focus."

"All right," the king said. "Tell me about the darkness in Samarkand . . . and how it has been defeated before."

And so Percy did. He still refused to define his exact nature, but revealed that he had worked to assist most of the Thousand Guardians in the Cave. In recent years, fewer of the Heroes bothered to visit the Cave to give their respects to their predecessors, and so missed out on the opportunity to have . . . whatever Percy was, serving them. "I've not been disturbed for a few centuries," he said.

The darkness, he said, was always changing. "Because the darkness feeds on hatred and fear, and every person's hatred and fear is unique." In its purest essence, it was as the king had seen it before—black, tarry fluid that had a direction and sentience all its own. And it was fond of using other sentient beings as its tools, corrupting them and using them to betray those they loved best.

"I am familiar with that tactic," the king said, his heart heavy.

Sometimes it tainted living things in other ways. It would seep into soil, poisoning the roots of plants so that their fruit was deadly. It turned clean water toxic, spreading its contagion to those who foolishly drank of it.

"We encountered that right before we met you," the king said. "We found a kannat of water that turned many of my men into jakala. Part jackal, part human."

"I see you are rather more experienced than I had anticipated," the dragon said. "That might actually give us the tiniest shred of hope."

"Your confidence in me is overwhelming."

"I'm glad you think so." The king was starting to enjoy the banter. After so many dangers and grim events, humor was as welcome as fresh water.

The worst manifestation of the darkness, and the hardest to defeat, Percival continued, was the nonphysical. You could fight the black goo. You could slay those who had unwillingly betrayed you. "But how do you fight your own thoughts?" asked Percy, presumably rhetorically. "It whispers in your ears, in your mind . . . that you have failed, that all are against you. That nothing you do will ever matter. That the darkness is eternal and can never be vanquished. And most of the time, you don't even realize that the thoughts aren't actually coming from your own head."

The king felt cold. He recalled traveling with Walter in Aurora, the whispers that were barely heard, the despair and terror they inspired. He, at least, was aware of what was going on, and no matter how convincing the evil words sounded, he knew they were not his own. How, then, could anyone overcome it when they *didn't* know?

"So . . . understanding what's going on. Knowledge of its methods. And hope," the king said. "That's what's needed to defeat the darkness."

"Fireballs and bullets help also," Percy provided.

"They often do," the king said.

The trip passed quickly. The king used the aerial advantage to correct and refine Shan's map, realizing how useful such knowledge would be in the coming battle. "You know, we can even scout out Zahadar once we get close enough," he said. "It would be amazingly useful to be able to see where the Empress has troops gathered and what the state of the countryside is like."

"It would indeed," said Percy, "if you'd like to advertise that you're on your way and you've got a dragon on your side."

"Oh," said the king. "I suppose you're right."

They reached the monastery shortly before sunset. For most of the king's life, Samarkand had been a place of mystery and imagination, of tales woven in rich hues and singing of marvels. Other than the Cave of a Thousand Guardians, little he had seen of the place seemed to support that notion. But now, gazing down on the several buildings that dotted the monasterial grounds, his breath caught.

Nestled in the embrace of the eastern mountain chain, reachable on foot only by a narrow, zigzagging mountain pass, the monastery lay in a fertile green valley. He could see the silver glint of lakes and waterfalls as they caught the morning sunlight. The buildings themselves were domes, their roofs gleaming almost blindingly as if diamonds had been inlaid upon them. Small figures were milling about, tending crops, performing what appeared to be ritual exercises, or simply seated in what looked like meditation.

"It's all right!" he cried happily. "The darkness hasn't found it yet. Neither has the Empress!" Even from above, the peace of the place was apparent, and the king no longer wondered why an elderly Hero might come here to live out his days. It tugged at him too, and he realized that because of the additional obligation as king, such an option would be denied to him. One didn't "retire" from being king.

"My, my," Percy said, genuine fondness in his voice, "it hasn't changed at all. I'm so pleased."

He flew in closer, and the figures on the ground grew larger. They had obviously spotted the figure hovering above them and were gathering.

"Um," said the king, "it's probably a bit late for me to be

thinking this, but—do you think they'll understand we're friendly?"

"Let's hope so," said Percy. "I intend on landing a fair distance away, to be on the safe side."

He suited action to words, coming to earth with a gentle *thump* and crouching so the king could easily slip off his back. A few grains of sand pattered down as the monarch did so. The monks, dressed in robes almost the same color as the dragon, were running toward them. They carried staffs, spears, swords, ropes, axes, hammers—

"They're much better armed than I thought they would be," the king murmured.

"Why do you think they call them warrior monks?" sighed the dragon.

"I just thought they'd be good with fisticuffs or something."

"Well, for goodness' sake, put your own weapons down and kneel."

The king wasn't used to kneeling to anyone, but in this instance he was willing to forgo his land's niceties. He quickly divested himself of his weapons and knelt as Percival suggested. The dragon himself did the same thing, folding his wings and crouching down in a nonthreatening posture.

The monks continued to race toward them, men and women both, slowing to a halt as they drew closer. They held their weapons at the ready but did not attack. One of them, an older man with a shaved head, approached. He was obviously the head monk. He carried no weapon; the king had the sneaking suspicion that the man really didn't need one to break every bone in the royal body.

"Who are you, who comes on the back of the hated enemy dragon, to disturb the peace of this place?" the head monk demanded.

"I am the King of Albion, and a Hero," the king said. "As was my father before me. This dragon is no enemy, but a friend, to me and to you all, if you wish it. He is an ally to all Heroes."

"He is . . . made of sand," a woman said, puzzled.

"He is not a true dragon. Merely the image of one. He is known as . . . Percy. I come not to show disrespect but to seek both your aid and counsel with one who lives here. His name is Garth . . . and he traveled with my father."

"There is no one here by that name," said the head monk. Startled, the king glanced over at Percy, who shook his head slightly. Garth was here, Percy was telling him . . . but the monks weren't going to reveal that. "What aid would you have of us?"

"Your land is falling into darkness," the king said bluntly. "And it is my understanding that your leader, the Empress, could be in league with it."

"So," another monk said, "you have come to overthrow our Empress. Perhaps you think to marry her and take the Emperor's place?"

The king shook his head. "I have a lovely queen awaiting me, and I think ruling one country is more than enough."

"I believe him," came a deep voice from the back of the crowd. Everyone turned to regard the man who had spoken. He was of average height but much older than even the head monk. He, too, had no hair on his face or head. His skin was quite dark, almost as dark as Page's, and his eyes were utterly piercing. But what was most arresting about him was that glowing blue lines adorned his face, scalp, and body—a testament to the power of his Will. He leaned on a staff, but the king suspected he didn't really need it for support, despite the age lines etched on his face. The king got to his feet.

"Garth," he said quietly.

"It has been a long time since I have been called so," Garth replied. "Here, I am Taron, the Seeker."

"Seeker? Of what? You were a Hero, one of the greatest masters of Will anyone has ever heard of."

Garth smiled. "I sought not to be that anymore," he said simply. "In exchange for food and a place to sleep, I teach the monks how to harness their own wills. It is something that everyone has, not just Heroes, and a strong discipline over one's mind can only aid the monks in their calling—which is battle in a righteous cause."

"Surely there can be no more righteous cause than the defeat of the darkness!" the king exclaimed. Garth's eyes clouded.

"So always speak the young," he murmured, more to himself than to the king. Recalling himself, he turned to Percy. "You are welcome here—I can sense the bond between us. No doubt this is how our feisty young Hero king found me when I did not wish to be found."

"No doubt indeed," said Percy, inclining his head. "He roused me from my centuries of slumber and gave me this form, and so he is my master. But I will also serve you, where such service does not conflict."

His voice sounded the same to the king, but richer, deeper; more formal, and certainly more respectful. The king was mildly irritated, then remembered just how important and powerful Garth really was. And then he wasn't offended at all but rather flattered that Percy was even willing to talk to him.

"The boy and I will share a meal," Garth said. "I will listen to what he has to say. And then . . . we will see."

Garth led the king up a gently winding stone path to a small dwelling that was revealed to be built partially into the mountain itself. Outside, there was a garden, where fragrant blossoms were blooming. When Garth opened the door, the king stepped into a cool and pleasant space.

To the right of the door, a woven rug lay near a window. Several colorful cushions were strewn on the floor, and the afternoon sunlight streamed in. Opposite what the king assumed to be a meditation space was a simple wooden chair and table. A small cot was placed on the floor to the left of the door, and a tall cabinet stood beside it. And that was it. The king had grown up in lavish surroundings, lacking for nothing, and yet the spare simplicity of the room was soothing.

"Please, sit," Garth said, indicating the single chair. "As you can see, I am not one for visitors. The community does much together, so in my private space I am . . . private."

"Thank you," the king said, taking the seat as invited. Garth moved about, reaching into the cabinet and pulling out odd-looking fruit, a selection of cheeses, and fresh-baked bread that smelled so good the king's mouth watered. Garth prepared a plate for each of them, gave one to his visitor, then settled himself on the cushions. He indicated no discomfort at sitting on the floor and folding his legs into what seemed to the king a very odd position as he began to peel a knobby fruit.

The king imitated Garth and bit into the fruit. It was delicious. He realized that he was actually ravenous and had to fight to not appear a glutton as he ate. At last, still hungry but needing to talk, he turned to Garth.

"In Albion, people think you are dead," he said. "There are rumors that Reaver killed you."

Garth made an annoyed face and waved a hand. "Of course there are," he said. "He tried. No doubt he was so embarrassed at his failure that he concocted some lavish tale about my demise at his hands."

"That certainly sounds like the Reaver I know," the king said. "We've not seen him around Albion for a while, thank goodness. He's smart, and he'll help you if it's in his interests, but he's—"

"Always out for himself, and has an ego larger than our friend out there," Garth finished.

"Exactly!"

"Well, he's off somewhere causing trouble if he's not doing so in Albion," Garth said. "Yet I think the trouble here is not of his making."

"What do you think it is?"

Garth paused in his eating and gave the king a piercing look. "What do *you* think it is? You're the Hero, not I."

The king bit back the comment, *but you live here!* and instead told Garth what he and Percy had discussed. "I don't know what form it is taking now, nor who or what is responsible for its being here. You might have a better idea than I."

"There is no doubt in my mind that if the Empress is not actually creating it, she is in league with it," said Garth. "And not just in league, but in . . . partnership, somehow. There is a personal feel to this darkness."

"You've been in this monastery for years, haven't you?" At Garth's nod, the king continued, "Then how can you know? You've been a hermit, not out in the world, and the darkness hasn't come here yet. Thankfully."

Garth smiled and tapped his temple. "I know here," he said. "When you open the mind and the heart, many things are revealed to you." He grew thoughtful. "Perhaps . . ."

The king held his breath.

"Yes," Garth said at last. "I will instruct you. We don't have that much time, and usually apprenticeships last years. But I will teach you the best that I can. Send Percy back to the army.

He will be able to protect them during their march. I will have one of the monks teach you what they can of their fighting style, and I will work with you on meditation and Will."

"I would be very grateful," the king said. "And . . . you will come with us? Against the Empress?"

Garth raised an eyebrow. "It depends. I am willing to be impressed, young Hero. But *you* have to do the impressing."

Chapter Eighteen

Page and Timmins walked along a narrow road, snow-covered save for the lines made by cart wheels and horses' hooves. Wrapped tightly in cloaks and shivering, she reflected that she was grateful that people seldom questioned what they thought they saw. They had only been intercepted once during their escape from Bowerstone Castle. Page had simply turned her face away and lifted a dark hand, and the guards let her through with a deep bow. They had assumed they were seeing Queen Laylah.

Reaver had been swift about putting up the Wanted posters. A mere two days after their disappearance, Page had spotted them going up on trees along the main roads. "He must really dislike you," she had commented to Timmins. "Look at that nose!"

"What about you?" Timmins had replied. "You look positively cross-eyed."

It was weak humor, but it helped. Their first task was simply to put distance between themselves and Bowerstone, and stick to side roads where possible. Last night, they had slept in a farmer's barn, their lullaby the lowing of cows and their food dried apples filched from said cows' feed.

"We probably ought to have a plan," Page said as they trudged along.

"Stay alive," Timmins said. "Prove our innocence."

"Ha-ha," Page replied. "I was thinking about something more immediate. We could go to Mistpeak. Sabine would certainly believe us over Reaver—or even over Laylah."

"I'm sure that's the first place Reaver has sent men to," Timmins said. "For the exact reasons you mentioned. Reaver knows Sabine would ally with us, and the Dwellers are not to be discounted in battle. So we need someplace—or places—that are less obvious. Someplace where Reaver wouldn't think to look for us."

"Good luck coming up with even one place," Page sighed.

"Blackholm, for one."

"Are you mad? You were arrested there, and several villagers along with you!"

"Which is precisely why Reaver would never expect us to go there. Page, you're a hero at Blackholm. And they know exactly what that cache was for—I gave it to them so they could protect themselves. Blackholm has good people. They won't turn us in."

"Even though some of their own were arrested alongside you?"

"The faster my innocence is proven, the faster those poor sods will be released," Timmins said. "And you know Her Majesty. Reaver might have convinced her to execute me, but she wouldn't execute anyone else without a fair trial, no matter how hard that rat pushes her. And trials can take a long time."

Page did know Laylah, and thinking about her was painful.

"All right, we can go to Blackholm. I remember there were a lot of little places that His Majesty had resettled. They were doing fairly well, as I recall. They'll likely be isolated enough so that those Wanted posters might not have reached them yet. And while we're on the run and figuring out how to convince Laylah that Reaver is the real culprit, we might as well do some scouting. I've not heard any evidence that the darkness has been encroaching anywhere in Albion yet, but at the least, we can observe for ourselves."

Timmins glanced at her and sighed. "I begin to think perhaps you were right, Page. I pushed the queen too hard."

Page shook her head. "You were trying to keep her safe, Jack. Nothing more. And Reaver's forgeries were masterful. Neither of us stood a chance once he got the idea into his head."

"Still . . . we played right into his hands."

"Nearly everyone does," Page said morosely. The sky was gray and she expected snow before the end of the day, and hoped fervently that they'd find another barn tonight.

They finally reached the outskirts of Blackholm. Timmins steeled himself. "Wait here," he told Page. "If this goes poorly, I don't want you caught in the cross fire."

"I think I should be the one to tell *you* to wait," she said. "As you pointed out earlier, I helped defend this town once at the risk of my own life, and they won't forget it. You, on the other hand, got some of their citizens arrested."

Timmins hesitated and Page rolled her eyes. "I'm nearly as good a shot as you are, and that's saying something. I can take care of myself if something goes wrong. And if it does—one of us needs to stay alive and free, or else Reaver will be running this country before you can say 'rat bastard.'"

"I despise your logic, Page. Because it is irrefutable. I'll be here with my rifle at the ready. All you need to do is shout."

Page gave him a reassuring smile. She was fairly certain she'd be welcomed, at least for a brief while, Wanted poster or no. The more she thought about that, the angrier she got. The artist *had* made her eyes look crossed. Confidently, she strode up to the gate and knocked.

"A traveler seeks a hot meal and a place to stay!" she called. For a long moment, nothing happened. There was a flutter of anxiety in her chest, but she reasoned, if the darkness had indeed started to threaten this little town, of course they would be cautious. She readjusted her grip on the pistol hidden in the fur muff. "I am an old friend of Russell's," she said. "And still a friend to Blackholm. Will you let me in?"

There was still no answer, but the gates creaked open. All of Page's senses were on heightened alert. Subtly she removed the pistol from the muff and dropped the hand by her skirts. No one was milling about, but she sensed eyes watching her. Were they all clustered inside, in the safety of their homes? What had happened to this place?

"I am Page," she called. "What's going on? What's happened here? Perhaps I can—"

The word "help" was never uttered. She heard the crack of a rifle and sensed movement behind her. Whirling, she fired directly into a falling body clad in a shirt, short trousers, boots, and a cap.

A very short, strangely shaped body, that was dead before she had even put a bullet in him.

"Behind you, Page!" shouted Timmins, running in the gate. Page heard giggling, chittering sounds, and by now she knew exactly what she faced. There was no time to reload the pistol, so she drew her sword instead.

Hobbes were always hideous, but there was something even worse about these. She'd seen them don bits and pieces of human clothes before, almost like trophies collected from their kills, but these ones were completely dressed. They carried guns and swords of their own, and they swept upon her like a wave. She heard the crack of gunfire as Timmins fired, dropping one of the grotesqueries with every shot. One of them reached her, brandishing a short sword and wearing a pink, frilly dress. Unnerved by the sight, Page hesitated almost too long before slicing open the creature's potbelly. It dropped, squealing.

More converged on her, all wearing the villager's clothes. She sliced off a long-eared head wearing a fetching bonnet, ran her blade through another wearing short trousers and suspenders, and again and again had the strange sense that she was fighting—

No, she couldn't think that, not if she was to defend herself. Even as Page gritted her teeth, she was careless in blocking a blow from a farmer's scythe, and it tore a gash down her arm.

The hobbe was felled before it could swing again. Timmins was beside her now, wielding two swords, his plain-featured face hard with determination. Back-to-back they fought, until at last, squealing in anger and disappointment, the remaining creatures fled.

There was utter silence in the town now. Page caught her breath and lowered the sword. Timmins noticed red seeping across the fabric of her arm. Grasping her other arm, he steered her back against the gate and sat her down. He tore a piece of fabric off her skirt and made a makeshift bandage.

"Hey, you realize that half yard of dress cost more than your annual salary," Page joked.

"Well worth it," Timmins said. If it had been any other man, Page would have thought he was flirting, but this was Timmins.

He handed her rifle, powder horn, and bullets. "Stay here. I'm going to make sure there aren't any more lurking about."

"No," Page said in a tone that brooked no disagreement. "I'm coming with you."

"I'm not sure that's such—" He sighed and held up his hands resignedly at the look on her face. In all honesty, Page wasn't sure it was such a good idea either. But she had a horrible suspicion, and wouldn't rest until it was either dispelled or confirmed.

They went to the bar and knocked on the door. No one moved to answer it, but there was a child's giggle from behind the door. Page let out a sigh of relief.

"Thank goodness," she said as Timmins turned the knob on the door. "I thought those hobbes were the village children and the parents had been—"

The words died in her throat. Before them were sprawled at least a dozen corpses. Some of them looked like they had been burned. Others had scratches on them, but no other signs of violence; still others looked as if they had been . . . chewed on.

And Page suddenly realized that it hadn't been a child who had been giggling.

"Nymphs!" she shouted. She pulled out her pistol and Timmins readied his rifle. Both of them looked around but saw nothing.

Another titter, as if there was a jolly good joke going on, and they weren't in on it.

And then Page spotted one, perching in the rafters. Its huge black eyes stared down at her, its wings moving slightly, its head cocked as if in curiosity. A soft, ethereal glow surrounded its green, bark-textured form.

Timmins blasted it with his rifle. It squealed, more in indignation than pain, and dropped to the floor.

The others attacked, wings buzzing in anger. It was almost

impossible to target them, as they darted back and forth, sometimes transforming themselves into small orbs of glowing light
that were impervious to attack, other times hurling little blasts
of fire that exploded into thornbushes.

"Retreat!" shouted Timmins. Page needed no second urging.
She raced out the door, Timmins at her heels. As soon as they
were clear, he slammed the door shut and leaned on it as angry
nymphs made soft, small *thuds* against it.

"Let me hold the door!" Page shouted. "You go find something to prop against it!" With her wounded arm, she wouldn't
be able to lift anything. Timmins nodded and a moment later
returned with a small bench, which he wedged against the door
under the knob.

"That won't hold for long," he warned.

"It doesn't have to," Page said. "Let's get out of here!"

There was nothing left for them in the town. The adults had
been slaughtered, and the malevolent nymphs had changed the
children of Blackholm into hobbes. They had no choice but to
flee this place and hope that the next town offered more hope
and less horror.

Laylah had awakened shortly after Page and Timmins had escaped. They had locked her in Page's cell, and the guard on
duty had himself been locked in the loo. She had to wait until
the morning shift came in, and of course by then, the two mis-
creants had made a clean escape.

She was devastated, and angry, and later, when Reaver had
offered her his deepest sympathies and asserted that he would
immediately have Wanted posters printed, she had told him,
"Offer a high reward."

How could Page do this to her? And furthermore, why, if she

was as innocent as she had claimed? Laylah had no doubt as to Timmins's guilt, especially not when Reaver had related how he had "caught that yellow-livered coward red-handed in Blackholme. Hmm . . . that's a colorful anecdote, don't you think? I rather like it."

He had cautioned her that now was not the time to show compassion. "The whole of Albion knows what a kind soul you are," he said. "But you must prove that you have a stout heart as well. Everyone will be watching what you do next. You must demonstrate beyond a shadow of a doubt that any acts of treason against you, or your council, which now consists solely of me, will not be tolerated. I suggest a round of lovely and graphic executions."

"No," Laylah had said. "I will execute no one without a fair trial. My husband would never do such a thing, and neither will I."

He had sighed. "Scruples," he said. "Such annoying things. As you wish. Then we must content ourselves with showing Your Majesty's untouchable power in other fashions." Angry, wounded, and eager to prove that she could rule just fine without traitorous babysitters, Laylah was more than willing to implement several of Reaver's suggested policies. She extended the curfew in Bowerstone that had gone into effect the day after Page and Timmins had escaped. Guards were recalled from distant places in the kingdom, sent there to watch for any appearance of the darkness, and instead reassigned to patrol the roads between towns. She raised the taxes on everything that came into and went out of Bowerstone.

As the days crawled by, Laylah withdrew into herself more and more. She no longer appeared daily to settle disputes, nor did she even leave the castle. She cloistered herself in her room, seeing only Reaver and Barrows, who brought her food, and, of course, the faithful Rex. She had expected being without her husband to be difficult, and ruling in his stead even more so. But she had never expected the horror of betrayal.

She was listlessly stirring sugar into her tea one afternoon when Barrows knocked on her door. Rex was looking at the scones with pleading eyes, thumping his tail hopefully on the floor. "Enter," she called.

"Madame," said Barrows, "Mr. Reaver is here to see you."

Laylah sighed. "Show him in. Oh, and Barrows, tell the cook to feed Rex. He's being a bit of a beggar today."

"Of course, my lady. Come on then, Rex, time for supper." The dog pricked up his ears at the word "supper," rose, and happily trotted to the door just as Reaver entered. Rex growled, but otherwise did nothing, following Barrows as Reaver swept off his top hat gallantly.

"Your Majesty," he said, and sat opposite her at the small table.

"What's happened now, Mr. Reaver?" Laylah tried to rouse herself to interest as she poured him a cup of tea. He accepted with a nod of thanks.

"Well," he said, "we've heard rumors of an insurrection in the Mistpeak area."

She stiffened. "That's quite impossible," she said. "Sabine is a friend, and more than loyal to Albion and my husband. Your informants, I think, are too eager for their pay and are making up stories."

"Possible, possible," he agreed. "But I would suggest sending several soldiers up there just to be certain."

"They're the closest to Samarkand," Laylah pointed out. Something was stirring to wakefulness inside her. Something wasn't . . . right. "Why would they choose now to alienate me?

We're the ones who'll be protecting them if the darkness crosses the mountains."

Reaver threw up his gloved hands in an exaggerated gesture of puzzlement. "Who can comprehend the mind of a Dweller?" he said plaintively.

"No," said Laylah. "I won't insult our friend like that."

"Then at the very least, I'd like for you to sign this," Reaver said, handing her a parchment and sliding the inkwell and quill on the table over toward her.

"What is it?"

"Nothing that you need concern your head with. Just a trifling adjustment to the current workers' composition, schedule, so forth and so on. I know how all this wearies you."

"Thank you, I think I will read it," Laylah said.

"I really don't think you need to—"

"*I* do, Mr. Reaver, and in case you've forgotten, I am the one ruling this kingdom." Her eyes fell to the parchment and landed on the words "child," "twenty-hour shifts," and "no further compensation for unfortunate incidents." She looked up at him— and saw a pistol staring her in the face.

"I am rather sorry to inform you, Your Majesty, that, actually, I am the one ruling this kingdom," Reaver said.

Laylah's eyes widened as fear shot through her. Even so, her hand dropped down to her thigh—and the pistol she always kept in a pouch there.

"You can't be serious," she said. Her voice quivered only a little. "You wouldn't dare kill me."

"Please put those lovely hands on the table right now, my dear," Reaver said, "and of course you are right." Without blinking an eyelash, he aimed his pistol at the closed door and fired. There was a sharp cry from Barrows on the other side. Laylah opened her mouth to scream, but somehow he had closed the distance between them and had her pinned to the floor, his hand over her mouth.

"You will do exactly as I say," he said. "I have plenty of bullets, and there are several dozen servants in the castle, are there not?"

Her eyes widened still further, and she nodded. "Good girl," he said. He lifted his mouth from her hand and moved away, permitting her to rise. In the brief time it took her to do so he had already reloaded the pistol. "I knew you'd see reason. Now. I understand there's a certain—Sanctuary that your husband likes to visit. You will take me there at once."

"I don't know what you're talking about."

His eyes went cold, and for the first time, Laylah truly saw the darkness in the man. Oh, if only she had believed Page and Timmins! "I quite enjoyed playing my little games with you, Your Majesty, but the hour grows late, and I am sure you are tired. Barrows?"

The door opened, and Barrows, unharmed, entered. Laylah couldn't believe it. "Barrows," she whispered. "You serve *him?*"

Barrows smirked. "Yes, Majesty. I've already told everyone not to worry—that you were cleaning your pistol and it went off. Best do as he says, my lady. There are plenty other servants here who aren't in his pocket."

"Good job, Barrows. Now, please make sure no one disturbs Her Majesty for the next little while. I'm guessing the Sanctuary isn't too far. I shan't kill you—I need you a bit too much—but Barrows is right. There's such a plethora of hostages I could choose from. Now. Take me to the Sanctuary, or we shall have to pay them a very unpleasant visit."

Chapter Nineteen

Jasper often felt as though he were the luckiest butler to ever live. Apart from that unpleasantness with King Logan, which was all eventually resolved quite satisfactorily, he could look back on his long life without complaint. He'd served the old king well and been treated well in return. And Jasper was utterly certain that part of the reason the current king had turned out as well as he had was due in no small manner to Jasper's care of him as a child and young adult.

Now, his care of the young king had been rewarded in a manner that made him feel joyful every day. No longer a mere butler, even a butler to a king, he was the keeper of the Hero King's Sanctuary. The place was intoxicating—every day, Jasper learned something new. And he had something he didn't know he craved—solitude. It was lovely having visitors now and then, mind you—while the king had been adventuring, the young Hero had returned frequently but briefly. And the lovely Queen Laylah had come a few times since her husband departed for war, often bringing him his favorite treat—peach cobbler from the kitchen. While the confection was always best with fresh peaches, he found the dried ones available during the winter an adequate substitute.

Tonight, something had been bothering him and he found himself rising from his rest. Donning his slippers, he padded in his nightclothes and cap to the three-dimensional map of Albion, wondering what had prompted him to do so.

He started violently when he heard Her Majesty's voice. "Jasper? I'm so terribly sorry to wake you."

Somewhat disoriented, the butler glanced about, wondering where the deuce Laylah was hiding, then belatedly realized she was speaking to him through the Guild Seal. He cleared his throat, feeling himself blush slightly with embarrassment.

"Not at all, not at all, Your Majesty! As it happens, I was already awake. Is all well?"

"Oh, yes, quite well, but there's something I need to check on in the Sanctuary. I was hoping you'd put the wards down so I could enter. I'm afraid I won't be bringing cobbler, though, not this time of year, so I'll have to make up for the inconvenience with something else later."

He opened his mouth to remind her that she could come and go as she liked, and also that one could prepare cobbler with dried fruit—

Oh, dear.

He hurried back to his room and began throwing on his clothes as he spoke. "Of course not, what a silly thought, peach cobbler in the winter, please don't worry your lovely royal head about it. I'll have everything ready for your arrival."

He hoped she would pick up on what he was saying—that, as he and the royal couple had once discussed, if anyone other than Laylah knew about the Sanctuary, Jasper was to pack up the most essential items and flee. He was no fighter; all had agreed this was how he could best serve.

"Excellent. I'll be there in a few moments."

"Lovely, Your Majesty, it's always a pleasure to see you no matter what the hour." He winced. Had that been too much?

No matter. He grieved to leave the lovely queen in possible peril, but he had his orders. He threw the Book of Heroes and a few other key magical items into a bag and hurried to the map. Where should he go? There was so much more the king would miss if it fell into the wrong hands. Maybe he should pack more.

His mind was a total blank. Suddenly he stood up straight. "Shake it off, Jasper!" he told himself sternly. "You have been butler to three kings. You know the politics as well as Their Majesties do."

He focused on Mistpeak Valley, realized it was too late to grab a proper overcoat, and activated the ring that contained a piece of the Guild Seal.

"How charmingly dramatic this all is!" Reaver exclaimed. "Descending into a chilly tomb, activating a hidden lever, a weeping angel giving you the Guild Seal . . ." He feigned a shiver. "You did well with Jasper. I think I shall enjoy having him serve me."

Laylah did not reply. In the frantic trip from her chambers to the tomb where the Seal was kept, she had been racking her brain trying to think how to warn her friend. She was fairly certain he had understood her, but she wouldn't know until they materialized in the Sanctuary

"Now," he said, "tell me how this works." When she did not reply, he sighed. "I thought we had reached an understanding. If you don't tell me how this works, we march back to the castle and I start executing chambermaids and groomsmen."

Tears welled in her eyes. To obey him would be the ultimate

betrayal of her husband. To defy him would be to murder innocents. But to unleash him on the Sanctuary, especially if Jasper had not been able to escape with the more precious items—it would give him yet more power. And how many innocents would die then?

"I grow weary of your balking," he said, with an edge to his elegant voice. "Choose, or I shall choose for you."

Courage stiffened her spine. She had betrayed the location of the Guild Seal, but so far, all she had done was warn Jasper. She could still protect the Sanctuary from this monster. She felt a smile curling her lips as she spoke.

"The Guild Seal is bound only to my husband, Jasper, and to me. Before that, it was bound to my husband's father, the king. You can't enter it unless I take you there. And I am *never* going to take you. I will kill myself before I let you use me."

He seemed not to have heard her last impassioned statement. "Bound to the old king and the three of you, eh? Not by blood, obviously. By loyalty and love, then. Obviously I don't have *that*. But now here's a fair question—is it bound to the king because he is a king . . . or because he is a *Hero*?"

He reached over, grasped the Guild Seal, and with a blinding flash of light, they both disappeared. An instant later, they were in the Sanctuary—a Sanctuary mercifully empty of Jasper. Reaver turned on her, giving her a mock bow.

"Clever girl. You managed to warn the old fellow, didn't you? Well done. Even though I obviously do not need you to operate the Guild Seal, I think I shall keep you around for a while longer. You may be very useful indeed." He looked around, marveling. "This place is extraordinary! Although your husband needs better taste in tailors," he said, as he eyed some of the costumes on mannequins with distaste. "However, the quality of these weapons make up for that. I can't wait to supplement my armory."

Laylah wished she had used the pistol on herself. Anything
not to have to watch this evil, smug dandy behaving in so propri-
etary a fashion with her husband's most precious items.

"Oh, and one more thing," Reaver said. "I did tell you if you
didn't cooperate, someone would suffer. I gather this map will
take me wherever I need to go in a jiff. Let's go back to Bowerstone, and you get to select who I'm going to kill."

They materialized inside the castle. Laylah's legs nearly gave
way when she saw seven chambermaids and footmen sitting on
the floor, each one of them bound hand and foot and staring up
at her in pleading silence. Only Reaver's steel-like hand on her
arm kept her from falling. They were overseen by the smirking
Barrows.

"Welcome back, Majesty, Mr. Reaver," he said. "I've assembled some of the staff as you requested."

Something inside Laylah broke. "Please," she whispered. "I
won't thwart you again. Just don't harm these people. They're
servants, not in any position to do anything for or against you.
Don't harm them!"

"Ah," Reaver said, "but you see, they *are* in a position to do a
great deal for me. As long as I hold them hostage, I have, as you
say, a guarantee that you won't thwart me again. However, I
think it incumbent upon me to prove that I am not the old softie
that my employees make me out to be. I will pick someone if
you don't, rest assured. You do understand I've got to be certain
of your cooperation."

How could she live with this? How could she pick an innocent to die? Who deserved life most, and who was she to deter-
mine it? She looked at the elderly footman Robertson, the shy,
mousy young kitchen girl Daisy, at Mary and Chester and . . .

"I have made my decision. I may choose any of the assembled
domestics, correct?"

"Quite correct."

"I have your word that you will not gainsay my choice?"

He put his hand to his heart. "I do have my own code of honor, Your Majesty. Choose someone to execute, and I shall execute him or her."

Slowly, she turned and locked eyes with Barrows. "I choose him," she said.

Barrows gaped, all his smugness gone. "What—Mr. Reaver, sir, that's ridiculous. I'm your servant, not hers!"

Reaver gave the queen an admiring look. "Well played, Majesty. That's twice tonight you've managed to thwart me, at least slightly, in my aims. I confess, I had thought you a simple little thing, but now I see you're made of sterner stuff. You should be aware you might have played your hand too soon, though. I shan't underestimate you again."

"You will honor your word?"

"I always do," he said, and even as Barrows gibbered and begged, Reaver calmly cocked the pistol, aimed, and fired.

No one took much notice of the queen's absence over the next several days. Since the arrests of Page and Captain Timmins, she had not appeared publicly much, and the populace, as populaces will, had adapted to her new schedule. There was some speculation over ales at the Cock in the Crown tavern and elsewhere, and not a little bit of complaining. Still, the end result of most such conversations, save the ones that were overly fueled by alcohol, was that the queen was a lovely and kind thing, and it must have been very upsetting for her to learn that her friends had betrayed her so. And as for the rules and taxes, well, war was expensive; better to tighten belts now than later, eh? Besides, spring was coming, and the almanac was predicting a lovely and fertile one. And wasn't it the other fellow's turn to get the ales this time?

When it was revealed that Her Majesty would be making a Very Important Announcement in the gardens of the castle, everyone was abuzz. Was there word on the war? Were there confirmations of some of those nasty rumors of the darkness lurking around the edges of the comfortable lamplight of smaller towns? Was there going to be a grand party or a new holiday declared? Well, a chap could always hope.

So they gathered in the gardens, filling it to capacity and beyond, eager to get a glimpse of Her Royal Majesty Queen Laylah after so long and hoping for good news. As she appeared, the crowd burst into cheers and applause. Goodness, had she always been so thin? It was hard to tell, but she seemed paler, didn't she? Of course, everyone was pale in the winter. Behind her walked Reaver, and a single loud "Boo!" uttered in comfortable anonymity wafted up.

The queen smiled and waved, then indicated they should quiet down. They obliged.

"My beloved subjects," she said, and my, didn't her voice sound subdued, don't you think? "It has been some time since I have formally addressed you—or even informally come to your places of work, or been welcomed into your homes. I regret the necessity which has kept me so cloistered. I will keep this brief, as there is still much that requires my attention on a daily basis.

"Some time ago, two people whom I considered friends turned traitor. They were arrested, and made their escape—by attacking me physically."

Gasps of horror and sympathy rippled through the crowd. Hurt Queen Laylah? How could anyone even *say* anything cruel to one so gentle, let alone harm her?

"They are extremely dangerous. I know that in times past, you all thought well of them. So did my husband—and so did I. But those times are indeed past. As of today, I am doubling the reward for information on them to five thousand gold, and to those who can find and bring them to me, d-dead or alive, I offer ten thousand."

Now that was some real money! Hadn't the pie maker over the hill said he thought he'd seen Captain Timmins the other day?

"Now, as to the war," the queen continued, "I have, regretfully, heard nothing from my husband the king as to its progress. But he is in a faraway land, and truly, none could reasonably expect to hear anything for a long time. I know all of you are doing your duties as good citizens here, and your helping your kingdom, and me, helps the king.

"To that end, Mr. Reaver has offered to expand Reaver Industries."

Ah, now, *that* . . . unhappy muttering went up. Queen Laylah lifted her hands imploringly. "I know that in the past Mr. Reaver has not been . . . popular. But hear me out! Our ruler is at war, protecting the interests of Albion. Can we do no less? If Mr. Reaver steps up production, it means more employment, more productivity, more weapons to protect us here at home if the darkness does choose this time, when we are depleted in our weapons and manpower, to attack."

Hmm . . . hadn't thought about it that way.

"Increase in farming tools will help you sow your crops more efficiently, which means more food come harvest time. I personally will be working with him to ensure what is best for all."

There was a smattering—just a smattering—of dubious but polite applause. After all, Queen Laylah would *always* do what was best for her people.

"Finally, until this war is over, we are ceasing all trade with

Aurora. While it is true they are our allies as my husband braves Samarkand, we cannot afford to support them at a time when our resources are already depleted due to tending our own populace and to the war effort. Albion must focus on its own needs until such time as we are victorious, at home and abroad."

More than anything, the general populace was puzzled. How was not helping Aurora, Albion's ally, helping the war effort? Then again, Aurora was helping itself by fighting alongside the Albion troops, wasn't it? So . . . it made sense. Kind of.

"I thank you again for your loyalty to the crown and your country. Long live Albion!"

"Long live Albion!" This, at least, was a thought easily understood and readily embraced.

"And long live Their Majesties!" shouted Reaver, speaking for the first time.

"Long live Their Majesties!"

The speech was over. Time for an ale. Maybe two.

"You were magnificent, my dear," said Reaver as he "escorted" the queen back to her quarters. "Even I would be hard-pressed to deliver so eloquent and impassioned a speech."

"I hate you," Laylah spat.

"Well, we both know *that*," said Reaver. "But it doesn't mean I can't appreciate and even applaud your thespian abilities. Keep this up, and I daresay you won't have that many jobs to fill at the castle. Have you hired a new butler yet, by the way?"

"You know I haven't. I'm waiting for one of your toadies to show up."

"I've not had much of a chance to interview toadies; I've been too busy with minions and lackeys." They had reached her quarters. One of Reaver's men stood guard at the door. As he opened it, Rex, who had been curled up on the bed, got to his feet. He glanced at Laylah, his tail wagging slightly, then at Reaver, and he growled.

"Now," said Reaver, "be a good little queen and settle in until I've need of you."

"I need to let my dog out first," Laylah said. Reaver frowned, clearly mistrusting the request. "Oh come now," Laylah burst out, "he's a dog. He needs to go outside. Or do you expect me to clean up when he goes inside?"

"Well, that would be rather untidy," Reaver said. "Let's let him out then, poor fellow." He smiled at the dog. The dog bared his teeth—a similar gesture, but an entirely different meaning.

"Come on, Rex, off you go," said Laylah. She gripped the border collie by the collar, leading him to the door that exited onto the gardens. Turning so her back was to Reaver, she quickly let Rex sniff one of her gloves. Rex wagged his tail, then bolted.

"Here now, what's this?" snapped Reaver. He hurried to the door and drew his pistol on the dog.

"No!" shouted Laylah, tugging his arm down. The shot went wild, and Rex was out of range and harm's way. Reaver turned on her, not bothering to hide his fury, and even after all she had seen from him, Laylah quailed inside at the look on his face.

"What mischief are you up to now, hmm?" He grabbed her arm and squeezed painfully.

"You've already got several innocents as hostage," she replied. "I'm not going to let you have a poor dog's life to hold over my head as well!"

"You and the king and your dogs," Reaver sighed. "I'll shoot the cur on sight if he returns, you know. You'd best hope he doesn't."

Laylah prayed he wouldn't. She stood, straight and silent, until Reaver departed, closing the door behind him. When she was certain he was gone, and she would not be heard, Laylah flung herself on the bed.

Oh, my love, I have unwittingly betrayed us all. But I will thwart him every way I can until you come safely home. I promise, I promise!

Chapter Twenty

The training with Garth began immediately after their meal and quickly took on its own rhythm. The king would rise at dawn, break his fast with something simple, then meet the masters of the various martial arts—the staff, the sword, the rope, and what was cryptically termed "*our* weapons." The king was most proficient with blade weapons and a variety of guns, but less so with the others. He recognized the uses of such things as the staff and the hammer, and the handiness of a rope, chain, or whip, though the proper usage of such things challenged him. He was, however, totally unprepared for the dangerous weapon known as:

"A rake?" the king said, staring at the pronged instrument used for breaking topsoil.

"A rake," the monk said. "We also have scythes, spades, and shovels with which we fight. You will notice this is no ordinary rake but one we have adapted to use for a martial purpose. Still, any of our monks could find any such tool and fight well with it. It is a higher art than the sword—being able to make use of whatever comes to hand. That is why we call them 'our' weapons—we make them ours, and they serve us."

"I do see how that could be useful, particularly if we are arming a populace," the king said. "Very well—show me how to fight with rakes and spades."

The monks did, and the king, who was no slouch when it came to battle, found himself marveling at not just the skill but the grace and seeming tranquillity with which the monks fought.

He held his own when it came to sword fighting. Even so, the monks taught him different parries and feints than the ones he had learned from Sir Walter or in the thick of combat, where necessity was a fine teacher. They taught him how to use his attacker's own force against him, and time and again the king found himself flat on his face when it appeared to him the monk sparring with him wasn't even breaking a sweat.

After the exhausting training sessions, he would meet Garth for the midday meal, which was the heaviest of the day—roasted meats, bread, cheeses, and fruits. Garth began teaching him ways to stretch, move, and hold his body that felt more like punishment than the actual sparring did. After the third day, the king asked, "I understand why I am learning to fight with different weapons. But . . . why am I learning how to do these?"

"So you can sit for hours and meditate," came the confusing reply. The king reasoned that Garth knew what he was doing— at least Percy hadn't indicated that the Will user had gone stark raving mad—so he obeyed.

Then came the sitting. It was the hardest discipline of them all. Just . . . sitting. At first the king fidgeted, trying to get and stay comfortable and clear his mind as Garth instructed him.

"Your mind chatters like a monkey," Garth observed. "I can hear it from here. You are thinking to yourself, why is this old man having me sit when we could be making plans?"

"Um," said the king, blushing a little.

"Because when you learn to be still in your mind, it will start opening to you. And you will discover things about how to use it you have never even imagined. I sat for a decade in Lucien Fairfax's hellhole of a spire, honing my Will, being still, and unlocking the secrets of my mind in order to escape. We don't have the luxury of so much time, but you are a Hero. Things come easier to us, more naturally. It is part of our heritage. So perhaps the little time we have will be sufficient."

The change happened almost from one breath to the next. The king was sitting, bored, his mind chattering like the monkey Garth had said it was, when all of a sudden—it clicked. He understood. His breath was energy, it flowed through him, and as if he had unlocked a treasure chest, suddenly he realized the full potential of his mind.

"I've got it!" he cried, and of course the focus shattered.

Garth had sighed.

After that, the king was able to dip deep into the resources of his brain. The fighting became easier as he learned to think like the monks. The meditation left him clear and refreshed instead of bored and twitchy. Garth began teaching him new spells, new ways of looking at old spells. It wasn't quite effortless, but there was a flow to it that the king had never quite grasped before. No wonder his father had extolled Garth as one of the greatest Heroes of Will ever known.

It all came together; calmness begat focus, focus begat harmony between thought and action. And by the time a monk hurried up to Garth with word that the army had been sighted and Percival had landed, the king felt as if he had barely known who he was before.

Percival landed in the same open area he had before, this time bearing Ben, Kalin, Shan, and Shalia on his back. The king strode up to them with a broad smile on his face, hugging Shalia and Kalin, clapping Shan on the shoulder, and giving Ben a thump on the back and a warm handshake.

"You seem . . . different, Your Majesty," Kalin observed.

"I am, and for the better," the king said. "Garth has been teaching me in many things."

"Garth," said Ben, suddenly subdued. "It's an honor to meet you, sir."

Garth inclined his head, accepting the compliment. "His Majesty has spoken well of all of you," Garth said, and when his eyes fell on Shan, he smiled. "I am especially proud of my young Samarkandian brother. And sister," he said, including Shalia in his smile. "But time is not our friend. The longer you are in Samarkand, the more likely it is that word of your arrival has reached the Empress. We must begin our strategizing and plan the assault."

He unrolled the map he had brought with him. Rather to the king's surprise, Garth sat down and spread the parchment right on the bare earth. At the king's expression, he said, "We could retire to my small home, but then our friend Percival would not be included."

Percy looked startled, then pleased. "I must say, you newer Heroes are a much more polite lot than the ones I served a few centuries ago. Thank you, Garth, I shall contribute as best I may."

They all sat in a circle, regarding the map intently. "I have been to the palace as a guest of the Emperor before it was fully corrupted by the Empress," Garth said. "It pains me even now to think of its beauty. I know not what we will find, but I have drawn a map of the city as I remember it. I would imagine the basic structure has not changed. I did not see the wall when it was completed, but I know it has a timber frame and is covered with hard-baked earth. It rings the city completely and stands forty feet high."

"How do you know all this if you've never seen it?" Ben asked.

Garth smiled. "I may have rejected the outside world for many years, but I still have my sources," he said, then turned back to the map. "Outside the city, wandering nomads and the farmers who fed the general populace dwelt. The river Zaha, which gives the city its name, flows through the center, dividing it in half. Zahadar consists of five parts: the northern and southern outer city, the northern and southern *inner* city, and the palace."

The king nodded. The city was very tidily structured, its geometry nearly perfect. "The outer city is where the ordinary folk live and work. Here you'll find markets, merchant stalls, that sort of thing. General food items were sold in the southern half, and mercantile and textile items in the northern. The northern inner city was reserved for government buildings, the southern part for private residences for the higher classes. And the palace, of course, was for the Emperor. As you can see—"

"All three parts have walls," Ben said glumly. It was true: one massive one about the entire city, one enclosing the more urban part, and one ringing the palace itself. "We're going to have to do a great deal of architectural redesign."

"Perhaps, perhaps not," Garth said. "The river flows through here and here," he continued, indicating Xs on the wall on the east and west sides. "The main gate opens to the south." He glanced up at his companions with dark eyes. "It would be my supposition that the walls are patrolled day and night, and the single entrance heavily guarded. Your Majesty, did you bring any siege weaponry?"

The king grimaced. "We have some," he said. "What didn't get sunk by hollow men or stolen by sand furies or just plain stuck in the sand."

Garth nodded. "A pity. Well, we'll just have to make do. Now, based on my knowledge of Zahadar, this is my plan."

The next town that Page and Timmins came to was a place called Thorndeep. Until recently, it had been abandoned for centuries, and many dark things had dwelt there. But once the king had defeated the Crawler's armies, he was determined to restore not just the damaged Old Quarter, but all of Albion, if possible. Hardy souls who were willing to clear out Thorndeep, build homes, and make a community there were paid well for their efforts, and the little place was thriving.

"Hard to believe this was once a bastion of evil," Timmins commented as they approached the outskirts of the town.

"Even in winter, it seems cheery enough," Page said. Cottages were nestled a few yards from the road. Most of them had candles in their windows and smoke from hearth fires streaming up into the afternoon air. Others, though, stayed dark, and Page noticed that there were no footprints in the snow around these. "Though it looks like some people have left for the winter," she added.

"Now that's a bit odd," Timmins said. "It's not really a summer town per se."

They exchanged glances. "Let's hope that the villagers are both alive and still human," Page said.

Alert now, they were cautious as they reached the town proper. It opened into what was clearly a market square, with government buildings, an inn, a tavern, and places of business lining it. No market in the winter, of course, but it still felt—and looked—oddly empty.

A door to one of the buildings opened and a cheerful-looking, stout lass emerged carrying several loaves of bread and what appeared to be a freshly baked pie, and they relaxed. "Looks alive and human to me," said Timmins.

"Me too," Page said. "And that pie smells heavenly."

They went inside. The pie maker was attending two other customers, a large, burly youth with his first growth of beard and a genial manner, and a slender, plain girl who stood closely by the man's side.

"The dried apricot pie was perhaps your best yet, Tabitha!" the young man enthused. "But I hear you've got a dried berry pie that will top that this week!"

"Peg, does Fergus butter *you* up like this?" the pie maker asked playfully. The plain girl smiled, and as she did so, Page thought her beautiful.

"He does," Peg said, leaning close to the man who was clearly her husband. "Young love is so sweet. By the time he's done, I think I'm the queen herself."

"Lucky, the pair of you," the pie maker chuckled. "I'll bet you'll be saying that the second month you're married, too! Here you go—and an apple tart on the house."

"Talented, lovely, and generous too," Fergus said. "What a blessing to have you here, my dear." He picked up the pie and tarts and turned his beaming smile upon Page and Timmins. "Well, well, new faces! What brings you to Thorndeep—other than Tabitha's superb pies?"

"What'll it be, loves?" Tabitha asked cheerfully.

"One berry pie, if you have any left," Timmins said. To Fergus, he said, "We're heading to Bowerstone, to see if we can get some work there." No one had to know that they had come *from* Bowerstone.

Fergus sighed. "And here I was hoping you and the young lady might stay on. You and the rest of the populace are heading for Bowerstone, it seems," he said in a melancholy tone.

"Several boys joined up when the king asked for recruits," Peg added in her soft, shy voice, "and since then many more people our age have decided to seek their fortune in the big city."

"I see," said Page. "And that's not really helpful to Thorndeep's continued success, is it?"

"No, it isn't," came an angry voice from the corner. A cadaverously thin man sat there eating a piece of pie. "This town needs stability; it needs good, strong, devoted people. Else those bal—"

"Hush now, Theo," Fergus scolded. "Finish your pie."

"Bal?" asked Page, then her eyes widened. "Balverines? Here?"

Fergus gave Theo a glare. "A few, now and again," she said. "They're under control, for now. But I do worry that if more and more people leave, what's to become of the rest of us? Can't go to the king for help, he's away fighting a war and I hear his captain of the guards has turned traitor."

"Indeed?" said Timmins blandly.

"Aye. Now Reaver will be running the place, I imagine. And I don't think we'll get any help from the likes of—"

Gunfire interrupted him. Page met Timmins's eye and with no words spoken, they rushed as one out of the shop.

Four balverines had charged into the square. One of them was attacking the woman they had just seen leaving with a pie. Two others had attacked other passersby, and the fourth had broken into one of the shops from which screaming could be heard.

Page drew her pistol and took aim at the one mauling the shrieking woman, but she wasn't in time. The balverine's teeth crunched down on its victim's throat, and her cries ceased. It threw back its head and howled its victory. The gooey red remnants of the smashed berry pie on the ground looked sickeningly like the blood on its hideous muzzle. Page dropped it in midhowl with a precise shot to the head. Timmins had already drawn his sword and was battling another balverine. Page quickly reloaded, aimed, and dropped the second one.

Both of them ran into the shop to find the balverine lying on the floor and a stunned blacksmith standing atop it. The man had felled the creature with a red-hot blade still being held by a pair of tongs.

"First time I've ever killed anything with a blade I was still making," he stammered.

"Well done!" exclaimed Timmins. "Are you sure you got it?"

The man peered at the balverine, at its elongated ugly limbs and hunched body, and his face hardened.

"Awful things. Better make sure," he said, and brought the hammer down on the creature's skull.

A sudden familiar sound reached Page's ears as Timmins checked to make sure the man hadn't been bitten. She hurried out of the shop to see a bedraggled black-and-white dog running up to her and jumping into her outstretched arms.

"Rex!" exclaimed Page, hugging the dog tightly. He was thin and trembling from the cold, and his coat smelled very rank. She didn't care. She was thrilled to see him.

"How did he manage to track us down?" asked Timmins, coming out of the shop and patting the dog himself.

"A long time ago, Laylah trained him to come fetch me, using a pair of gloves I'd left behind," Page said. "She must have sent him."

His expression hardened. "Why? What does that mean?"

Page noticed something fastened to the dog's collar. "I bet this will tell us," she said, forcing her voice to stay calm. She placed Rex down and with trembling fingers untied the tightly-rolled-up note, unfolded it, and read:

To my true friends—

I have discovered, to my anguish, that I should never have doubted you. All is indeed as you tried to warn me. I send this stout fellow to you, both to ensure his safety and to let you know—I know. I am unharmed and believe I will stay so . . . he needs me too much.

Forgive me, my friends, and know—I will not let him win!

"Nice and mysterious, in case someone caught Rex," Timmins said approvingly. "Smart girl."

Page was overcome and held the letter to her heart. Laylah believed them now—and was on their side. "She's going to put herself at risk if she tries to defy Reaver and he finds out," Page said, clearing her throat and rising. She tore the letter into small shreds and tossed them into a nearby brazier.

"Well," Timmins said, "we'll have to make sure that someone's working on her behalf on the outside. That would be us."

"Indeed it would be," said Page. "We'll stop Reaver and the darkness—the three of us, and anyone else we can find who believes in our cause. Somehow. We've got to!"

Chapter Twenty-one

There were two more oasis villages along the Great Road between Zahadar and the monastery. The vast majority of the monks had agreed to accompany the king; a few remained behind, to tend to the crops and the animals. The king thought that, with the legendary Hero Garth and several dozen warrior monks as allies, the villagers might be persuaded to join in the fight.

"They live closest to the heart of darkness," the king had said. "When they see their countrymen joining with me, they may be inspired to offer their aid."

"And they may not," said Garth.

"We have a dragon," Ben pointed out.

It was decided that the effort at least would be made at the first village. It was met with success beyond the king's wildest imaginings. There was no true loyalty to the Empress this close to the capital city. The outlying towns were obedient only out of fear. When the king and Garth arrived on the back of a legendary creature, along with an already-assembled army and several of the famed warrior monks, the villagers wept happily and ran to get their own weapons, simple though they might be.

"Before you came," the leader of one village said, "we had no hope. Now, we see two Heroes and a mythic beast, with an army behind them, ready to put an end to this evil that has cowed us for so long. Yes, we will fight with you. With pitchforks and scythes and our bare hands, if need be."

"That is what *we* will be using," one of the monks said, shrugging.

The king was glad of the extra supplies the monks had contributed as the army expanded as they marched. By the time they were ready to depart the second oasis town and head into the final stretch of the march on Zahadar, their ranks had increased by over five hundred able-bodied and willing villagers.

Scouts who had gone ahead reported what Garth had feared. "There is a standing army. Our numbers are greater, and our weaponry similar, but they are rested and well fed and watered. They also have many mounted units. We could not tell what sort of military presence is inside."

"Do they appear to have been there for some time?" asked the king.

"Yes, Sire. There was a familiarity and ease among the men as they went about their business."

"Well, that means that she didn't bring them in just for us, then," the king said.

"Which is both good and bad," Garth replied. "It means that the Empress probably isn't aware of our presence yet—but it also means she's been prepared for some kind of attack for a long time. And it also means those fighters are highly trained and deadly. And, no offense, but yours is largely a volunteer army."

"Many of them saw action when Albion defeated the Nightcrawler nearly ten years ago," Ben said. "The rest have more than gotten their feet wet since they've been here. Maybe this

Empress does have more professionals than we do—but don't count out the Albion army yet."

"Plus," put in Kalin, "we have two Heroes."

Garth looked pensive. "I'm not sure what the Empress is, exactly," he said, "but she certainly is more than an ordinary woman. Let us hope that she, too, is not a Hero."

The river Zaha flowed westward from the eastern mountains, through farmlands, then into the city. Most of the Empress's soldiers were stationed to the south and west of Zahadar, where they could keep a sharp eye on the main roads. No army would approach from the east; they couldn't march sufficient numbers through the mountains. So it was here, with the silhouette of the great Samarkandian capital looming up against a skyful of stars, that the attack began.

The king and about a dozen others selected for this first mission were strong swimmers capable of holding their breaths for much longer than usual. They would have to be to complete their tasks. They were naked, carrying their clothing—traditional Samarkandian wear offered by the villagers—in empty, pitch-sealed water gourds. The gourds were weighted, so the swimmers would not be overly buoyed. The vanguard waded into the river, shivering a little at the cold, then slipped in fully and began to swim.

They were not fighting the current, so the first part was easy—swim steadily, keeping their heads above water so as to navigate by starlight. After a time, the king could see the wall of the great city looming. He raised a hand, and they all halted, drifting over to either embankment.

Here was where it got tricky. From this point on, all was an unknown. The king handed his gourd to one of the other swimmers, inhaled and exhaled a few times, then dove straight down.

He was completely blind, and went slowly, his arms out-stretched. Questing fingers brushed up against an expected obstacle—a gate of metal bars. The gaps were large enough for water to flow in easily, but the bars filtered out larger items. Such as human beings, the king thought. But, they had ex-pected this. His air was starting to run out; he would have to act quickly or else surface and try again.

The king extended his gauntleted arm and summoned his Will. He tried to concentrate, to remember how to augment the spell as Garth had taught him. A shock rippled as an invisible force pushed hard against the gate. He heard it groan, the sound muffled by the water. He tried again, and again it gave—but not enough. His lungs burning, the king shot to the surface.

"There's a gate, like we expected," he said to the waiting sol-diers. He was gasping a little and slowed his breathing to nor-mal. "It's weakening. One more good one should do it. Four of you—come down with me. We'll need to hide it once it's free."

He dove again, accompanied by the others. Once more he concentrated, focused, force-pushed—and the gate gave way. The four others seized it and bore it a safe distance back up-stream. The others would have cheered if they'd dared.

The way into the city was now clear.

Ben wasn't the most patient of men, certainly not right before a battle. He kept stealing sneaking, admiring glances at Garth, who sat cross-legged on a small rug on the sand. In the darkness, the strange symbols on his skin glowed bright blue. Ben had protested against the king's being one of the initial scouts. "We can't take the risk of anything happening to you," he had said.

"We can't *not* take the risk, Ben," the king said kindly, dropping a hand on his friend's shoulder. "I need to know what it looks like in there. And I have abilities that no one else but Garth has. You know I want to do this as efficiently and humanely as possible."

"You're too good for your own . . . well, good," Ben had muttered. He still didn't think they should risk the king in this way, but his liege was adamant.

The first group was to find a way in through the river entrance, scout out the city, and report back before dawn. And dawn was on its way.

There was a soft squeeze on his arm, and he turned to see Shalia sitting beside him. "It will be all right," she said. "The king is very wise. He will take all precautions."

"Suppose some overeager guard spots him and arrests him for something stupid, like a broken curfew? Or loitering with a water gourd?"

Shalia smiled. "He will have gotten rid of the gourd," she said, her voice holding a hint of amusement.

"I know, I know, I just—"

Garth's eyes snapped open. "The scout returns," he said, getting to his feet. Ben looked in the direction of Zahadar, and saw nothing for several long minutes. How had Garth—never mind. He didn't want to know.

"Good news, I hope," he said as the man hurried up. It was one of the monks, Sohar.

"Very good," Sohar replied. "We were able to assess the climate. The people here are not happy but they are obedient, and when they obey, their lives are tolerable. The military moves among them freely. There are several Palace Guards stationed at key areas. But the best news is that the king has found a way to slip into the palace itself. Here is his plan."

Shortly after delivering his report, Sohar led a second round of expert hand-to-hand fighters through the river to enter the city. They would meet up with the others, prepare, and await the next phase of battle. As soon as Sohar had gone, Garth gave the orders, and the army, siege engines in the front, began to move on Zahadar.

Under cover of the night, they would not be sighted quite as soon as they would have been during daylight hours but they would be detected eventually. The men kept pace with the oxen as the beasts steadfastly pulled several small cannons, the single surviving catapult, and the ballistae. Ben cursed the fate that had robbed them of so many siege weapons. He was well aware it could mean the difference between success and failure.

They were spotted when they were still two miles out. A moving line appeared on the horizon, and Ben realized he was looking at dozens of mounted soldiers.

"The jig's up," he cried to Garth. "Here we go!"

"Indeed," muttered Garth. "Shan—you stay behind me and do everything I say. Do you understand?"

Percival's shadow fell on them, then the sand dragon landed. "Yes, sir," Shan stammered, his eyes wide at the approaching tide of riders. He followed Garth, scrambling atop the dragon and clinging tightly. Percy made a vertical leap upward, bearing the two Samarkandians aloft.

"Line one, formation!" came Garth's voice from above the fray. "Take aim, and fire at will!"

As if it were a choreographed performance, several dozen armed soldiers hastened into a line. Almost simultaneously, their rifles cracked. The soldiers dropped to their knees, reloading.

"Line two, formation! Take aim, and fire at will!"

This was Ben's line, and he joined the others, mowing down

the onrushing soldiers before they could get close enough to attack. There were a few stray shots from the Empress's army, but a man standing—or kneeling—on the good solid earth was always going to have the advantage over one on horseback.

Percival wheeled above them, dove in low so that Garth could attack, and then bore the Hero out of harm's way. For a moment— a very short one—Ben felt sorry for the guards. They had no idea they were attacking a Hero and looked more stunned than anything as vortices of wind whirled them about, scouring them bloody with sand the eddies had picked up. When at last the dust devils Garth controlled threw the hapless soldiers aside, they were easy for the king's foot soldiers to pick off.

Cannon fire roared, blasting a cluster of the enemy. The drivers of the oxen pushed the frightened beasts onward grimly, the heavy weapons making their slow-but-inexorable way to the wall of Zahadar. The fighting was largely hand-to-hand now that the two armies had closed on one another. The advantage the Empress's army had—horses—had all either fallen with their masters or else, terrified beyond anything they had been trained for in battle, had bucked off their riders and, very sensibly Ben thought, galloped the hell out of the way.

Percival swooped low again. This time, Garth's Will manifested itself in pillars of lightning that paralyzed and killed, cutting a swath through the soldiers.

On the army of Albion and Samarkand marched, the oxen bellowing in protest as their drivers forced them to tread on the fallen bodies and bloody sand. Finally, the enemy's numbers diminished. When Percy and Garth bore down on them for another attack, the soldiers of the Empress turned and fled back to the safety of their walled city. A ragged cheer went up and some made as if to give pursuit, but Garth called down, "Fall back! The battle has only begun, do not squander your energy!"

He landed and dismounted, Shan scrambling down after him. "Scout ahead, Percy, and let us know what's waiting for us when we get there," Garth instructed the sand dragon. Percy inclined his head and took off, his great wings carrying him swiftly upward.

"They'll have men on the wall," Ben said. "Hoping to pick us off."

"Most likely," Garth agreed. "But we have a dragon and a Hero."

"Two Heroes," Ben corrected.

"Of course, two of us. I pray our second Hero is able to take advantage of the distraction we will be providing him."

"Funny, when you think about it," Ben said, "a dragon, siege engines, rows of firepower, a Hero throwing magic about—and all this is just a distraction. The real battle will be going on inside there."

"Not if we don't get that gate down," Garth said. Percy was returning, dropping to the sand a few yards away and striding over to them.

"Marksmen on the walls," Percival reported, and Ben tried hard not to look smug.

"Let's remove that threat right away, shall we?" replied Garth. Percival lowered himself so Garth could climb atop his back. Shan started to follow, but Garth stopped him.

"We'll be flying lower this time and will present the main target," Garth explained. "You're safer here, at least for now."

Shan nodded. He was disappointed but trying not to look it. Ben clapped a hand on the boy's shoulder. "Don't be overeager to see war, my young friend."

"Everyone is doing something except for me," Shan said, uttering the classic complaint of young boys. "I want to help!"

"Shan, if you didn't do a thing from now till the day you died, hopefully at a ripe old age, you've already been of tremendous help to His Majesty and your own people. We'd never have gotten this far without you."

"Then—you don't think I am a tool of the darkness?"

Ben felt a stab of guilt, remembering that once he had indeed had such suspicions. "Lad," he said, "if you're of the darkness, then I'm the poorest marksman in Albion."

Garth sat astride Percival, his body relaxed, his mind tranquil and focused. He breathed deeply, summoning his Will, and as Percival dove, roaring fiercely, the Hero shoved his hands in front of him. Blades whirled, wielded by invisible hands, slicing down the Empress's marksmen. Those who were not cut to pieces he simply forced off the wall. Those who were out of range fell with a swipe of Percy's tail. A few lucky ones tumbled down inside the wall. The rest were quickly defeated by the encroaching army.

"Now!" yelled Garth as Percy flew back. There was a volley of cannon fire.

The siege of Zahadar had begun.

While cannons and the battering ram pounded mercilessly against the gate, others of the king's men were placing ladders provided by the diligent monks up against the north, east, and west walls. Percival's shadow fell repeatedly upon the streets of the city; he knocked off those of the enemy who had climbed atop the walls and carefully dropped some of the army's best hand-to-hand fighters literally on top of their foes. Once he had done that, the sand dragon clutched the Empress's men and dropped *them*, much less carefully, outside the city walls.

The streets below were chaos. Civilians screamed and sought shelter in their homes while the battle raged right outside. The king's men had been told in no uncertain terms that they were not to fight anyone who was not clearly in the pay of the Empress.

Boom. Boom. Boom.

The city's weak point was the size of its gate. The walls itself would have been nearly impossible to fell. They were made of rammed earth and designed to last for centuries. If the gate had admitted only one or two at a time, there would have been no hope. But the gates to Zahadar, one behind the other, were made of wood and steel, and would yield to the relentless onslaught of cannon balls and the pounding of the battering ram.

Garth, on the ground now, made his way through to the gate, gazed at it, then smiled a little. The siege engines fell silent. He spread his hands, closed his eyes, and a fireball, half as large as he himself was, flew from his palms to slam into the wooden gate. Fire licked greedily at the dry wood, its heat eating through.

Boom. Boom. Boom. Again the battering ram swung back and slammed into its target. There was a groan as the iron gate shuddered. A second time Garth focused his Will, and another orange ball of flame exploded. This time, the wood was completely consumed, and even the iron bars were starting to glow orange. The cannons fired again simultaneously and the gate could no longer offer any resistance.

Garth strode through the main gate of Zahadar, the lines of blue dancing across his body with the strength of his controlled and focused Will. Casually, he extended a hand and lightning crackled, killing six would-be attackers at once. A sweep of the other hand hurled a dozen enemy soldiers out of the way, slamming them hard into the wall they had thought would protect them.

Shan kept close beside him, and Garth glanced back and winked at the boy. Siege engines were maneuvered into position to bring down the wall to the inner city.

"One wall down, two to go," said Garth.

Boom. Boom. Boom.

"That's our cue," said the king. He, Sohar, and the other monks darted out into the chaotic streets, blending in with the frightened citizens rushing about. Most were running to their homes, seeking shelter, and as the king glimpsed a woman clutching her baby trying to evade the clatter of carts and horses, he felt a pang of regret. If only this attack weren't necessary.

The plan he and the others had come up with was designed to reduce loss of life among civilians, but there would still be casualties. There were always casualties. He set his jaw and turned away from the terrified inhabitants and focused his attention on the wall encircling the palace.

The chaos, and the dust stirred up by it, served them well. There was a single entrance, well hidden, where the water from the Zaha was channeled into the Pleasure Gardens. In the panicked crush of people, no one noticed as he and the monks dropped down, removed the small metal gate much more easily than they had its larger cousin outside, and squeezed through. The lean, wiry monks had no trouble, and the king was glad that he still had the slenderness of youth. Even so, it was a tight fit, and he thought of claustrophobic Walter as he edged along the narrow passageway.

They emerged in the small reservoir at the base of the garden, cautiously poking their heads up. The two monks at each end shook their heads.

No guards.

Slowly, carefully, the king and the monks emerged from the shallow water, and the king beheld the Pleasure Gardens.

They were as beautiful as Shan had described them. There were three tiers, each stretching for several yards in a semicircle that enclosed a flat area at the top. Sweetwater trees grew at each end of the first level, their roots dipping into the life-giving water. Benches and small tables invited one to sit and reflect. On the second level, flowers grew in every hue imaginable. Their fragrance was lush and heady. Vines twined about the walls, and small stairways connected the three tiers. From this angle, the king couldn't see the final tier clearly and gestured to his men. They nodded, also wary of a trap.

Utilizing cover where they could, they climbed up to the next tier. Still no one raised an alarm. After a few moments, the king gestured, and they ascended to the third tier.

Here, a table draped with an intricately embroidered cloth and a single chair sat alone, a multicolored pavilion providing shade. A half-eaten meal of fresh fruit, bread, and cheese was left on a plate, along with a single goblet. Someone had been disturbed at his—her?—meal.

They had come for the Empress, and it seemed they had come close to finding her.

If the king and his small, elite group could capture the Empress amid the chaos and confusion of the siege, there was a good chance his goals could be achieved without bloodshed. She would not be expecting so brazen an attack within the very walls of her own palace. Once they had her, the king would do his best to see if she could be reasoned with. If she refused, he could keep her prisoner and negotiate with those who stepped in to fill the power vacuum.

His ears strained to hear over the sound of battle raging outside. The booming of cannon fire was coming closer now, which meant that Garth had succeeded in breeching the main gate and was now attacking the wall of the inner city.

Behind the little pavilion area with its single chair and table was an open door. It could be that the guards had rushed their mistress off and neglected to close the door behind them in their haste, perhaps never thinking of attack from the gardens.

Or it could be a trap.

A soft sound—the quivering intake of breath.

The monks heard it too, snapping to attention but awaiting his orders. The king lifted a hand, staying them, and gazed at the cloth-covered table. "They must be inside," he said, and jerked his head in the direction of the open door. "Let's go."

The monks nodded and headed for the door. Their feet slapped on the stone tiles while the king stepped backward quietly and waited.

For a moment, nothing happened. There was a rustling sound, and a slender, blue-draped, veiled figure emerged from where she had been hiding beneath the table. Quick as a snake, the king dove, snatching her by the arm and whirling her to face him.

Her veil fluttered to the ground, revealing a face so exquisite, so perfect, that—

He heard gunfire, then there was only darkness.

Chapter Twenty-two

The king had come to realize that no matter how exotic the country might be, or how much money and fame one's captor possessed, prison cells, everywhere, were much the same.

He had been given a cot, filthy and flea-riddled, and a chamber pot that wasn't emptied nearly often enough. Food and water were offered and the chamber pot removed by means of a small second door at the base of the cell door. It had its own lock, and the king knew that even Rex would be hard-pressed to wriggle through it.

After the first hour of attempting to sleep on the cot, he found the stone floor much more comfortable. There were no windows; the king estimated, given the coolness of the place—the only positive thing about it—he was deep underground. The guard, a large man who resembled Boulder but without his gentleness, spoke only to offer such comments as "Get up, you jackal" or similar pleasantries.

The king remained silent as well. He went over what had happened, trying to figure out how it was that he had been captured. He remembered entering the Pleasure Gardens and something about a table . . . and then nothing. His failure to recall the events was disturbing, but not as much as other things he didn't know: Had his friends survived? What about Percy? Had the sand dragon forsaken the Hero he was supposedly bound to serve? When the king couldn't fight off the bleak despair any longer, the questions became as dark as the evil that was plaguing Samarkand itself: *Will I ever escape? Do they all think I'm dead?*

Will I ever again see my Laylah?

His brooding was interrupted by the arrival of the Boulder look-alike . . . and a companion. This man was as slender as the other was bulky, well-groomed, and smelled pleasant.

"I am Ayar," the smaller man said. "It seems our Great Empress has taken an interest in meeting her royal prisoner. She has ordered that you be made presentable, so that you are fit to enter her august presence."

"You tell your Empress she'll see me as I am, or she'll not see me at all."

Ayar chuckled. "How amusing you foreigners are! Let me phrase it this way: I am providing you with hot water, soap, towels, a razor, and clean clothing. You may avail yourself of them freely. If you choose not to, Harul and I will clean you up ourselves."

The king glowered at them, then nodded. "All right. I'll pretty up for your Empress." He remembered Ben's comment about the Empress probably looking like a horse, and added defiantly, "Provided she's prettied up for me."

The two men exchanged amused glances. "You may be a king of another country," Ayar said, "but even you will fall to your knees once you behold her beauty."

"I doubt that very much," the king said, and accepted the toiletries passed through the small aperture. He looked down at the steaming bowl of water, scented with fragrant herbs; at the round cake of soap, the small mirror, the neatly folded towel and the long, sharp straight razor.

In his ravenous and weakened state he briefly fantasized seizing it and cutting his own throat. They would not be able to enter the cell in time to save him. He would thus deny this evil Empress any access to him. But he couldn't do that to his people. So many of them had died already, fighting for a cause he convinced them to believe in. He could tell himself that he was doing it to protect state secrets from being tortured out of him; that he would remove himself as a game piece in her strategy. But in the end, it was a coward's way out, at least this early on. Perhaps the Empress could actually be reasoned with; perhaps he would learn some valuable information. As he lathered up the soap and began to shave stubble off his chin, he realized he would never give up hope.

He was the King of Albion. He had a whole nation relying on him and one woman whom he adored. And that was more than enough to keep him going for now.

The monarch had to admit, he felt much better having had a chance to clean up. There was no guarantee that another such opportunity would come his way again for a good long while, and at least he would meet his fellow royal looking like a king.

The clothing was clean and of high-quality fabric, but simple: tunic, breeches, and sandals. He was led up a winding stone stair, then down a long corridor through several doors, then up stone steps again. When the door was opened, he blinked from the brightness after so long belowground with only lamplight for illumination.

As his vision adjusted, he had to struggle to conceal his awe.

Before him was an enormous open chamber. Vaulted ceilings made of carved whitewashed stone arched high above. Frescoes adorned them, a riot of colors in glorious geometric patterns. The pillars were exquisitely carved in meticulous detail, depicting geometric shapes, leaves, and flowers. Healthy foliage grew everywhere, from flowers to fruit trees, and an exquisite smell suffused the area. The sound of bubbling water filled the air, pouring with reckless generosity from an enormous fountain in the center of the room. The chamber opened onto a patio, where clear blue sky could be glimpsed. Comfortable-looking chairs, lounges, and cushions were provided, with low tables that bore platters of fruits and other delicacies.

All was harmonious, bright, beautiful—Samarkand at its best. Except for the fact that she who dwelt here epitomized Samarkand at its worst.

He turned to say something to Harul, who had led him up here, but the huge man had somehow vanished. The king looked around, puzzled, then saw the cunningly hidden doors set into the white walls.

"So this is the King of Albion," came a soft voice. It was warm, husky, almost purring, and the king steeled himself as he turned around.

He bowed low. "I am indeed," he said, straightening. "And you must be the Empr—"

The words died in his throat.

She smiled at him, red lips parting over pearl-white teeth. Her skin was a shade of soft golden brown, her eyes large, deep, and expressive. Gleaming black hair, covered partially by a jeweled scarf the shade of the sky, tumbled to her trim waist. Full breasts, demurely covered, swelled as if in rebellion against the restraining drape of lavishly embroidered silk. Rings, simple but elegant, adorned hands that were decorated with ink made from a local plant. The king swallowed hard, his mouth having suddenly gone dry and his brain empty of thoughts.

Her smile broadened. "I am she," she said in that purring voice. She lifted a hand, and with a dancer's movements indicated that he might sit on one of the lounges.

He nodded. "Th-thank you," he said. His voice cracked on the last word, as if he were an adolescent again. Indeed, he felt like a gawky teenage boy around this composed, graceful woman. Unable to tear his gaze away from her, he felt for the couch and managed to sit down without falling on his arse.

She sank down beside him. She wore some kind of perfume or oil; the scent was sweet, clean, and intoxicating.

"I hope you have been treated well," she said. "I regret that circumstances have prevented our meeting ere now."

"So do I," the king blurted. Inwardly, he frowned. *Get ahold of yourself! She's beautiful, yes, but she's just a woman. Focus, dammit.* "Thank you for permitting me to clean up a bit before our meeting."

Her smile became mischievous. "I know how I would feel about meeting fellow royalty in such a disheveled condition. I dressed my best for you." The last was almost . . . shy. The king tried and failed to suppress a sense of achievement. So, she found him attractive too. *Use that*, his logical self told him.

Her smile faded, and she turned away. "I wish our meeting were under happier circumstances," she said. "Your effort has failed, and in the most sorrowful of ways. I understand that you fought not just with a devoted army, but with friends as well. We found among the fallen a fair-haired man, an Auroran female, and a teenage boy too young to really fight." She turned eyes to him that glistened with compassionate tears.

Anguish twisted his gut. Ben, Kalin, and Shan? All of them?

"Your—beast?—has fled, along with the aged Hero he bore. I

do not know how you managed to tame a dragon out of legend, nor where you found Garth, but as soon as it was clear which way the battle had turned, they both took to the sky and vanished. I do not think such creatures are capable of understanding true loyalty. Nor, it would seem, does a once-famous Hero."

Percy and Garth, too? The king clenched his jaw, hard. He didn't want her to see how badly this had affected him. He wanted to say something dismissive, but he couldn't speak.

She reached and laid a gentle hand on his cheek. The perfume from her wrist wafted about him, and he closed his eyes. "We had to defend ourselves. I know you must understand that. But believe me, I grieve that the loss was so personal to you."

"I want to see them," he said hoarsely. "The bodies of my friends."

The Empress looked even sadder. "It is our custom to burn the bodies of the fallen, both our own soldiers and those of our adversary."

"*Burn?*"

"It is a way of honoring them," she said, looking confused and retreating slightly, as if hurt. "There was no disrespect. To burn the bodies of your soldiers is to honor them as worthy foes—to give them the same courtesy we give our own fallen."

He looked down. He lifted a hand to his temple. He felt dizzy, slightly sick. It had to be the news of his friends' deaths. What else would make him so rude to a lovely lady?

She's not what she seems to . . .

And the vague thought was gone, replaced with chagrin at his discourtesy. "I'm sorry, I didn't mean to snap at you. I'm just . . . shocked. And saddened."

She seemed to be thinking. "One moment, please," she said, and rose with a soft rustle of clothing. She went to one of the doors in the wall and knocked. Another guard the king did not recognize appeared, nodded, and withdrew. The Empress returned. "We have not yet honored the boy. You may see his body if you wish. As for the others, it seems my guards did retrieve some of their personal items. Shall I have these brought in?"

No, he wanted to shout, *I don't want to see Shan. I don't want to see proof that my friends died because of me.* Instead, he somehow managed to say, "Yes."

A few moments later, the door opened again. Several guards, looking solemn and respectful, entered. Two of them carried a stretcher covered with a white linen cloth. Another carried a crate, which he put on the ground and proceeded to open.

Slowly, with jerky movements, the king made it over to the stretcher. Steeling himself, he pulled the covering off.

Shan's face was pale. He had died from a single, well-aimed shot, right to the heart. At least death had come swiftly for him. "I'm sorry," he whispered to the still figure. "I'm so sorry. Garth was supposed to take care of you. You deserved so much better than this." He turned to look at the crate, and his heart ached even more.

"Vanessa," he murmured. Ben would never let his beloved rifle be taken from him, not while he was still—

"Who?" The Empress stepped beside him, offering comfort.

"The gun," the king said. "Ben named his gun Vanessa." He forced himself to continue looking through the items and grew still when he found one of Kalin's distinctive bracers. Gone. All of them, gone. And Percy, apparently released from his duty, had fled to freedom; and Garth, to return to the peace of his monastery.

His shoulders suddenly bowed from the weight of it all. "This was a fool's errand," he said. "I never should have come."

"Leave us be," the Empress said to the guards. They obeyed, silently bearing Shan and the crate back through the door in the wall, vanishing as if they had never been present. The Empress slipped the king's arm through hers and guided him back to the lounge. He sat heavily, guilt threatening to crush him.

Gentle fingers touched his chin as the Empress turned his face to hers. He felt a quick, inappropriate jolt of pleasure at the touch. She was so beautiful . . .

"I grieve for all that you have lost," she said, "but . . . perhaps some good may yet come of it. Now that I have met you"—and she smiled softly—"I see that we were not truly ever meant to be enemies. Let us then be allies—Samarkand and Albion."

He couldn't look away. He was falling into the pool of leaf brown that were her eyes, breathing in her scent, hearing her voice become huskier.

"Perhaps . . . more than allies, if you would like," she whispered. Slowly, her face drew closer to his, her breath sweet. "We can rule together. No one will be able to stand against us. All will be ours, to enjoy and share . . ."

She was so beautiful, and the king found himself enraptured by her red lips as she spoke. He leaned forward, his heart pounding, and bent to kiss—

—*Laylah*—

He didn't love this woman. He loved Laylah—wise, gentle, strong, brave Laylah. He didn't want to surrender his kingdom— he wanted to rule it well, keep his subjects safe . . .

His eyes, half-closed, snapped fully open, and he drew back. He felt as though cold water had been thrown on him, but he welcomed the refreshing, purifying shock of it. Suddenly, the rich scents, so pleasant before, seemed cloying; the luxury over the top when so many in Samarkand were dying terrible deaths from the darkness.

"My, my," he said, anger sharp and cold in his voice. "You are quite the little temptress, aren't you?"

Her eyes fluttered open and her soft expression, all warmth and surrender, grew cunning.

"I am," she said, "and all you need to do to satisfy that temptation is to yield. All will be given unto you, Your Majesty. I find you pleasant to look upon, and the power we can wield together will please him as well."

He felt like he was awakening from a deep sleep. "Him?" he said, seizing on the word. Was she merely a tool of some larger, darker power? "Of whom do you speak? Is the darkness not yours to command?"

Now even the cunning playfulness vanished. "I tire of the game," the Empress said abruptly. "You had your chance. Years from now, when you are old and your joints scream in agony, when the only sight left to you is the inside of your prison cell, you will remember this day and weep for all you could have had."

"Somehow I doubt that."

"Well, lucky you, you'll get to find out." Her mask of superiority cracked, and he knew that he had judged correctly. She was offended she had not been able to seduce him and bend him to her will. So this was how she had tamed the Emperor, once a good man and adored by his people. She would not claim a second monarch.

"You're not in charge, are you? You're just a puppet. Someone else is controlling the darkness, aren't they? Isn't *he*, I should say?" Anything he could get from her right now would be useful, and he knew he had precious few moments to goad her into slipping.

"You think you're so clever," she snarled, "marching in here with your sand castle of a dragon, a Hero of yore, your loyal troops. You haven't the slightest idea what you're up against. The only reason I don't kill you now is—"

Her jaw closed with an audible click. So, the king realized, he was still valuable. But before he could hound her with more questions, the Empress was on her feet.

"Guards!" she cried, and they hastened in. "Take him back to rot in his cell."

There was no pretense of courtesy this time as the guards roughly grabbed his arms, removed his gauntlets, and started to haul him away. "Do what you will with me," he said over his shoulder. "You can't have killed us all. And even if you did, there will be others to take my place. There are still Heroes in Albion!"

She laughed, with what appeared to be genuine amusement. "Are there? Are you sure? You have no child, Your Majesty. Nor does your brother Logan. And as you are in prison now, it is unlikely there will ever be an heir. The royal bloodline is dead. Albion is *his* now! Think on that, alone in your cell!"

He was stunned. She was right. Could it be true? What would happen to the Hero lineage in Albion if there was none with the royal bloodline anymore? So shaken was he by this thought that he didn't even struggle as he was brought back in and thrown, bodily, into his cell, landing hard on the stone floor. The cell door creaked as it was slammed shut, and he heard the key turning in the lock.

No more Heroes of Albion. No one knew what had happened to him, if he were even still alive. And if they did believe that he was, how would they find him? He was in the center of the walled city, in the depths of the very palace itself. The Empress was right. He would rot here, growing old, with not even hope to sustain him through the long years. While she and her mysterious commander would continue to release the darkness upon innocents.

Upon Albion.

His heart ached within him, and he could almost physically feel his spirit break. Unable to bear it, he fell into the sleep of the wounded and exhausted.

Chapter Twenty-three

"All right, sharpshooters, to me!" Percy bellowed. Ben raced toward the sand dragon with Vanessa, an ammunition bag, and a powder horn draped across his body. He and seven others who had been selected for the honor scrambled aboard the dragon's broad back. "Careful, don't scrape me to pieces," Percy scolded as a bit of sand crumbled from his side when an uneasy rider dug his heels in too deeply. "Now hang on!"

He crouched, gathering himself, and sprang skyward. Ben was unable to stifle a whoop of excitement. The king had tried to describe the ecstasy of flight, but the description had fallen far short of the reality. His stomach seemed to need a second or two to catch up to the rest of him, and the wind on his face—

"Wind," he shouted over his shoulder. "We'll all have to calculate for the wind from Percy's wings!"

Delight in the experience would have to take second place to the reason they were all here: To fire on the enemy below.

Percival flew over the first wall while the battering rams and cannons continued to pound at it. "Lower," Ben shouted, and the dragon obliged, dropping smoothly. He picked his targets—

the ones who looked like they were in charge—and began firing.

Kalin had dropped her sword and was fighting with one of the monk's staffs. Four soldiers surrounded her. She was fighting well, beautifully in fact, considering how little practice she had with the weapon, but it was clear to Ben that she would be downed in a few seconds.

"Percy, Kalin—to your right!" Ben shouted.

"I see her," Percy said grimly. He folded his wings and dove into the fray. One of the soldiers saw him approaching and screamed, no doubt thinking his demise was upon him. His cry alerted the others, whose eyes went enormous as they froze in sheer terror.

They seemed flabbergasted as the dragon reached for Kalin instead of them. Emboldened, one of them broke his paralysis and grabbed Kalin's arm as Percy lifted her up.

Ben tried to line up a good shot, but it wasn't possible. He was afraid he'd hit Percy, which wouldn't matter all that much, or Kalin, which would. "Dammit, let go of her, you son of a cur!" Ben yelled in frustration. Kalin's face was contorted in pain, and Ben imagined her arm felt like it was being yanked from its socket.

The Samarkandian soldier snarled at her, and, impossibly, drew a knife from his belt and tried to stab at Kalin. But the Auroran leader was doing something Ben couldn't see, and to his delight, the man's face turned from an evil leer to an expression of horror as he suddenly fell, Kalin's bracer still clutched in one hand.

Shan stuck close to Garth, as per their agreement. It was likely the safest place to be. Garth was making a trail of destruction, hurling bodies left and right, calling lightning down and directing massive fireballs. Shan followed in the great Hero's wake, taking his time aiming his shots, making them count, as Ben had instructed him. He felt almost giddy, invincible. He fired, reloaded, fired a few more shots, reloaded while his dark eyes scanned for the next target. Out of the corner of his eye, he saw several men, unarmed, racing toward him and Garth. The old Hero, intent on directing whirling magical swords at another cluster of attackers, did not see them.

"Garth!" he called. "On your right!"

Garth whirled, incinerating most of the men. Two of them, though, veered directly toward Shan. Even in the thick of battle, Shan realized there was something strange about how they ran, and when he saw that their eyes were completely black, his sudden fear was confirmed.

We ssspared you once. We shall not ssspare you again.

He froze in terror. The Shadows—the darkness—it was inside these men, as surely as it had been inside the statues in the Cave of a Thousand Guardians. His mind flashed back to the confrontation on the *Queen Laylah.*

We've heard the stories . . . how you claim to have been "released" by the Shadows to come warn us. Well, maybe you are one of them . . . !

"No!" Shan shrieked. He lifted his rifle, tried to take aim with shaking arms, but the thing—it was no longer a man, not really—slapped it out of the way. The weapon flew out of Shan's grasp, and the twisted creature grabbed Shan's shirt and spat a thick, gooey black glob at his face.

Shan wailed, feeling the darkness devouring him, not physically, but deeper inside; chewing at his soul. Sound went away as he fell in slow motion to the sand. The only thing Shan could hear was his own heartbeat thudding in his ears. He lay on his back, feeling the darkness seep inside him, eating away at him like cancer. Tears streamed from his eyes. He stared up at the sky, and a dark shadow passed over him. Percy. The dragon dropped lower, and Shan realized that Percy was reaching out with his foreclaw. The great beast was trying to save him. Ben's face peered over the dragon's side, concern on his face.

Shan forced his lungs to work, to speak while he still could, while his mind was still his own. He reached up a hand as if he were swimming through mud, thumped his chest, and cried a single word:

"Darkness!"

It sealed his lips, now, the darkness; it would never let him utter anything but what it wanted him to. But that was all right. He'd seen understanding and sorrow on Ben Finn's face as the blond soldier lifted Vanessa and aimed her at the Samarkandian boy he had called friend.

Garth had turned just in time to see Shan's body collapse, blood blossoming in his chest. There was no time to mourn the boy, for even as Garth realized what had happened the two "men" who had truly been the ones to slay Shan attacked. He blasted them with fire and both stumbled backwards, limned in orange-and-red crackling flame.

Where had they—or more accurately, the darkness that had inhabited them—come from? Garth reached out, his senses heightened, trying to figure out the source. Up until this moment, the Albion army had been closing in on victory, even if the king hadn't been able to find the Empress. But if she had summoned the darkness—

The river rolled past, enemies locked in combat struggling on the banks. Sunlight glinted on its surface, but something seemed—off. More of the corrupted soldiers rushed at him, more like animated dolls then men. Garth summoned the vortex spell and a whirlwind appeared, keeping them at bay while he studied the river.

The sunlight was no longer glinting on its flowing surface. It was being absorbed by it.

Even as Garth watched, inky tendrils, like a stain, merged with the once-pure water, and within another heartbeat, the life-giving river had been turned to poison.

Globules of foulness extracted themselves from the flood of darkness, splashing unerringly on those who served a king, not an empress. Other tendrils, snakelike, oozed up the banks and undulated their way to their victims, twining up their bodies. And Garth realized with a sick anger that victory, so close a few moments ago, had been snatched from them.

There was no choice. "Retreat!" he cried. "*Retreat!*"

There was utter pandemonium. The darkness wasn't targeting the citizens of Zahadar, but they were too frightened to realize it. Even the Empress's own soldiers were turning tail. People were screaming and rushing forward, trampling one another underfoot in their mad dash for escape. There was a tide of humanity from both sides racing for the exit, racing to flee the city that had suddenly become a nightmare. Garth did what he could to help the king's army retreat, using his Will to force aside soldiers and civilians alike.

The darkness kept coming. The globules shifted, re-formed, became shadows. Instead of tendrils, they now took on an even more alarming shape. Giant hands, the fingers long and spidery, slammed down on screaming soldiers. They swept away clusters of living humanity as if they were nothing more than insects, unworthy of notice.

Garth turned. It would be his last stand; on foot he couldn't hope to outrun these evil, shadowy hands. He calmly summoned his Will, mind and heart at peace, and extended his hands to Force back the shadows.

A shadow fell over Garth. But it was a natural, welcome one, and he found himself borne aloft in Percival's foreclaw. Like a sentient being angry that something had escaped its grasp, the hands reached skyward. Again Garth concentrated, and his Will exploded in a Force so strong that the shadowy claws actually dissipated.

For the moment.

A few flaps of the great wings and they were clear of the city. Percy landed where they had camped the previous night, and Ben and Kalin, along with several of the marksmen the dragon had been carrying, climbed off him.

Ben's face was pale and he clutched his right arm. Blood was seeping out from under his fingers. "Sit down," Kalin ordered, "I can at least bandage it quickly."

Percival turned to Garth. "I can carry more out," he said.

"Do so," Garth said. "Bring them here." Percival inclined his golden head and leaped skyward again. The army was arriving by ones and twos. There was no fear of pursuit; those lucky enough to have escaped the darkness in Zahadar would not be interested in hunting down their enemy and continuing the fight. They would be fleeing as fast as their legs could carry them.

"We should have expected this," Garth said, clenching his fists in anger. "How did we *fail* to expect it? We played right into her hands!" He paused in his pacing and eyed Ben. "You going to be all right?"

"I think so," Ben said. "Dropped Vanessa, though. Dammit." He seemed to Garth to be more upset at losing the rifle than getting shot. Unduly upset, in fact, and Garth realized Ben was, in his own way, mourning Shan, not the lost weapon at all.

Percival returned, carrying more survivors. He placed them down gently.

"Ben!" cried Shalia, hurrying toward the blond soldier and dropping down beside him. Ben grinned, relief spreading across his face as he and Shalia exchanged a fierce kiss. Garth recognized his friend Sohar among the others, and felt a chill as he saw how gravely wounded the monk was.

"Garth," Percival said in a grim voice, "you need to hear this."

Garth knelt beside Sohar, making a quick, sorrowful assessment. Sohar was too badly injured for any healing Garth could offer to save him. The monk clutched Garth's hand with his bloody one.

"The—the king," Sohar whispered. "She has him. It was—a trap—"

He struggled to continue, blood bubbling out of his mouth. But no words came. Gently Garth placed a hand on Sohar's cheek. "Rest, my friend. Rest peacefully, and forever."

Sohar gave him a grateful smile and Garth eased him down to the sand. The monk coughed once, then was still.

His head bowed, Garth said, "Percival. Can you tell if the king yet lives?"

The dragon nodded. "He is still alive," he confirmed. "I would sense it if he were . . . not."

Garth nodded. "That's good, at least. Even so, the dark Empress has both defeated us and stolen our king. Her city is broken and her people panicked now, but she will regroup. And when she does, she will send the full force of the darkness after us." He eyed Ben and Kalin. "We cannot permit her to find us."

"Wait, what?" Ben said, trying to get to his feet. Shalia eased him back down. "Are you suggesting we just turn tail and leave him?"

"Garth is correct," Percival said. "If the Empress laid a trap to capture the king, it is highly unlikely she wishes him dead."

"But she could torture him—torment him—give him over to the darkness!" Ben sputtered.

"Ben," Kalin said in her calm, quiet voice, "I too agree with Garth. We are the ones at risk here. We are the last hope of defeating the Empress and the darkness. That was the king's desire. If we try to mount a rescue now, we could doom all of Albion. Is that what you wish?"

Ben looked from Garth to Percival to Kalin. His blue eyes held a world of anguish.

"We are not going to abandon him," said Garth. "But we must survive. Regroup. Have a strategy."

"I for one literally *cannot* abandon him," Percy said. "I know you understand, Ben."

"I do," Ben said, his voice cracking slightly. "Damn your eyes, I do."

Theresa stood before him.

The king had not seen her in years, but the blind Seer seemed exactly the same to him. She wore her usual garb of ivory and maroon. Her eyes glowed white, gazing down at him from her cowled face.

He moved himself stiffly into a seated position, but was unable to stand. "Theresa?"

She smiled but remained silent, and lifted both arms out beside her. Suddenly a bird appeared on each arm. On her right was a dove. It cooed, content, and fluffed its snowy white feathers. On her left arm perched a raven, cocking its head impudently at the king and peering at him with yellow eyes. It opened its mouth, cawing harshly.

Now, at last, Theresa spoke. "Born a Hero you were, and a Hero you are. Darkness has indeed come to Albion, and few there are and will yet be who can stand against it. But do not despair, King of Albion. The world has changed. The time approaches swiftly when Heroes are not born . . . they are made."

Theresa flung her arms upward. The birds took flight, then vanished.

"Theresa—"

The king awoke sitting upright, one hand reaching out to the empty cell. Despair knifed through him. Just a dream, then. A ridiculous, foolish dream. He cursed his sleeping mind for the false hope it had given him. Sighing, he pressed down a hand to help himself rise.

It touched something very soft.

A feather—no, two of them. One white . . . and one black.

His chest swelled with joy. Not a dream—a vision! He picked up the feathers with hands that trembled, gazing down at the promise in his palms.

The Empress was wrong! More than wrong, tragically, fatally mistaken. She would fall, as all darkness must fall to the light. Maybe he would not be the one to engineer her destruction, but others would come, to take up the torch, to save their land. To save their world.

Theresa had shown him.

There *were* still Heroes in Albion!

Epilogue

The fires had been extinguished, and Gabriel walked slowly back to his caravan. Maybe Katlan was right. Heroes hadn't been seen in Albion for a long, long time. Decades. Maybe they did exist in history once, but not now.

Still . . . the stories . . .

Time to grow up. Time to get some sleep. He climbed into the caravan and pulled the blankets over him.

Gabriel closed his eyes and dreamed of Heroes.

. . . To be continued

About the Author

CHRISTIE GOLDEN is the *New York Times* bestselling author of more than thirty novels, including *Star Wars: Fate of the Jedi: Ascension,* and several short stories in the fields of fantasy, science fiction, and horror. Her media tie-in works include *Vampire of the Mists,* which launched the Ravenloft line in 1991, more than a dozen *Star Trek* novels, and multiple Warcraft and StarCraft novels, including *World of Warcraft: Thrall: Twilight of the Aspects* and *StarCraft II: Devil's Due.*